Will the Morning Be Any Kinder Than the Night?

To Marvin:
With great affection, remembrance
of our time together in our
writing group and hope that
we be part of an important
human transformation

Irving

Will the Morning Be Any Kinder Than the Night?

And Other Stories by

IRVING WEXLER

The Sheep Meadow Press
Riverdale-on-Hudson, New York

For Marlene
whose encouragement and insightfulness
were indispensable from beginning to end

All inquiries and permission requests should be addressed to:
The Sheep Meadow Press
P.O. Box 1345
Riverdale-on-Hudson, New York 10471

The book is set in ITC Caslon 224 by Keystrokes, Lenox, Massachusetts
Printed by Princeton University Press, Lawrenceville, New Jersey

Library of Congress Cataloging-in-Publication Data:

Wexler, Irving.
Will the morning be any kinder than the night? : and other stories / by Irving Wexler.
p. cm.
ISBN 1-878818-07-4
I. Title.
PS3573.E974W55 1991
813'.54—dc20 90-27063
CIP

Contents

Will the Morning Be Any Kinder Than the Night?

Enlightenment

Steve Feld is sunning himself in Washington Square, beached on the steps of the fountain like a piece of driftwood. He likes being lost among the rest of the nondescripts—the alkies, hustlers, blue-haired old ladies. On days like this, stretched out in the noonday blaze, he can be alone with his freedom without in the least feeling lonely.

Ambition, career, dreams that drive one crazy, they don't mean a shit to him now. It's been this way since his wife died two years ago. Finally, the last of his ballast gone. Three grown kids on their own. Old friendships long ago disintegrated, bridges crossed, plans forgotten, commitments cancelled—every last one of them.

If he were to raise his head and turn left, he could see the sandbox at the far end of the park, where he played in the fifties with his youngest, Josh, the only one he really misses. His son the spiritualist—one year Yoga, the next Zen Buddhist, after that Shaman, or whatever. If not one, then another prescription for enlightenment.

God, how Josh had tried to indoctrinate him in those days: "Dad, why are you hung up on straight thinking? I mean, petty cares like money, power, yea, even fear of death. They're only illusions of the egocentric mind. Once you give them up, you will awaken to the nature of your true self. Why can't you grasp this?"

Even after he left home, Josh would send his father articles, letters, notes with spiritual advice from God knows where: "As Christ walked on the waters, so you must learn to walk the sea of nothingness, buoyant in the absence of absolutes." Or words to that effect. Steve was cynical then, but at times now he wonders: Maybe a little of Josh has rubbed off on him. This very moment, for example, he leans back motionless, inhales, exhales slowly, his mind an alpha blank, hypnotized by the rainbows of spray gushing from the fountain.

From far off—maybe nirvana—weightless voices are humming on the loose above the grass. Vaguely he grasps that they are the sounds of children playing in the water. Without warning, a sharp tug at his shirt violates his calm. It's a little girl, six at most, staring at him coldbloodedly. "Mister," she asks, "how does it feel to be old?"

Steve glances down to see her naked feet, like white stoned fish, resting on the bottom of the pool. "Don't ask me," he says. "It's too early in the game to tell."

His answer perplexes her. "Really, Mister," she insists, "does it make you sad to be old?"

Before he can invent an answer, the mother whisks away her child. "Susan," she chides, "is that a question to ask a stranger?" She turns to Steve, apologetic: "Oh, I'm so sorry," she gushes, "you never know what they're going to say next."

Steve looks at her smiling, sunburned face. She and her child have utterly unbuoyed him. He imagines his joy hissing out, as from a punctured tube. "Forget it," he barks and turns his head away.

He wanders, discombobulated, no longer innocent of time, through the arch out of the park. It's not his terrain, lower Fifth Avenue, never has been. The elegant buildings. A uniformed doorman whistling for a cab. The whole stinking business of life swimming into focus again.

He lingers on the corner, confused, his will as rusty as an old nail, his depression the color of lead. What is he supposed to do now? Go home? Home is a sublet decrepit flat on Thompson Street. Returning in the afternoon this way—indigo blue—is always a bad omen.

Steve starts back west, crisscrossing streets and avenues aimlessly, except that his feet have, by themselves, taken him to the basketball court on Third Street and Sixth Avenue. He leans forward, pressing his face into the mesh fence. Some kids are practicing hook shots, faking, weaving, letting the ball fly gracefully toward the basket.

Thirty years ago, he tells himself, small but shifty he had some good moves too, floating loose and lovely in his dirty Keds. Oh Christ, the ache of it, never again to barrel down the court, faking his man out, then swish—through the nets! *Mister*... he hears that damned child's voice again... *how does it feel to be old?*

Precipitantly, his heart a pump gone wild, he walks through the open gate onto the court. At the sight of him, the players stop to eye this graybeard coolly. Dimly, through a surge of exaltation, he perceives that he may be making an asshole of himself.

"Can I take one?" Steve asks, as hip as he knows how, his hands held out to the young man with the ball.

The man shakes his head, unbelieving. "Fuck, man," he says, one huge palm encircling the ball, "we're playing."

"Only one?" Steve cajoles.

"Oh, hell," another player says, "let the guy shoot."

The first player shakes his head, spits and bounces the ball viciously in Steve's direction. Steve twirls it in his hands to get the feel of the leather. Only it's not leather, and far heavier than he can recall. His legs are trembling beneath him like fragile stalks. Hope to God, he prays, my body still remembers what to do. He raises the ball high over his head to shoot a two-hander. A dozen pair of hot eyes are watching through the wire fence. He lets the ball fly skyward toward the basket. It rises in a weak arc and falls short of the backboard. Several onlookers applaud derisively. "Hey, grandpa," someone calls out, "let 'em play ball."

Steve's face has begun to burn. He knows he should stop the farce but it's too late to retreat. He holds his hands out imploringly to the player who has retrieved the ball. "Second chance," he wheedles. Before he's ready, the man whips a bullet past his hands into his belly. Steve curses himself for his clumsiness. Dribbling unsteadily downcourt, he goes in for the lay-up—the kind of shot he could have made once with his eyes shut. As he leaves the ground, he feels himself catapulted, without control, toward the wire fence. The side of his face hits the steel mesh hard. His legs twist from under him and he careens face down across the concrete floor.

As he lies on the ground dazed, he notes that a rivulet of blood is dripping down his chin. One of the players slips his arms around his shoulders to help him up. Steve shakes him off savagely. "No, I don't need any help," he half screams. With his fingers hooked through the fence, like a monkey in the zoo, he pulls himself slowly to his feet. Tentatively, he limps—his right knee wobbly—through the gate.

"You're bleeding bad," a young woman says. She offers him a tissue, but he waves it off. Dammit, he thinks, no handkerchief, not even a scrap of paper in his pockets. With the inside of his sleeve, he wipes away the line of blood from his chin.

"Want me to get a cab?" the woman asks.

"I'm okay," he says, "just fine." Turning away abruptly, he hobbles across Sixth Avenue and painstakingly makes his way home. In the hallway he stops to look for his social security check. Except for a leaflet announcing a new Chinese take-out restaurant, the mailbox is empty.

As always, his tiny living room is a semidark cavern in its north light window. Steve undresses and stands nude before the bathroom mirror. His knee, bruised and purpling, is beginning to swell. He washes the gash of skin on his forehead with alcohol. The shock of pain, he chastises himself, is no more than he deserves.

Throwing a blanket over his shoulders, Steve sinks to the floor and slithers to the mattress. On his back, in the gloom, his eyes fixed on a crack in the ceiling, he pulls the blanket over his head. At once, in the dark tent, the image of a grotesque old man sprawled on the basketball court forces itself into his consciousness. He lets the sickening flow of humiliation flow freely over him. There is no way he can stem it—until sleep finally engulfs him.

Later in the afternoon, the doorbell shatters his twilight sleep with a shrill series of high-decibel rings. He tries to ignore the carefully spaced, nagging stabs. Nobody knows where he lives, and even if they did, who would bother to come? Nevertheless the rings continue.

Maybe it's a drunk, he thinks. The super? A Jehovah's witness? An errant finger? A kind neighbor? A mysterious caller? Why don't they screw off, all of them. He's in no condition for a visit. He's regrouping his defenses. His dreams need rewriting. There are lunatic shutters over his eyes. For Christ's sake, he is out to dinner with his deadliest enemy!

He smothers his head in the blanket, but the vibrating tongue of sound is prodding him with guilt, like his mother's voice railing at him through the bathroom door. He lies there, heart racing, knowing that he must confront the one who is mounting the stairs, that he will open the door and that a face—one that he has no desire to see—will be there to greet him. He gets up, blanket trailing the floor, presses the bell and waits. Soon, a knock at the door, a timid rap he cannot recognize or divine.

"Come in," he says, breathing deeply, drawing—as Josh once tried to teach him—the zen bow of indifference to psych himself up for the unknown face. The door opens tentatively and, before the visitor steps in, he recalls with dismay the letter he sent Josh months ago, carelessly revealing his new address.

Josh comes slowly into the room, wearing the familiar dirty-red parka, a torn backpack on his shoulders. As always he is trailing clouds of gentle sadness, the same pale halo around his eyes, the sunny, open, pre-epileptic look—as Steve once told his wife in a fit of pique—like one of Dostoevsky's saintly idiots.

"How the hell are you, Dad?" Josh asks, the familiar heartbreak smile playing his lips, his eyes plugged into Steve's with the irresistible flow of his love.

"Great, Josh," Steve says, a fleeting touch of his hand on his son's shoulder, a flick across his hair and then withdrawal. As he steps back, Steve thinks gratefully, it could have been his older son or daughter.

That son would have, in one pained glance, sized up the situation—the unshaven face, the wound on the forehead, the grungy father in his tenement flat, one of the golden-age desperadoes who can't in the first place accept that the counterculture is dead and in the second place that it was never meant for geriatric clowns like Steve.

Or, just as bad, it could have been his daughter's low-key entrance, one eye imperceptibly cocked, coolly taking in the squallid scene without comment, regarding her father with a masked irony compounded of pity, contempt and obligatory love.

So it's you, Josh, he thinks, perpetually down on your luck, contemptuous of worldly goods, trusting that if you authentically seek, you will find, what is it, you kept explaining to me—zazen, satori, self-realization, Dharma, the peace of spiritual awakening?

"Can't you see," Josh would expound patiently, "once you let go of your values, preconceptions, points of view, you can begin to experience the oneness of existence? It's a whole new framework of perception."

"But I'm kind of fond of my old values," Steve would parry, "even if they're old hat. Besides, at sixty, I'm too far gone to slip into a new framework of perception."

Josh would shake off the levity and say, with a deadly seriousness that chilled his father, "Do me a favor, Dad, if you can't as yet accept my beliefs, at least take them on faith. This is the time to begin preparing for your next incarnation—your coming rebirth."

"Thanks," Steve would answer, trying to defuse him, "but one birth was more than enough for me."

"Please don't condescend me," his son would insist. "Unless you awaken in this lifetime, you could end up in your new cycle of existence as a blank wall, a pebble, a toad, a particle in space."

Stung by Josh's evangelical fervor, the implacability with which he announced his father's karmic doom, Steve would argue, "Okay, let's assume you're right. It's my fate to be bottom man on the reincarnation ladder. So why don't I just gracefully accept it."

"It's never too late," Josh would assure him. "If you open yourself, you can learn to breathe, meditate, clear your mind, experience the Void." He would begin to chant, his voice strident with zeal: "No hang-ups, no hate, no suffering, no illusions, no death. Only calm, grace, nothingness! Don't squander your life, Dad . . . transform it!"

And peering into his son's glazed eyes, he could see that he was as rapturous in his faith as the highest Hare Krishna. Yes, he had swallowed it all and was offering his poor unrealized father—out of the purity of his own love—a fling at oneness everlasting.

Now, in his ordinary mind-warp, Josh slips out of his parka and drops his coat onto the floor. The two stand awkwardly peering at one another in the dim light. "Hey, Dad," Josh says, noting Steve's bruised forehead. He grins shyly. "Can't stay away from the rough trade, right?"

Warily Steve arranges his face into a pinched smile and allows himself a grudging laugh. He must be careful to fly his flag of distress at half mast. Not low enough to signal that he's sinking. Not high enough to suggest he can take his son on as cargo.

"Missed you like crazy," Josh says. "When you didn't write, I knew it was because you couldn't. Anyway, thanks for the letter."

"Hard times," Steve says, "for the two of us."

Josh looks around at the wooden crates, the catastrophic pile-up of books, the sticks of furniture, the beat-up mattress on the floor. "Nice pad you have here, Dad." Not even a hint of distress at his father's complete disorder. Indeed, why should Josh take notice of the chaos? As a child he could live in perpetual dishevelment with a serenity that would drive Steve into a frenzy between rage and envy.

Even as Josh tosses his sweater, gloves, hat and scarf onto the floor, Steve remembers him as a ten-year-old relentlessly overrunning his bedroom with an impenetrable tangle of dismantled toys, a menagerie of pets in open cages, the pellets of defecation scattered over the rug, the acrid urine-smell hanging in the air, the stripped-down electronic gadgets and rebuilt inventions, the rocks, shells, molds, found objects, humming fishtank and, hanging by nails driven into the walls, a maze of graphics, doodlings, hieroglyphics, posters, cut-ups, pictures of the Beatles, Marilyn Monroe, Humphrey Bogart and, unaccountably, Huey Newton—machine gun in lap—staring ahead with snake cool eyes from a high-backed Victorian wicker chair...

Surely, it crosses Steve's mind, his son must wonder amid all this banter why they haven't embraced in their usual quick rush of love. And Josh must already sense, with his incredibly tuned-in antenna, that his father is deliberately holding his son at bay. Josh folds his hands together into a gesture of prayer, as he did when he was a little boy. It was his way, Steve remembers, of revealing despair. "This year has been a bummer," he says. "I'm on my way to some friends in Vermont. Maybe my luck will change."

In the pit of his gut, Steve feels a wild impulse to be a proper father... to hold, rock and console his son. Ah, but there's the rub. His son's need is too heavy. He must stifle it, stomp on it, murder it in its tracks.

Then suddenly, in an image of total recall, Steve sees his own father seated at the window of the living room, his bespectacled eyes riveted on a Jewish newspaper. Steve tiptoes behind him, and leans over gently, so that his dad will notice him and, tousling his hair, flash for his benefit an inexpressibly tender smile. Face uplifted, he stands there waiting, a presence too palpable to be missed. But his father, staring at the newspaper, never once glances down. And the scary thing is, he realizes, it's far too dark to read.

In the faded evening light, he sees his father's eyes swimming huge and helpless through the thick lens. The yellowish skin on his forehead is stretched tautly over the skull. Almost as if he has taken leave of his son, he seems to be wrapped in a cocoon of silence. Now the boy knows for sure—the vision is startlingly precise—what his dad will look like on his deathbed.

Steve's impulse is to move closer, slipping his body through the ring of arms that hold the newspaper. He senses, however, that his dad will only stiffen and turn away, that he cannot give recognition or love (dimly the boy understands and forgives), because at this moment their combined anguish is too much for this one father to bear.

Josh slumps down onto one of the wooden crates, his hand nervously curling and uncurling the stringy locks over his brows. They are in tacit agreement—father and son—not to probe each other's wounds with questions: How Steve fills his days; does he have friends and lovers; how he has come to this desolate pass? Steve, in turn, will not inquire where Josh has been wandering; why he is without job, hope or home; what he seeks from his father after this long hiatus.

Josh remembers that he is famished. "Do you have anything to eat?"

"Whatever your heart desires," Steve answers. He opens the refrigerator. It is a morgue of forgotten food. Inside, the tomatoes are oozing pale blood; the one cucumber has dissolved out of its moldy skin. He sweeps the rotted vegetables into a paper bag. One of these days, he promises himself, he must scrape the green gook from the bin.

All that remains is a pale-yellow apple. Washing it with painstaking care, Steve slices it into neat little chunks and places them in a cracked bowl. They sit without speaking in the gathering darkness, Josh on his parka, his father on the mattress, munching the mealy slices. The only sound is the muted hum of the traffic. They are immured in this quietude, steeped in a viscous stillness.

He is painfully thin, the son, his fine frame wasted, his unkempt hair overpowering a small-boned face. Only the eyes are fully alive, huge, feverish, violet flecked, the pupils dilated, the whites veined with tiny flecks of blood. How many unslept nights, Steve wonders, pot-smoking vacuums, vacant downs, crash pads, bus-stops, park benches? Oh, what an inept moment to show up with his burnt-out offerings!

As they chomp away at the apple, Steve feels the tension between them stretching thin like a rubberband. Several times Josh rubs his forehead and looks up at his father, expectantly, as if he were waiting for the magic word. Steve knows just what his son wants . . . daddylove, a passkey, a hint, an unfreezing, a direction. If only he, Steve, could cry out: *Sorry, my darling, I have nothing up my sleeves, trash in my purse, ice in my heart, slop in the refrigerator.* Holding his breath, he sees through half-closed eyes his son in silhouette moving across his field of vision in slow, translucent, jellyfish motion.

"Dad, I need a place to hang out for a while." Josh's high-pitched, anxious stammer brings Steve back to himself. "Is it okay with you?"

Steve bends over the mattress, draws the blanket closer and rocks mournfully like his own father in shul. In this position he feels oddly disembodied. Josh's words, though lucid, seem hardly to be reaching him at all. It is essential that he suck his son's words and the urgency behind them into the quicksand of his own silence. In this way he will muffle not only the sounds and sense of Josh's voice but the memory of his having spoken at all.

Glancing up, Steve notes his son's trembling lips, the blue vein pulsing in his neck. Josh regroups his small energy, his voice barely above a whisper. "I'll be here only a week at most"—a hesitation—"anytime you want me to, I can stay out of your hair."

He's trailed him, his cunning son, and thinks he can trap this wily old fox in his own lair. Not me, Josh—he warns his son silently—I have my own wounds to lick, there is not enough room, sustenance or pity for you or anyone else, for that matter. And astonishingly Steve discovers with a mixture of shame and satisfaction, he can lie to his son brazenly, shrewdly, obscenely.

"Christ, Josh," he says affably, holding his open palms up in mock despair, "Sally's with me. It would be awkward for her with you here."

Sally abandoned him ages ago. There isn't a hint of a woman's presence in all this chaos. Surely Josh has noted this, but if he does, he gives no sign whatever that he is aware of Steve's deception. He is on his father's grounds, he must play by the rules of his game, he must be as quick to dissemble.

"You know me, Dad," he pleads. "Have sleeping bag—will bed down anywhere." He watches his father's expression for an opening. Steve lowers his head and fixes his eyes on Josh's heavy climbing boots. Compared to his shabby clothes, they are remarkably well-kept—oiled, tightly laced, the heels and soles almost unworn. For some reason, the special care Josh has taken with his boots comforts Steve. He shuts his eyes and pictures Josh at twelve climbing a steep rock hill in New Hampshire. He is one rock above his father, his boots so close Steve can admire the heft, the grain, the gleam of the leather in the sun. With a tug of his arms, Josh hoists himself to the crest of the hill. Steve watches him wave down, flushed and cocky at his little triumph. Ah, the innocent grace and bravery of him, Steve remembers crowing to himself, the separateness of his son filling him with a dizzying elation.

Josh's voice, breaking his reverie, is hoarse with urgency. "The fact is, Dad, I have no friends here, no bread, nowhere to sleep."

If he gives in, Steve knows for a certainty, the two of them will suffocate in mutual pity. Isn't there a way he can make that clear? "Try to understand, Josh"—somehow the words are pouring out on their own—"I'm psychically unable to deal with another human being in this space . . . you included. Someday, maybe, when I'm healed, but not now, not now! It's a matter of survival. Does that make any sense?"

Josh tries to clear his voice. "Oh, hell"—the words are thick, as if mixed with phlegm—"I'm sure I can find a place to crash."

I am over the hump, Steve thinks gratefully, I have disarmed but not crushed my son. He will hang in like me . . . make it on his own.

Josh leaps up and says breezily, almost in an afterthought, "Can you spare some bread? I got a job lined up in Vermont."

"Sure thing," Steve says, reaching for his trousers. Turning the pockets inside out, he empties the contents onto the mattress: some singles, tens and twenties and change, including a new Kennedy coin.

Josh puts his hand down tentatively and picks up one, two, then a third single and the new coin. "Did I take too much?" he asks.

"No, no," Steve shouts and presses the tens and twenties into his palm. Josh tries to pull back, but his father curls his hand around the bills. Now their fists are tightly locked, Josh's clammy; Steve's hot. The embrace of flesh on flesh is total; their tremors reinforcing eath other's, their arms rigid to the shoulders.

Josh stuffs the bills into his shirtpocket. His face is chalk-white, his jaws clenched against tears. As for Steve, he is amazed at his cool. If he were to glance at the mirror, he thinks, the color of his eyes would be gun-shot metal, like Huey Newton's.

"Guess I'll be going," says Josh. "Give me a call real soon," Steve replies. "Stay well," says Josh. "You too," Steve says. "Keep out of trouble," Josh says. "Try my best," Steve says. "Love you, Dad," Josh says. "Likewise," Steve says. "Take good care," Josh says. "Will do," Steve replies. "Hold the fort," says Josh. No answer from Steve.

Josh slips on his parka, then his backpack. He stands without making a move. What is he waiting for, Steve wonders, a change of heart, a last-minute reprieve? They embrace briefly, lips brushing. Josh puts his hands on Steve's shoulders and pulls his father toward him. Steve feels himself melting under the petal touch. Without resisting, he lets his son wheel him around until their eyes meet.

"Dad," Josh says, as if they were back in the old days, "if you feel yourself slipping... no matter how deep down, no matter how heavy... realize that I am aware of what's happening." Steve tries to pull away but his son holds fast. "I knew you were in trouble," he says. "I was in touch with your negative energy. That's why I came—to be your spiritual guide, your healer, if you accept me!" His eyes are luminous with fervor. They seem to be floating in liquid flames, free from their sockets. "Have faith in me, Dad," he sings out, "believe that I can show you the way!"

Steve tears away from his son and stumbles backward, almost falling into the mattress. Josh opens the door and, stepping into the hall, skips three steps at a time down the stairs. Frantically, Steve lifts the windowblinds and looks down at the street.

He sees Josh standing shell-shock still, near the curb. For one moment, Josh glances up at the window, then turns away. He hesitates, shudders, lifts one leg, his weight hanging on the ball of the other foot—a giant, hump-backed frozen bird. What am I doing, Steve berates himself... have I gone out of my mind? There's time enough left to shout out, come home, Josh, please! I'll be a proper father and, yes, you can be my path, my way, my enlightenment!

Steve lifts the blinds higher and tugs open the stuck window. Leaning forward into the early night, he rehearses the words in his head: Josh, my son, forgive me! When he tries to call them out (later he will swear to himself how hard he tried), they stick in his throat.

He can see Josh, transfixed, without a will, waiting as if for a sound, a signal, a wind—anything, to point his way. Then swiftly his free leg comes down, he turns, walks down Sixth Avenue and disappears—will Steve see him again before he dies?—from the line of sight.

Steve takes in deep gulps of air, *prana, the breath of life,* and lets them slowly, rhythmically, out of his lungs. As Josh once taught him, he centers his rapt gaze on an imaginary candle glowing at the far end of the room. Swaying in gentle arcs from side to side, he empties his body and mind of all feeling.

Look in on Your Sister

I like to imagine I can tell from the ring of my telephone (its resonance, pitch, volume, intensity) whether or not Rachel is at the other end. It's a mad game, of course, but what's curious is the number of times I'm right. When anyone else phones, the sound is steady, evenly spaced out, inhumanly detached, as you would expect from normal people's. My sister's rings, however, seem to come in clusters of evil bells, each one more nerve-wracking than the one before. Between rings, each of the intervals becomes longer, so that—waiting—you feel your heartbeats stretching out filament thin, to the breaking point.

Almost always, Rachel telephones me after midnight, just as I'm about to tumble into that abyss of horror which of late has been my nightly sleep. At first I lie there semiconscious, trapped in an echo chamber of metallic jangles. Then, as the jolts persist, my left hand—an animal entirely on its own—finds the phone in the dark and hauls it over the blanket to my reluctant ear. Almost always, too, the sounds that greet me are not words but muffled caterwauls, as if her voice were wrapped in layer after layer of absorbent cotton.

"What is it, Rachel?" I speak with deliberate slowness into the phone. Fifteen years ago, when her crack-up (oh, that lovely word) began, I would listen to each call with utter paralysis, a rabbit waiting to be garroted in her words. After much practice, I have trained myself to listen temperately, even with insouciance. It is my mouth, however, that betrays me to myself. Dry and thick, the breath sticking like mucilage in my throat. Then, breaking over me, the torrent of her complaints:

"I want you to get that bastard Jerry"—her ex-husband—"put away where he belongs. You hear me, I want him in jail. You don't desert a woman and a sick child. Don't they have laws for pricks like him?"

Or: "Come right over, Robbie, this very minute. I can't get Susan"—her ten-year-old daughter—"to dress. She sits there staring at me, eating chocolates, waiting for them to take me away. Are you going to let her eat that crap for breakfast? Hell, you listening, Robbie, you listening?"

Or: "There's a rat trapped in the wall. He keeps running up and back, crying, so we can't sleep. You don't believe me? Here, Susan, tell your uncle we're not lying..."

Or, more quietly, her agonized voice humming high and dry over the wires. "Oh, my darling brother, what am I supposed to do with all these hours? Why did you let me piss away my life, why, why?"

Why did *I* let you piss your life away? Credit like that I don't need. You done it all by yourself, sister mine. After such brave beginnings too. Wunderkind of East New York. Cute as a button. Golden girl of the block. Papa's sveethartz, Mama's right hand with the housework. Public School 88, teacher's pet, most popular girl in the class one and the same time. Junior High 62, English, French, Typing medals. Thomas Jefferson High, valedictorian. Queens College, straight A's first three years. Perfect widdle baby sister. So seamless you slipped into puberty without a hint of tits. So invisible you never even hid a menstrual pad in our garbage pail. Hey, girl, how did you ever get the chutzpah to run real red blood down your legs?

So wha hoppen? I often ask the misty photo of you in your high school graduation gown, sweet as a lollipop, with your hair parted in the middle, forever immured in your last heyday as the girl most likely to succeed, before you gave up your promise in order to play nice girl, for which Mama had been grooming you all the while you were wasting your time winning honors and swallowing whole books at night like alcohol, writing little gems of term papers in your fine Spenserian handwriting Papa showed for the neighbors to oooh and ahhh at the precision, the letters flowing into words, the words into sentences dancing across the page gracefully to the tune of your fine mind. Oh, honeybun, it had to be nothing but downhill from then on in.

Why is my image of Rachel in the mid-fifties—the years just before I left home—so evanescent? Whole chunks of our ordinary life—what we talked about... whether I showed her affection... how she slipped overnight from a girl to a grown woman—seem to be fogged over by willful amnesia. The few memories of her that do remain are those etched in the track by the acid of small crises, silences, humiliations:

Rachel late one night trying to sneak a date into her room past the merciless eyes and ears of my mother. From the kitchen, I hear the door softly creaking open to admit a skeletally thin stretch of a young man—sandy-haired, goyish, nervously giggling. A wraith of a wire-haired Medusa in her white bathrobe storms into the living room. "Three in the morning you break into the house?" Mama greets the intruders.

"It's one, not three," parries my defiant sister. "Ma, I'd like you to meet Warren." Then, to soften Mama, she tosses her a scrap of information. "He's in my philosophy two class . . ."

Warren, ruffled, extends a gallant hand. But wait, it's his left hand, twisted awkwardly around to engage my mother's right hand. Motionless, Mama watches the gesture, then glances at his right hand. What she sees is a curl of crippled fist, hiding like a mouse halfway up his sleeve. Wheeling, Mama brushes past his hand and bangs the bedroom door shut behind her. Later, I hear Rachel and Mama hysterically raging at one another:

"Don't you ever do that again," my sister hisses. "Don't you ever humiliate a friend of mine again."

"Okay, then," my mother shoots back, from behind her unshakable code of what's right or wrong for her daughter, "then don't bring me home damaged goods three o'clock in the morning."

Rachel, in her cubicle of a room, slumped over the old Underwood, chain-smoking the afternoon away. The commingling of stale tobacco, cheap lilac perfume, a waft of her body. Overflowing the desk, piles of assorted books—Joyce, Gorky, Allen Tate, Jane Austen, Henry Miller, Marx, W.H. Auden. She types, as she conceptualizes, in quick spurts, furiously machine-gunning whole paragraphs at a stretch. Turning, she motions me in. "What do you think?" she asks, handing me a freshly typed sheet.

Glancing up, I see it's an overwrought diatribe against McCarthyism on her campus. "I didn't know you were such a hot-shot radical," I remark.

"Don't lecture me," she says sharply. "I asked for a criticism, not a personal evaluation."

Stung, I point to the crude bookshelves Papa built her, crammed with volumes of Marx, Lenin, Engels, Rosa Luxenburg, left periodicals and papers. "Be careful," I say, "these are rough times."

She swings around, one leg crossed over the other, and appraises me coolly. "My, my, brother, isn't it a little too early in life for a failure of nerve?"

I feel myself reddening. "Don't be so snotty, Rachel. Papa blew every last cent on your college career. That goddamned leaflet could get you blacklisted."

Her thin shoulders quiver; she bites down hard on her lips; she tries to breathe calmly. Between us is a volcano on the brink. Is this to be our first explosion? She thinks twice, spins in her chair and puts her head down on the desk. It strikes me that this tableau of Rachel, still life of a girl, her head buried in the coil of her arms on a summer's afternoon, is a metaphor of her utter vulnerability. Oh, "I could lie down like a tired child, and weep away the life of care . . ."

"In case you're interested," I say, "the leaflet is terrific." Then, I softly close the door behind me.

Me, at twenty-three, finally clearing out of the house for good. Rachel comes into my room as I'm packing. She rolls towels, underwear, socks, into tight little bundles. "So you're cutting out on baby sister," she says lightly.

"What's left for me here?" I ask.

"What's left for me?" she echoes.

"After you get your degree, you'll get a teaching job. Wait and see, it'll be a ball."

"God," she says, stroking my hair, "it'll be gruesome here without you."

"You'll visit me often," I assure her. "Hell, maybe we'll even become good friends."

As we pack in silence, the BMT train across the block roars by, setting the house atremble. "You'll be sorry," says Rachel. "Where else do you get free vibrations in your living room every twelve minutes on the hour?" The air seems to have gone dead in the wake of the passing train. Rachel sucks in a huge gulp of breath, as if she were trying to hold back a scream in her throat. Before I can draw away, she reaches over to enfold both my hands in hers. They lie there in her palms, hot and trembling, two living birds. She lets herself slide limply, like an empty rag doll, to her knees beside my bed.

"Rob," she cries, "help me, I'm in trouble!"

Firmly I free my hands and lay them on her shoulders. "C'mon, I say. "Things can't be that bad."

"Not that bad?" she mocks. "Wanna bet." Dumbly I wait. "Know what I am? I'm a scumbag, the kind you see floating in Canarsie Bay."

The intensity of her despair is palpable—it rises in waves. Curiously, I feel no pity for her, only loneliness—an old loneliness asleep in my bones she has just reawakened.

"Where do you suppose I go when I disappear nights at a time?" She flings the question at me with the force of a concussion.

As for me, I seem to be floating in the air, impenetrably frozen within a crystal cube. "Why lay this on me when I'm leaving," I ask in a querulous voice I can barely recognize as mine.

"Because you're my favorite—my one and only living brother," she answers.

"Christ," I say, touching her hair, "if I could help I would, but I'm way, way, over my own head."

Rachel gets up stiffly from the floor. She watches me frantically rearranging the clothes in my suitcase. There is not a trace of agitation left in her. "When I settle in, a couple of weeks from now, we'll talk," I say. "Maybe we can figure something out . . ."

She stares at me coldly, impaling my eyes with hers, and smoothes her hair. From her jacket, she hands me a brightly wrapped package. "Good luck, Rob," she says, and leaves abruptly.

A week goes by before I tear open the package in my new apartment. Inside is Rachel's deftly drawn sketch of me, staring disconsolately out of my window. On it is written in her impeccable script: "To my favorite, my one and only living brother. From Rachel with love."

Shortly after this episode, a bizarre telephone call awakens me in the middle of the night. "You Robert Weiss?" The voice is at the same time chummy and frightening.

"Yes," I say, "that's me. Anything wrong?"

"Yea, man, your fucked-up sister is in a hellava lot of trouble. Get your ass over quick," the voice instructs me, "and bring a bundle of cash. Mucho money."

"What's this," I say, "a gag or something?"

For a moment the connection breaks. I hear his voice shouting from afar. "Lady, do yourself a favor. Get your brother here—on the double, right?"

Rachel's voice comes over the phone, as I have never heard her, piping thin, quavery, a terrified child's. Not to ask questions, she begs me. Come quick, to a hotel (the name escapes me now) off Coney Island Avenue. She'll explain later, she says, please, brother, hurry!

I dress, take my last fifty dollars, grab a cab to Coney Island. All the way there, I fight down the ball of fire that burns in my chest whenever I feel physically threatened. Violent images flicker across the screen of my mind. Rachel, white belly up, raped and razored in bed. Rachel, a man with a stockinged head behind her, his hands around her throat. Rachel, on her back, legs open, a bunch of circus freaks taking turn. A flickering movie of me as a child, fishing for eels in Canarsie Bay. I feel a tug on the line, whoop with delight, only to pull up a condom that breaks with the weight of water as it surfaces. "Whitefish, comefish," my friends sing out, "Robbie's caught a scumfish."

I let the images race by until the screen behind my eyelids goes blank. Then, trembling, I force my eyes closed until I fall into a mindless, timeless, sightless semi-torpor the rest of the ride. It is a magic trick I discovered as a child to keep out the bad thoughts.

The hotel is bottom-of-the-barrel—a fleabag for derelicts, prostitutes, drunks. A bile-green lobby reeks of sour piss and Flit. Before I can ask, the clerk propped up behind the desk points a thumb upward. "Third floor, room sixteen," he barks.

I mount the stairs, heart cavorting wildly as I do. Standing before 16, I fight back the impulse to turn and run. Luckily my hand with a will of its own pushes open the door. I look in at a long coffin of a room, with a bed at the far end; a table near the door. On it is a crumpled heap of Rachel's clothes. As I step in, the bed seems to have retreated into the distance, as through the wrong end of binoculars. On the bed Rachel lies undressed, a dirty sheet wrapped around her. Beside my sister a huge, powerfully muscled man is draining a bottle of beer. Nude from the waist up, he wears jockey shorts and dirty white sneakers. Inexplicably, he has on long black stockings held up around his calves by elastic garters.

Seeing me, Rachel pulls the sheets over her tear-bloated face. Gently, almost with affection, the man uncovers her head and tousles her hair. "Ain't you glad to see your brother?" he asks. For the first time I see that a circle of broken beer bottles surrounds the bed. "She's a real kook, your sister," he says. "She tried to run out on me when I was sleeping."

"For God's sake," Rachel cries out, "get me out of here."

"You got no manners, girl," the thickset man says, "pickin' up strangers in bars, shakin' your ass, showin' your tits. You think it's nice," he addresses the question to me, "your sister talkin' dirty, leadin' me on, and not puttin' out?"

Rachel puts both hands over her eyes. She lets out a dry wrenching sob. From the corner of my eye I notice a short lead pipe leaning against the wall. With one move I could swoop it up, leap over the bottles and bash his head in like an eggshell. Meekly, I take the folded bills from my pocket.

"You know what they call girls like her," he continues, smiling broadly. "Tell her, Rob—that's your name, ain't it? Cockteaser. Ain't that right, Rob?"

I hold the bills out toward him. "How much you bring?" he asks.

I shuffle the fives and tens. "Fifty," I say.

He shakes his head playfully. "That's cheap, brother, real cheapo. You gettin' away with murder." He counts on his fingers. "Cab fare, dinner, beer, pretzels, hotel room. And you know what she tells me when we both strip down?" He raises his voice into a mocking squeal: "I'm scared, mister, I wanna go home. Lemme call my brother."

"She's sick, man," I shout, waving the money frantically. "Let her go!"

He tilts his head back, empties the bottle, breaks it on the radiator and throws it into the circle on the floor. Abruptly, he slips his arms around Rachel, lifts her and carries her toward me, the sheet trailing down his elastic garters. When he comes to the broken bottles, he motions for the money. I put the bills into his huge fist. I clear my throat and ask thickly: "Can I have a few bucks for a cab?"

"Fuck off, man," he shouts. "Take the goddam subway like the rest of us." With this, he dumps her into my arms, tearing the sheet from around her body. As I carry Rachel the few steps to the table, my eyes carefully averted from her nakedness, I am amazed at the lightness of her body. I put her down quickly near her clothes. I hear her feverishly dressing. On the bed the man seems to have lost interest in us. He lies back, staring at the ceiling, the bills unrolled beside him.

When we leave, I catch a last glimpse of him stretched out flat, one stockinged foot with the elastic neatly in place, dangling onto the floor. For a fleeting moment I visualize my own father, dressing for work, his long white stockings held snugly in place by elastic garters. For no reason that I can think of, it strikes me that the coincidence is of profound significance.

We sit side by side, wordlessly, all the way home on that hour-long subway ride. Every so often Rachel tries to slip her arm through mine. Each time I press my elbow against my body like a vise. I can feel her body brushing mine, then recoiling when I stiffen. Without turning, I can guess that her face is a mask hardened against her suffering. If I could, I would embrace her, comfort her, assure her the nightmare will dissolve in the morning. Instead, I stare stonily ahead, devouring the subway ads with murderous intensity. In this manner we hurtle through the dark tunnel, station by station. When we get to my home, a faint dawn light streaks the mouse-gray sky. Rachel falls into my bed, with her clothes on. I throw a blanket over her shivering form. In a few moments she is asleep.

I lie on the couch, my legs curling and uncurling to find a comfortable position. If I close my eyes, a procession of pictures dances by: Rachel on the soiled bed under the man's heavily muscled torso . . . the black triangle of pubic hair as he swung her nude into my arms . . . a swollen condom floating on the water. Suddenly a shock of rage jolts me. Damaged goods! Mama, did your chickens come home to roost. When I awaken, Rachel is gone, the blanket neatly folded. There is a brief note:

"Dear Rob: Thanks a zillion. I do what I do not because I want to, but because I need to. It's the only way I can feel anything. *P.S.* Not every little adventure of mine ends so sordidly. Bless you. Forgive me. Rachel."

These days Rachel rarely writes, calls or otherwise confides in me. I have to patch together, from a few strained conversations we do have, a portrait of my sister working hard at self-annihilation. I try not to think of her often—it frightens me, the poignancy of the old memories flooding back.

Periodically Papa reports on his daughter: She hangs around the house weeks at a time. Has stopped reading. Slumps around all day in rags. Mama is aghast at Rachel's descent into dishevelment. Her unkempt hair, chalk-white face, mismatched clothes. "*Mieskeit* (ugly one)," she rails, "once you had a personality. Now you forgot how to smile? Look at your cousin Esther. She got herself a permanent, dolled up like a painted bird, went Friday nights to socials. She smiled back when a young man smiled. What was she? . . . a nothing, a piece of spongecake plain. And you know what? She caught herself a live-wire husband—an accountant. You, fresh mouth, with your chain smoking and no nails. You think you're too good for boys?"

That winter Mama suffers a major stroke. When she returns from the hospital, her crystal-clear mind is completely fogged over. She sits up in bed, rubbing her hands together, calling out: "What time is it? Did my brother Itzig come back yet from the field?" I watch Rachel at her bedside, washing, feeding, tending this stranger, her mother. Eyes riveted on her face, Rachel floats over Mama on gauze wings, like a tender bird of prey. Feverishly she goads her on, throwing out associations, questions, stories, names.

"Please, missus," Mama pleads, "tell me the time."

"Never mind the time," Rachel answers. "You recognize us, don't you? I'm your daughter Rachel. That nice man is your husband Julius. And there's your favorite—your son Robbie."

Appalled, I say, "Let her be. You can't bring Mama back."

"She's doing it willfully," Rachel insists. "She's dying ahead of schedule out of sheer fucking spite."

A month later Mama is gone. Rachel shows up at the funeral dressed in a rainbow assortment of old clothes. "A regular gypsy," my mortified father whispers as we file past the body. In the Queens cemetery, Rachel wanders away from the open grave as the rabbi intones the burial prayers. She returns moments later with three strange women in mourning black, their eyes puffy with tears. They kneel, Rachel and the trio, while the body is being lowered. Their wails, bitter and piercing, shatter the muted air, drowning out the polite grief of the other mourners.

"Not yet, Mama," Rachel moans, leaning into the mouth of the hole to grab a handful of earth from the disappearing box. Two second cousins rush over to keep her from falling into the grave. After the earth has been patted down, Rachel opens her purse and divides a handful of bills among the professional mourners.

"One for each of Mama's dead sisters," Rachel explains, as we drive home in the long-finned limousine. "I chose the ones who look most like them. For sure," she adds, "Mama appreciates the gesture."

I observe her closely. There is no irony, no self-mocking in her voice. She's deadly serious. For the first time, the question occurs to me: Are you mad, my sister. Can it be you're really out of your mind?

A double blow. My father follows his wife, in a few weeks, with a massive coronary of his own. Before he dies, he arranges a secret meeting with me at the hospital. "Do I have to tell you," he asks, through the tubes dangling from his nose, "something has gone wrong with Rachel? She's mental—a very disturbed girl. Was I born yesterday? Don't I know about the nights she stays away? The bums she goes with? Swear to me, Robbie, you'll look in on your sister once in a while. An orphan, a skinny girl who cries her eyes out through the wall?" "Okay, Pop," I assure him. "I'll look in. I swear." It's the last time I see him alive.

It's startling, the domestication of Rachel the wild, in a few short years. Evidently she took Mama's advice seriously: Dolled up, went to a bar, smiled and hooked a husband. A graduate student in mechanical engineering. Maybe not as live a wire as an accountant; still, considering everything, not half bad. They have a linen shower, a Sunday afternoon wedding on the Island, set up home sweet home in Rego Park. A few years later, she has a child—Susan. To Rachel I remain a distant brother; for Susan, an invisible uncle.

I receive an upsetting letter from Rachel's neighbor: "My heart goes out for your sister. Poor girl, she wanders around night after night, while her kid's alone in the house. She has no friends, no money. Right now the electricity is off. Worst is Jerry, her husband. He used to screw anything in skirts. Now he's got a blonde spring chicken from the Island. Believe me, he's about to dump Rachel. Everybody knows but her. Somebody should tell your sister, How about you?"

It's excruciating, getting involved again. I swore on the Bible I never would. Instead, I call Jerry at his office. Opening gambit: He blusters and denies. Who told you that garbage? Stage Two: He shifts to domestic tragedy. We haven't slept together for a year. Being with her is a living hell. She's poisoned my kid against me. New tack: He mollifies. Not to worry about child support. We both deserve a crack at happiness. She's better off without me. Upshot: He and Grace—his new love—are flying to Mexico for a divorce. I counterattack: Just like that, you run out on your wife and kid without even a note. One man to another: Try to understand, Rob. She's off the wall. It's my skin or hers. Coup de grace: Jerry, you cocksucking deserter, someone ought to blow your lying balls off.

That night, when I get to Rego Park, Rachel's garden apartment is dimly lit with candles. We hug, the pain of it after so long an absence almost too primal to bear. Sitting beside me in a broken chair, Rachel runs on nonstop about her existence: "It's the pits, dullsville—but all we can afford." Even in the semidark I can see that despondency has ravaged her face. "Jerr's away most of the time working. Susan and I"—her head is a metronome falling from side to side—like my mother praying, "we're two animals by ourselves in a cage . . . biting, scratching, picking lice. We've hurt each other too much. It's too late." She lifts her arms toward a closed door. "Susan baby, a little space? A nice black hole for mommy?"

In the gloom the apartment—with its clutter of boxes, its furniture in disarray, is a blur of chaos. I have the impression nothing was—or will ever be—unpacked. "What happened to the lights?" I ask.

"You know how I am," she answers. "A total mess with bills."

"Come off it, sis," I say gently. "Why not admit it? Jerry gives you barely enough to live on."

"No," she pleads. "It's me, the world's worst housewife. Really, he's very generous."

"Leave us not lie," I press on. Better get it over with quickly. "When was the last time you slept with your husband?"

Her huge eyes float out toward me into the darkness. Without meaning to, I turn away.

"You want to punish me?" she asks. "Step on me like a rag?"

"No," I say. "Just get you to stop conning yourself."

In one movement she crosses her arms, pulls her shoulders together and doubles over, as if to crawl into her own lap. She lies there, her whole body shaking. Why did I swear, why did I promise Papa to look in on his daughter? I can still pull out, make some excuse, let her sink by herself. I lay my hand lightly on her shoulder.

"Why did you come?" she says. "We don't need you, Jerry and I, we're doing fine." Somehow she goads me on, my sister the hausfrau, little loyal patsy, Jerry's dishrag, breakdown kid, everybody's easy lay. A demon has taken me over! I'm afire with rage . . . the ill tidings I bear are burning to be told—

"Listen, dreamboat," I spit out. "There is no Jerry and you. There is no happy family. No home sweet home. Your husband is cutting out, that bastard, for a new love. Bye bye? On a plane? For Mexico? You hear me, am I getting through?"

Rachel raises her head. Her voice is disconcertingly calm. "The time of darkness is past," she recites, "the winter solstice brings the victory of light. After a time of decay comes the turning point." Her eyes are luminous with belief.

"What the hell are you talking about?" I say.

"These were dark lines," she intones. "Misfortune from within and without. Selfish tendencies . . . separation . . . mistakes. I threw the I Ching, Robbie, and the judgment told me: 'It's the turning point' . . . for Jerry and me." She fumbles for a book on the table, and holds it out open toward me. "You listen, Rob, you listen. 'The powerful light that has been banished returns. After illness comes health; after estrangement comes understanding. Everything must be treated with tenderness and care, so that the return may be a flowering.' "

Her voice has taken on a messianic ring. A mechanical smile holds up the corners of her mouth. I hear my heart thumping violently. It wouldn't take much for me to sink to my knees and puke.

"Oh, Rob, we weren't tender enough. Jerry and I didn't make a caring home." She folds the book ecstatically to her breast. "You'll see, Rob. I'll find the strength to pull myself together. Keep the house ship-shape, neat, in place, the way Jerry loves it." She waltzes lightly around the room, pushing her path through the boxes, her hands dusting off the disordered piles. When she reaches the closet, she slides the door open. Inside a panoply of Jerry's clothes—suits, sports jackets, coats, ties, immaculately tailored, are lined up stiffly like martinets. Rachel unfolds a box of freshly laundered shirts, fingering the collars lovingly. "A place for everything," she sings out, "and everything in its place."

Out of the blue, a picture leaps to my mind: Jerry in a hotel suite, his spotless shirt, suit, underwear scattered on the floor, humping away at his little blonde suburbanite.

I leap across the room at Rachel, tear the shirts from her hands, hurling her backward into the closet. Down come the crossbars, the suits, ties, sweaters sliding from hangers into a tangled heap. I dismember the shirt in my hand, ripping his neck open, his chest apart, his arms off, his waist into shreds. Rachel is at me with a roar. She beats at me with one fist, opening the other to scratch a bloody gash across my face with her nails.

Rachel's screams bring her daughter running from her bed. I hear Susan sobbing in a thin, sleepy voice: "You're scaring Mommy, Uncle Rob. Leave us alone."

As suddenly as it rose, the fury between us dies. Rachel and Susan lie back on the fallen clothes. I open my palms to let a strip of shirt fall to the floor. They watch me wordlessly. Before I leave, I empty whatever money I have in my wallet onto the table. Rachel opens the door behind me and hurls the dollar bills into my face.

I stand for a moment in the patio, listening to the sounds inside. "It's all right, angel," Rachel croons. "We don't need them—not Grandpa, not Uncle Robbie, not Jerry, not God. We have each other."

"I want my daddy, I want my daddy," Susan cries out. Her noises, convulsive, unrelenting, drift out at me through the door. Turning, my cheek aflame with the pain of the wound, I stumble away from her keenings into the night.

Fifteen years now she's been falling apart. Some track record, eh? God knows, I've made every effort to keep her away from my two wives, my children, the woman I live with now. As for me, I've tried to quarantine her as much as possible, avoid getting ensnared, do the minimum I can as a decent brother. How come, then, for all of my efforts, she manages—present or absent—to insinuate herself into every pore of my being?

Take the matter of her midnight crises: if it isn't one, it's the other.

Example: Susan decides at twelve to live with her father and stepmother. That very night Rachel's at me, howling over the wires: No hellos. No how-are-you's. Not even an Oh, Rob! Only a relentless cascade of lamentation that swirls me helplessly into the vortex of her panic. "Little bitch," she rants. "Jerry's girl, opportunist, cutting out on me when it suits her purpose, same as her traitorous father." When I calm her down, frenzy gives way to self-blame, self-blame to terror at being alone. "What am I without her, Rob? A nothing living with a nobody."

"Don't worry," I say. "We'll work something out." The words take me by surprise. Why this big brother bluster? I have nothing in mind. Too late—she leaps at the live bait:

"You'll stay with me a while? Be my friend, like you once promised?" The woman who is my current love tugs at my sleeve. "Don't get involved," she whispers. "It's no use." Quickly, I pull my arm away.

"How will I ever make it?" Rachel says. "The days are ghastly enough. Imagine the nights? Do you know what twenty-four hours add up to? I figured it out once. Fourteen hundred and forty minutes. Eighty-six thousand, four hundred seconds. God, Rob, I'm already stretched paper thin. What am I supposed to do with all that time? Drown in it?"

I hear in my voice the timbre of my mother's contempt: "You don't know what to do? I'll tell you. You get up, you wash, you dress, you eat, you laugh, you cry, once in a while you breathe, you go to work, you come home, you talk, you yawn, you sleep, you dream, you wake up, you start all over again. Simple, isn't it, Rachel?"

"Please, Rob," she begs, "Don't make fun of me. You'll come over, sleep here, watch TV. We'll talk the way we used to. Whatever you say, I'll do, whatever you want. Only don't let me be by myself."

What I despise . . . what I dread most about Rachel . . . she's a master of. Emptying herself of pride—abandoning to me without shame the last remnants of her will. For this, she is beyond forgiving. I breathe in deeply, hold it as long as I can, to quiet the spasm in my gut. "Take two valiums," I command. "Rock yourself to sleep. In the morning we'll talk."

These days my woman friend complains I'm in a very bad place—not fit, she insists, to be lived with. Why don't I see an analyst she's heard good things about? I myself don't see the point of therapy—in any shape, form or fashion. To me the idea of a grown man confessing his intimacies to a paid listener is ludicrous—of no value whatever. If

I do see the analyst—and one session at that—it's only to placate my lover. That is the sole reason I find myself in a chic apartment in the East Seventies.

The analyst is a handsome woman, radiantly tanned, in her late thirties—and very, very pregnant. Some masks, clay fragments, a silver chalice are hanging on the wall. On the floor—between the chairs—is an exquisite Persian rug. Every piece of furnishing—this I recall distinctly—has been chosen to create a low-key elegant decor.

Right off, facing her blonde, unflinching gaze, I draw a blank. I just sit there, forever it seems, staring ahead, overcome with drowsiness. Out of embarassment, I try to dredge something up to break the impasse.

"Really," I say, "I can't think of anything special to say. There's no crisis. No burning problems. Nothing I can't handle. I probably shouldn't even be here."

"Is that how you feel?" she asks.

"Well," I say. "Maybe I am a little low lately. But, then again, who isn't at one time or another?"

"Is that what you think?" she asks. Her lips are slightly parted, revealing two flawless rows of teeth. At the flash of white, Rachel's teeth float into mind—pulled, decaying, root canals, gold caps loose and leaky.

"My sister's mouth is a disaster area," I blurt out. Immediately I regret the remark. "I can't imagine," I say, "why I should have brought Rachel up."

She leans forward, playing with her thin wedding band. "Why do you think you did?"

I push the question aside. "I suppose," I say, "I should talk about my own life. Isn't that the point of therapy?"

"What do you think the point is?"

"I'm not sure there is any," I say sullenly. And then silence again. Finally, I say, "There's not much to tell. I'm sixty, twice married, both washouts. I have two kids, on their own. Technically I'm what you might call a supportive father. Actually, I'm not the daddy type. I know it, they do too. We keep our distance." She peers at me expectantly. "Should I go on?" I ask. "Is this doing you any good? Or me, for that matter?"

"What do you think?" she asks.

I'm tempted to answer, "I think it's a fucking waste of time." What I do say is, "What's so significant about a marginal character like me shooting off his mouth?"

"Is that how you see yourself?"

Her questions infuriate me. "Hell, no," I flare up. "I'm a freelance indexer. A pro . . . one of the best. With me, making an index is an art." I can sense her perking up, all attention. It excites me that she's hanging on to every word.

"Without an index," I lecture, "any book—even the best—is not organized, not complete. That's my skill—to take a raw set of facts, to extrapolate the essence, and pin it down on index cards."

I'm showboating. It's clear what I'm going on about hasn't the slightest relevance. But I can't stop myself: "When I'm finished, everything's arranged, categorized, unified. My index, the backbone, the structure, a to z, in perfect order!"

Abashed at my grandiosity, I slump back into my chair. "An anal personality," I remark limply. "A compulsive hoarder of facts. Isn't that what you call my type?"

"What do you think," she says.

"Better anal," I snap at her, "better to hold back, than to pour your shit out, messing up everything, everyone in sight."

"Is someone doing that to you?" she asks softly.

Before I can control the words, they're out: "Yes, it's my sister."

"Is that why you're here?" she presses on. "To discuss your sister?"

"No," I groan. "I want no part of my sister. Enough, I had it up to here with her depressions . . . her crying jags . . . her paralyses. Sick, I'm sick to death of her self-pity. The way she sucks up to perfect strangers for a few nice words . . ."

"Is that how you feel?" she asks.

Rachel's piss-stained face rises up before me, her head tilted, her black eyes pleading, promiscuous as a beggar's cup. "Can you understand what it's been like?" I shout, "seeing her latch on to anyone who will listen—children, old people, drunks, bagwomen, loonies. Wherever she can—in bars, subways, streets, elevators, yes, toilets too. How do you think I feel lying in bed, knowing she's out at night licking around, hanging on to someone's neck, spilling her guts out to some poor sucker she's hooked. Yes, and the guys she ends up with, screwing them for a pat on the head, a little sympathy."

When I open my eyes—have I been in a hypnotic trance?—my fists are clenched, my body is shivering. If I let go, something terrifying will happen. My skeleton will collapse. I'll pour out on the ground through my own membranes . . .

My eyes meet the analyst's. Hers peer back at me brown, bright, tender. It would take only the merest movement to melt me—a flutter of her eyelid, a turn of the head, a hand extended, one word. I see myself on my hands and knees, crawling toward her. She reaches down to stroke my hair, the unfamiliar gentleness of her fingers, the animal sounds of my grief pouring through the plaster cracks, her voice caressing me back from numbness, calling me, Robbie, back to life...

Do you read me, Doctor, will you pillow me in your lap, let me sink into the mother softness of your belly? Cradle me, Doctor, in your brown bare arms? ...

I've stepped out of my skin. There is nothing to hold me together but you. Undone, Doctor, on the brink, ready to grovel, lick it up, spill my guts, suck around... if you give me the sign.

In one spasmodic gesture, I turn my palms down and thrust them toward her. They hang, for a split second, vibrating on their own, in space. Instinctively, she pulls back, into her chair, her breath drawn in.

I lower my arms, put my skin back on, and sit up alertly. The room comes back into focus. She tugs nervously at her sleek ponytail. Shifts her feet. Straightens her skirt. She is unruffled again—all in one piece. It galls me—she and her flawless room, married to one another. I take them to be personal affronts.

I get up stiffly, reach into my suit pocket and pull out my wallet. "How much do I owe you?" I ask.

"You still have another thirty minutes," she says. I take some bills out of the wallet. "I don't think you should leave now."

"How much?" I repeat. "Fifty dollars," she says.

"Was it something I said—or did?" she asks.

I place five ten-dollar bills on her desk. Turning toward her, I say as pleasantly as I can, "Is that what you think?"—and walk out the door.

Somehow or other, as the weeks and months go by, Rachel manages to hang in by herself through each of the 86,400 seconds of the day. "Would you believe it, brother," she calls to tell me, "the fog is actually lifting. When I looked at myself in the mirror, I said, 'Who is this zombie, where has she been?'" Miraculously, Rachel explains, she rediscovers the movies, the taste of food, how wind feels in her face, that plants die unless you water them. She scans the piles of newspapers in her house, realizes that history has been happening without her all this while. "I know we've got this asshole for a president—Richard Nixon. But fill me in, Rob," she says, "who the hell is vice president—John Nance Garner?"

Not much of a joke. Still we roar with laughter at the sheer wonder of not being our sad and usual selves. "Look at me," she mocks, "don't

I sound exactly like a normal person?" Hearing her chat away so blithely, it dawns on me that for all these years of her exile I have done nothing but bully, chide, humiliate, condescend, rail at or pity my sister. At this moment I haven't the faintest idea of how to treat her as an equal. It shouldn't be hard for me to learn. I could say, Rachel, love, from now on things are going to be different between us. Instead, I blurt out awkwardly, "You're doing great, kid; one of these days we ought to get together just for the hell of it."

I feel myself being pulled into the dead silence at the other end. Then I hear a sharp intake of breath, as if Rachel is trying to hold together the fragments of her that keep breaking apart.

"It's not necessary," she says. "I'm doing just fine."

"No, no," I insist. "I'm free tonight. Is it okay if I come over?"

"Sure you want to?" she asks.

"Sure, I'm sure," I banter, "if you're sure."

We laugh tentatively, each of us uneasy with our new roles.

That evening, Rachel, did it begin as self-consciously for you as it did for me? You were wearing a new dress—the first you had dared to buy on your own in years. It was turquoise-blue, a color—I had always warned you—that brought out the sallow in your complexion. There was a bare suggestion of transparent gloss on your lips. You had added one new decorative note—a sparkle of gold-and-purple glitter on your eyelids. As shyly as if we were on our first date, I held out a bottle of wine for your approval. I remember how you blushed when I placed it on the table. Unexpectedly, it was set for dinner—sweet and sour shrimp, I think. You had served the meal in Mama's blue dishes, the ones you had saved as mementos, together with those of her clothes you could cram into the still-unopened boxes cluttering up the room.

At first everything seemed—at least to me—stilted, somewhat of a farce, the way we chewed the food and drank the wine with lugubrious deliberation. There were long silences one could drive a truck through. When you finally did speak, did it strike you as odd that I listened and weighed your every word carefully instead of overriding you with my usual torrent of ironic commentary, judgment and disdain? If you noticed the difference, did you have any idea that I had changed my pattern with you in honor of your new start . . . because I wanted to relate on this occasion as I had not been able to in the past?

Later, when we sipped wine on the couch, listening to scratchy records of fifties pop tunes, our reserve melted entirely away. Nat King Cole, Frank Sinatra, Patti Page . . . you followed their love lyrics aloud, word for word, sighing and swaying like a teen-ager at a pillow party. How could you ever get through the nights, you told me, without these oldies? You pulled me up from the couch to dance. We stood in one spot shuffling our feet rhythmically. Then you raised your arms high above your head, did a charming two-step of your own, and sang in a surprisingly affecting voice:

> The wind is blowing, the snow is snowing;
> But I can weather the storm.
> What do I care if icicles form;
> I've got my love to keep me warm.

God, your eyes were glistening! It was like watching a rerun of you at seventeen carrying on like wild at one of the rare boy-girl parties Mama let you give in our house. "I can weather the storm?" Maybe the words were prescient. You were, after all, barely forty, still attractive, smart, full of spunk and fire. Before I could control my words, they were out of my mouth:

"Rachel, why don't you let me help you redo your place? We'll clean it up, get some shelves, furniture, rugs." I kicked at one of the tumorous growths of yellowing newspapers—*Sunday Times, New Yorker, Life Magazine, New Republic*—that were heaped along the walls. "First thing," I said, "we'll throw these out. They're starting to rot."

Half-serious, half-playful, you leaned over to embrace the pile of papers. "No, no, Rob," you cried out, "I haven't gone through them yet. Know how many unread years of my life they represent?"

If I heard the alarm in your voice, I was too far gone to stop. In my head I already saw the room neatly decorated, you clicking away at the typewriter, the books lined up on their shelves. On a sudden impulse, I lifted one of the sealed boxes onto the couch and tore away the tape. The cover was marked "English Literature." Taking out a few books I opened one at random and read aloud:

> I wandered lonely as a cloud,
> That floats on high o'er vales and hills,
> When all at once I saw a crowd,
> A host, of golden daffodils.

"Who wrote that poem?" I asked you. Hands over your ears, you shrank bank into the couch.

"I haven't read a book for fifteen years," you wailed. "There's nothing but sawdust in my head."

"Just think hard," I said. "It'll come back."

"Golden daffodils, golden daffodils," you repeated. You put your palms together and stretched your hands out before you, as if in prayer. In a second the answer flashed into your inner eye. "Wordsworth," you yelled, "William Wordsworth!" Both of us together—we let out a roar of triumph.

"Beginner's luck," you purred, pleased as could be with yourself. "Let's quit while I'm ahead."

I ignored you and turned to another page. "Ah, here's another one you should eat up like pie."

"Do I have to?" you said, but now you were all attention, a whippet eager to go. I spoke very slowly, pronouncing each syllable:

> Heard melodies are sweet, but those unheard
> are sweeter. Therefore, ye soft pipers, play on,
> not to the sensual ear, but, more endeared,
> pipe to the spirit ditties of no tone.

"Wait, wait," you said, "I should know that!" And again it came to you, out of some residue of memory you thought forever gone. "John Keats, of course," you shouted. "Ode on a Grecian Urn."

"Right on both counts," I said. We hugged each other, giddy with success.

Do you recall how revved up you were, Rachel, how you urged me: "Try something harder, Rob, more modern!"

"Okay," I said. "Finish my next quotation, give me the name of the poem—and the author:

> I have heard the sea nymphs singing each to each . . .

Without so much as a wink of hesitation you called out: "I do not think that they will sing to me! It's from the poem 'Prufrock'—a satiric portrayal of spiritual emptiness in contemporary society, by Thomas Stearns Eliot."

After that, Rachel, I wouldn't let up. I hurled the questions at you one after another, and you threw the answers right back at me, hardly missing a quotation. It was as if I had opened a sluice in your head.

We lost all track of the hour. One by one the overlays through which I had for so long perceived you darkly had fallen away. Before me was Papa's golden girl again, bursting to show teacher what a straight A student was like. When I looked up, it was time to go. The books were scattered over the floor, the dishes still on the table. We were a little drunk, both of us, reluctant to end the night. You helped me on with my coat, we clasped hands, leaned back and circled the floor in a sarabande of love. You were glowing, Rachel, as happy as I had ever seen you. I held my hand out, finger pointing at you sternly. "Young woman," I said, "can you identify the author of this astonishing statement?"

In the midst of our laughter we discovered that we were happy.

You stood silently, lowering your head before you answered: "It was Gertrude Stein."

Maybe I should have said good night then and there, but I realized this was the moment that had to be seized—now or never. "Rachel," I said, "Hear me out. They need English teachers bad. You have a degree, courses in ed, a good basic background. You saw that for yourself. We'll get some review books, I'll study with you every day. In five or six months, you'll pass the emergency exam in a breeze. What do you think?"

I suppose on one level I believed that what I was saying was in the realm of the possible. I might have even thought at the time that my suggestion was irresistible. In any event, I never did get an answer to my question.

Without saying a word, you got on your knees, painstakingly collected the books and slid them back into the box from which I had taken them. I saw the tears splashing down your cheeks and heard the terrible sound of your weeping. When I reached out to touch you, you pulled away sharply.

"Why do I keep these stupid books around?" you said to no one in particular. "They only mess up the room." That was the last time, Rachel, you or I ever mentioned the subject again.

Rachel has worn me to a frazzle. Her plunges into despair are too deep, too hopeless; her demands more and more incoherent. Worst of all are the frequent episodes from which I can no longer rescue her—the last one even more unnerving than the rest.

Until recently Rachel has been working at temporary office jobs in marginal companies as a means of augmenting her welfare checks and the little extra I can spare. Invariably she is fired—despite her remarkably intact typing skills—within a few days or weeks when her crying bouts, outbursts or pouring her woes on anyone she can collar disrupt the office.

Not too long ago I get this call from a co-worker at her final job—a group of orthodox rabbis who collect charity for Jewish orphans. "Your sister complains," the woman informs me, "that she feels completely abandoned. Can't you find it in your heart to comfort her?"

"My sister is also a Jewish orphan," I answer, surprising myself with my spontaneous venom. "Let your rabbis find it in their hearts to comfort her."

The next call is, however, too distressing for me to ignore. Rachel has locked herself into the storeroom, poured coffee into the file cabinets, and is heaping abuse on the chief rabbi. "Make your sister open the door," the bearded patriarch shouts at me when I arrive, "before the guards arrest her."

Though I persuade her to come out, Rachel is still defiant. "Think you can buy me," she rants at the rabbi, "like one of your little religious slaves at three dollars an hour! . . . Get you your coffee . . . type your asinine memos . . . listen to your pompous lectures. Not me, you asshole."

"Watch your tongue, lady," warns the rabbi. "You should be put away."

"Please, Rachel," I say meekly, "there's no point getting upset."

"You, you worm," she turns on me her withering scorn. "You're no better than the rest. How can you let those bigots get away with it. . . Making Mama sit in the balcony while they beat their hypocritical breasts down there praying away to Mr. God. Who are you to tell me I'm inferior, I'm dirty when I bleed, not fit to sleep with." She jabs a finger at the rabbi: "You fat-assed pervert, feeling me up, getting a good look down my tits . . ."

When the guards lift her up bodily, I try to pry her away. They grab me by the scruff of my neck. They carry both of us down the stairs, along the length of the hallway, and out into the street. The force of their push sends us sprawling to the sidewalk. We lie there stunned, a crowd gathering around us to stare. I lift Rachel from the ground with as much dignity as I can muster and hurry us into the first passing cab. She sits back quietly, the fight gone out of her, aware now that she has overstepped even her bounds. My well has run bone-dry. Finally, I know it. In her heart, I think Rachel knows it too.

For a short while Rachel's telephoning stops—out of fear of me, I guess. At first, I luxuriate in the absence of her shrill voice. After a few days, however, the silence becomes menacing—even more than the rings. I never realized before how hooked I am on the expectation of the one phone call that will desolate and deliver me at the same time.

No such clear-cut announcement arrives—only an intimation in the form of a letter in which are enclosed four index cards, inscribed respectively in Rachel's beautifully chiselled script: "A. *Arsenic,* as in "Arsenic and Old Lace." Uch! I couldn't stand the taste of it. B. *Blood,* as in cutting my wrists. Hell no, I faint at the sight of the stuff. C. *Cyanide.* What! And be my own holocaust! D. *Drowning.* And have to watch my dreary life flash by a second time? That's all for now. Any better suggestions, brother?"

When I get to her house, I see that Rachel has let it fall into total disorder. In the kitchen roaches are swarming over the unwashed dishes. An acrid stench of cat's urine hangs in the living room, which is overwhelmed with furniture, boxes, papers. Rachel, in a torn nightgown, lies in bed, the curtains tightly drawn.

The moment I put on the light she greets me with a "Hi, Rob," and a wave of her arm. The animation of her welcome is so unearned, it disconcerts, even infuriates me. On the bed is an open container with all of the prescription drugs she has ever tried—tranquillizers, anti-depressants, sleeping pills, mood stabilizers, downers. "Oh, don't give it a thought," she purrs. "Pills are definitely not my thing. I'd only throw up." Watching her closely, fascinated by the absurd energy of the performance, I find myself unable to come up with a coherent reply.

Beside her on the floor, Rachel has neatly arranged a circle of index cards in alphabetical order, some written on, others only with a large question mark. "I'm so glad you came, Rob," she says. "I need your expert advice." She slides into the center of the circle on her knees and begins to read the cards: *"A,B,C,D,* you already know. *E,* all I can come up with is *Euthanasia.* F. *Freezing* to death. G. *Gassing. H? I?"* Rachel turns to a sitting position, holds the cards up to me and asks: "Clue me in, my clever brother. You know what a coward I am. Give me a perfectly painless way."

As she rattles on airily, it occurs to me there is a good reason why I am not horrified. The truth is I have—fleetingly, to be sure—allowed myself the thought of Rachel's suicide many, many times. I have—all the while appalled at myself—rehearsed the exact moment of receiving the news: the initial shock, No, no! . . . the numbing grief, Oh my darling sister . . . the rush of elation, at last, I'm free!

Without a word I gather the cards, tear them up by twos and threes, and toss them disdainfully into the corner. I slide down heavily into a torn slingchair. By now, Rachel has come down catastrophically from her high. She squats on her knees, shaking back and forth, her hands clasped tightly, bowing in my direction. The noonday sun frames her cruelly, lighting up the black pouches under her eyes, the chinline eroded by fat, the lips limp, fallen open and twisted. I notice for the first time it is a torrid day. I am sweating profusely.

"What do you want me to do?" she asks, her words more supplication than question.

"Whatever you want," I reply, not unkindly.

My answer frightens her. She will accept anything from me gratefully—like a faithful dog—so long as I give her explicit orders.

I lean back and close my eyes. In the darkness I have made for myself I am as walled off from Rachel as I ever have been. I could sleep forever with a pillow shielding my head.

Rachel begins to sniffle, fighting to hold back her tears. I feel no pity at all. If I have any emotions, they are muted, subliminal, stupefied almost to zero. It bothers me, the way my mind insists on drifting along in slow motion. Shouldn't I be considering the options that remain? But why can't I face it? There aren't any left. She has gone to, thrown herself at, sworn by, badgered, denounced, and eventually discarded a small army of analysts, psychiatrists, social workers, group therapists, masseurs, healers, even layers-on of hands. She has hallucinated, had the shakes over, vomited, hyperventilated, been reduced to apathy or somnolence by a whole spectrum of drugs. We have spent, Rachel and I, lunatic midnights in emergency clinics, sprawled on hard benches with the addicts and knife-wounds, the weirdos and lonelies. I have walked off her hysteria, talked her out of paranoia in all-night diners, kept her company night after insomniac night. We've come to the end of the road, Rob, the options are closed. It's all over now, baby blue.

When I open my eyes, my mind is made up. "Rachel," I say, "there's nothing more I can do. Serious or not," I point to the cards, "I can't take a chance. You're better off in an institution."

"No, Rob," she cries out. "I don't belong in the cuckoo's nest. It's for real crazies!" *One Flew Over the Cuckoo's Nest*—it's an old joke between us. Rachel wept through the whole movie when we watched it together on the late show. After the scene where the Indian died, she kissed my hands and made me promise, word of honor, I would never commit her against her will.

"Why don't you let me finish what I started," she says. "I'd be better off dead." But there's no real conviction in her words. I can see she'll go like a lamb.

The arrangements are easier than I imagined. It's a semi-private institution outside of Yonkers. Excellent staff, the psychiatrist assures me, lovely grounds. Bring your sister as soon as you can. All through the packing, the long subway trip and the cab ride, Rachel doesn't betray a hint of apprehension. At the hospital she seems quite disoriented. She turns from me, without protest, when they take her off for an examination.

While she's gone, I wander through the public spaces for the inmates. In the parklike enclosure they sit around reading, playing checkers, rocking quietly on the patio. A man throws pebbles into the pond. Two visitors console a distraught woman. I pass another woman painting a childlike picture of bright flowers, with puffs of clouds and a huge sun in the background. The sun, I notice, has its mouth wide open, showing jagged blood-red teeth.

It bothers me vaguely, this omen, yet there's nothing, I tell myself, to give the slightest cause for regretting my decision. Why is it, then, I have this naggy feeling something is askew? It's the solitariness of the patients. The way this one lets his hand fall in a gesture of renunciation; and that one stares into his own emptiness, a slow dying-away in his eyes.

And of course not a drop of breeze on this burning day. Certainly this can't be faulted. Only, why this feeling of suspension that I have, people holding their breath, the wind motionless—no, lobotomized! Of course this morbidity on my part, it's guilt, overreacting, looking for flaws, it's perfectly natural. Rachel will have the best of care . . . she'll rest . . . be out in no time.

As I walk back to the office, the scene that opens up before me is curiously familiar: the people standing around in peaceful clusters, the long rows of trees on either side, the haze of light dappled yellow and green. Of course, a Seurat painting—holiday in the park. Without warning, the woman painter hurls the canvas to the grass, poking at it furiously with her brush. Two attendants amble over, put their arms around her and lead her away. The canvas of painted flowers lies undisturbed on the real flowers, which bend under the weight. Seurat? Yes. Something amiss though. Not a holiday in the park. A day like all the others, in a garden of cuckoos.

In the office Rachel slouches on the bench in a white-hot fury. She holds on tenaciously to her bag of clothes when a nurse tries to cajole it from her. Behind the desk—the lemon sun pouring over her shoulders—the superintendent reads a sheaf of papers. She looks up and says, pleasantly but all business, there seems to be no reason why you shouldn't sign the papers. Are there any questions?

At the sound of her voice, so official, so irrevocable, my sister opens her mouth to let fly out a savage shout. It falls like glass on the air, shattering the placidity of the scene. I had hoped that Rachel would be a compliant girl, letting me off with a few tears and hurried goodbyes. But no, I will not be allowed to walk away from her abandonment, with Rachel shuffling off under the wing of the nurse.

Rachel is up from the bench, stomping from one foot to the other. "If you leave me here, Rob, you'll come back to a vegetable." Her words are singsong, mocking, icy with threat. "What kind of vegetable would suit me best, brother dear?"

"Calm down," says the nurse, reaching out for her hands. My sister pulls away sharply and backs off, her tirade unabated:

"How about a carrot, Robbie, grated, sliced, boiled, soaked till I'm all mush?" The images, so cruel, so funny, so apt, pour effortlessly out of her feverish mind: "An onion, maybe, wilted, weepy, slimy as snot, like me? . . . Better yet, Rob, your favorite, fresh asparagus, au jus, smothered in cream sauce. You could eat me up alive, mmmmm, couldn't you, brother?"

"They sometimes act up like this," the superintendent assures me. "She'll be fine as soon as you leave."

The nurse is behind Rachel, holding her firmly around the waist. "Where do I sign?" I ask. The superintendent marks an *X* on several sheets. I glance up to see that Rachel has run out of defiance. She sags limply into the nurse's arms—like a vegetable, the thought occurs.

"Sign me in," she sobs, "and don't ever bother to come back."

"Shouldn't I read the fine print?" I ask.

"It's routine," says the woman behind the desk.

I pick up a pen. A moist gray film has formed over my eyes, obscuring the print on the papers. "If anything should happen," I ask, "will you call me immediately . . . ask for my permission?"

"I'm not clear what you mean," she says.

"Well"—a stream of clichés leap from my mouth—"shock treatment, a straightjacket, thorazine, lobotomy . . ."

She puts both palms firmly onto the desk. "Our staff is superbly trained," she says. "They use the utmost discretion."

"Maybe so," I persist, "I still want the right to give permission."

"We use standard procedure." Her tone has turned doctoral—edgy with impatience. "Emergencies can come up at any time. We can't always wait for approval."

"I'd like to think about it," I say.

"There's absolutely nothing to think about!" She slams a hand down hard on the papers.

It's out in the open now. One on one. She has all the cards—the power and the persuasion. Why don't I do myself a favor and sign?

Incredibly I no longer feel the weight of Rachel pressing in behind me. Her whimpering noises have stopped. A turn of my head lets me see that she is lying inert in the nurse's arms. I pick up a pen, stare blankly through the window at the green panorama outside. When my fingers are ready, I tell myself, they will do their work.

The superintendent pushes the sheaf of papers forward toward me. She rolls her chair backwards a few feet and waits. A chirp of impatience escapes her teeth. "Well," she says, "do you want your sister in or out?"

Her question, thrown out so baldly, fans the last spark of resistance in me that still remains. The look of disdain I read in her face fans it into a roaring fury. I race over to Rachel, pull her out of the nurse's grip, toward the door.

Aghast, the superintendent shouts after me: "She's a self-destructive girl. If anything happens, will you be responsible?"

"Screw you," I hurl back. "I've been responsible my whole goddamned life." Rachel in tow, I drag both of us along, beyond reason or shame, without the slightest notion of where I'm taking her or why.

All the way home Rachel scans my face for a clue to my intentions. She will not find any. I am devoid of expression—my muscles frozen—to hide from her whatever it is that I feel. If I were to turn my face toward hers . . . let her see the bewilderment underneath my granite set . . . I would let out a howl before all of the astonished passengers.

As the train rumbles along, the enormity of my act becomes increasingly manifest. "If anything happens, will you be responsible?"

Of course I will. I do indeed take this madwoman, huddled into a ball of woe beside me, to be my lawfully wedded burden, to have and to bear, till death by suicide do us part. The people across the aisle, reading, chewing, smiling, frowning, how I envy their banality on this most ordinary of days. Only Rachel and I, the ones chosen to be nowhere, returning to a small stifling room where I will want to tear her hair out by the roots when she washes her palms one against the other and asks again and again, "What should we do now, Rob?"

On 42nd Street, where we have to change, Rachel and I drift along aimlessly in the rush-hour crowd. I keep searching my mind for any way out of the cul-de-sac of my own making.

Rachel, picking up on my confusion, tugs dolefully on my arm for attention. "Rob," she pleads, "tell me things are going to be all right."

"You wanted out," I snap at her viciously. "Well, live with it!"

She reels backward under the force of my contempt. Leaning against a steel girder, with people streaming by on both sides, she holds her arms out to me: "Be kind, my one and only brother. Take me to the clinic in East Tremont? You remember, the one with that nice black nurse who hugged me and said for me to come back?"

Is no one aware of this absurd family conversation? Shouldn't someone, anyone, step in to call a halt? I could easily batter her senseless to shut off the words of a story she has told to death.

"She'll let me live with her, Rob, I swear she will. I'll wash her clothes, take care of her house. She'll let me. I told her she looks just like Mama."

The downtown train pulls in. The door opens. A crowd pours out of the train, like grains of coffee, leaving an opening for the people on the platform to refill. Rachel's lips are still moving, but her words are no longer audible above the noise. She is lost in her fantasy, oblivious to the crush around us. Her face is tranquil... almost rapt.

As soon as the doors begin to slide shut, I make a dash and squeeze myself in. There's just enough room for me to be swallowed up by the mass. Rachel, alarmed at my sudden rush, tries to follow me in. I reach out and press her back firmly, so that she cannot enter. "Don't leave me here, Rob," she implores, thrusting her hand through the narrow opening.

"Go home, Rachel," I shout as the door leaps open again. She makes one final effort to enter the train. This time I push her against the shoulders until she stumbles backward into a girder. The passengers look at me curiously. I hear a few mutterings. No one moves.

The train pulls away slowly, in stops and starts. Rachel runs alongside, pressing her face against the glass. She looks astonishingly unperturbed. I can barely hear her shouting, "I love you, Rob, I love you very much," but there is no mistaking the clear enunciation of her lips. When she can no longer keep up, near the ladder at the end of the platform, she stops and throws kisses with both hands at the departing train.

For the next few days, I hole myself up in my house, breaking off all communication with the outside. In the cocoon I have created, I enjoy my longest stretch of serenity in many years. The first time my phone rings, each stab reevoking Rachel, I disconnect the plug. I work, eat, wash, read, lie in bed, watch TV around the clock, without regard to night or day, luxuriating in my own self-indulgence.

By the fourth day I become too jittery to maintain my isolation.

At midnight, out of morbid curiosity, I replug the phone. As if they have been waiting for me all along, the telephone rings instantaneously resume. It is her voice, of course, only this time shadowless, cheery, floating feather-free into my ear.

"Can you come over?" she asks, practically singing out the request. "There's something I want to show you."

I hesitate—I have learned to be wary. Is this some ploy she has never played before? A pre-suicidal composure I don't know how to recognize? The stunning revelation I have secretly awaited all these years? I dress and leave the house.

As I have done so often in the past, I take the almost deserted express to Rego Park. Riding there, I am aware of something quite extraordinary. Why am I not in my usual state—upright, rigid, laced in anxiety? I have let my body go slack with the sway of the train, my head falling effortlessly from side to side. Below me I hear the click-clack of the wheels grooving the thin bright ribbon. We catapult cozily along, the express and I, with only the steel shell between us and the darkness.

When I get off, I stroll leisurely through the Queens night toward the clump of dreary houses where Rachel lives. At the end of the pebbled path that becomes her patio, the door stands half-opened. A swath of light from inside the house flickers on the patches of grass. Coming closer I can make out heaps of boxes, plastic bags, old suitcases, papers, furniture lined up in neat rows under the window. Tacked onto the door is an index card on which Rachel has printed:

"I have been swimming in the same stagnant stream for far too long. This is my ultimate realization, brother. *Change is possible!*"

I stand there, fixed to the spot, wondering what it is I feel. Rachel, risen from the dead, is promising me surprises, and for all of my cynicism the tripping beats in my chest tell me how pathetically eager I am to believe her. When I walk through the door, Rachel is not inside. What greets me instead is an empty room—except for a table and couch—the floor swept bare and washed immaculately clean.

It stuns me, the transformation she has wrought, the purity of that space, the thought of my sister sacrificing her beloved garbage, piece by piece.

As I look around I see that Rachel has placed a photograph of Mama, herself and me—the three of us heartbreakingly young—on the table. Near it a candle of remembrance burns in an old-fashioned glass—the kind my mother used as teacups. In the photo Mama and Rachel stand behind me, arms touching, a glazed smile hung on their faces. And there I am, a skinny college boy kneeling in the center, between them, caught with my eyes half-closed, smoldering, faraway, lost somewhere in a void.

"Where are you, Rachel?" I call out.

"I've been waiting." Her voice wafts out of the bedroom. The door opens and she moves gracefully into the room. Over her shoulders is the long woolen shawl Mama wore on holidays. She has redone her hair exactly like Mama's—meticulously braided, pulled back, parted in the middle, and crowned with my mother's tortoise-shell comb. Around her neck is Mama's silver brooch; on her feet, Mama's patent leather pumps, cracked but polished bright as new.

Rachel turns herself around in small mincing steps. It is only when she faces me full on that I realize she is entirely naked under the shawl. "Don't I look exactly like Mama," she asks, lifting her arms and tapping nervously, with her left heel, as my mother did whenever she was too excited to contain herself.

I move back until I touch the edge of the couch and let myself slip down. Rachel wraps the shawl ecstatically around her shoulders. "I did it for you," she says. "Every last piece—the shit I was saving . . . the books, the papers, the clothes, God knows what else . . . I threw it all out for you."

I sit motionless, without will, at the edge of her black hole. The dark pit where she waits beyond reach. Her hands held out toward me, and mine towards hers. To draw her out . . . to be pulled in.

She lifts the photo. "You'll see," she says, "I'll make things be the way they were. Your baby sister. No more trouble, Rob. You won't be ashamed of me any more."

She comes toward the couch, photo in hand, the look on her face, at this moment, so unlike my mother's. The shawl has fallen open. She stands before me, waiting, the candle throwing pools of light across her pendant breasts, the bulge of her belly, the fleshiness of her thighs. There is nothing between us but a faint corona surrounding her nakedness.

Rachel sinks to the floor, sliding her knees to the couch, where I crouch back as far as I can in my shadow. She burrows her head into my lap. Her breasts pin down my thighs. Her arms bracelet my waist. My sister and I, we are altogether entwined. It crosses my mind, vaguely, that I must disentangle, push her away, run for the darkness beyond the door.

"Sing me the song that Mama loved so much," she says.

As if Rachel has touched a memory key, I hear myself resurrecting a Yiddish tune buried in me for half a century:

To our home there came a little cousin,
Greenhorn she, yes green as that full moon there,
Cheeks she had like rosy pomegranates,
Tiny feet that pleaded to be danced with
Tiny feet that needed to be danced with . . .

I glance down to see that Rachel has turned her head toward me, an ineffable glint of joy in her half-glazed eyes. Before I can dissuade my fingers, I see them tenderly drawing through Rachel's curls the comb of Mama's that had so long ago unsnarled my sister's hair and mine.

The Side of My Face

For my fifty-ninth birthday, Katie gave me a framed print of a Barbara Kruger collage showing a woman's plaster bust, on which is written: "Your gaze hits the side of my face." As soon as she had seen the piece in a gallery, Katie flipped out. "Wow," she raved, "what an elegant commentary on the way in which women are reduced to sexual objects."

Of course I told Katie—who is my lover—that I was delighted with her gift. Still, I had to admit to myself, I was feeling a twinge of concern that she was making some kind of statement, at least subliminally, relating to me. To show my appreciation, I hung the Kruger poster on the wall opposite my bed. There it looms over me, night and day, the sad-eyed woman brooding off into space, the eight-word sentence reading from top to bottom in bold warning type. Wherever I turn, I can't possibly escape its message—terse, imperative, brooking no opposition.

Katie teaches women's studies at a small college outside New York. Not only a scholar, she's been an activist-feminist from way back. It startles me, sometimes, the anger with which she skewers the men she considers male supremist. I've even heard her stoop to clichés, like: "Fred, he's a sexist pig. He'll screw anything that moves. Or stands still, for that matter." No mediations at all when she goes after a man who peeves her. Katie just loses her intellectual cool.

Nowadays Katie and I rarely watch TV or see most Hollywood films. The slightest suggestion of violence—of women being sexually used or demeaned—she takes as a personal affront. Do you remember the scene in "L'Avventura" where the newly wedded hero slips a bill with his foot into a prostitute's vagina? Well, when we saw this revival recently, Katie dug her nails into my palm and began to tremble. "I'm going to be sick," she said. When Katie came back from the bathroom, she was chalk-white and withdrawn. She barely watched the rest of the film. What were my reactions to the scene? Out of empathy with Katie, I wish I could say I saw it objectively, purely as an aesthetic experience. The truth is, I felt—how can I describe it?—a small erotic throb in my loins.

Which brings up the question, through a convoluted link I can't understand, of how it is that Katie and I are lovers. After all, what would a forty-five-year-old woman like her—attractive, accomplished, popular—see in an older, marginal man like me? I'm not an intellectual, have no career (right now I work as a free-lance proofreader), and am socially quite clumsy. On top of that, I have a bad track record of previous relationships. Once, when we were in bed together, I asked her bluntly, "Why have you stayed with me all these years?"

She waited a long while before answering. "Frankly, I don't very much like most men. They frighten me. Like my husband. By the end of our marrige, every love-making was a compliant rape. . . . Why I stay with you?" She reached over to touch my face. "I guess I'm with you because you are a gentle man. I'd trust you, yes, even with my life."

Gentle? Didn't she really mean passive, floating like a jellyfish wherever the tide took me? My ex-wife—our marriage lasted less than a year—knew that from the beginning. "Nothing happens to you," she said to me one day without the slightest malice. "Or between us, emotionally, for that matter." How right she was. She slipped out of my life painlessly, as if we had never been together.

With Katie it was different. She needs psychic room, breathing space to be her own person. Living apart as we do, I left her that space willingly—to come and go as she wanted. I was the glove she could put her hand into for warmth, and withdraw if she felt too possessed. Both of us thrived in this no-clutch ambience. "Every time you open my door," I once told Katie, "it's as if you're coming home."

"Are you trying to tell me something?" she asked, smiling.

"Yes," I said, "I love you," for the first time ever with no reservations at all to a woman.

As for love-making it has been from the start a slow healing rather than a grand passion. The first time we made love, my cock went limp. "Don't worry about your little wounded bird," she said, "I couldn't care less." Gradually, things improved. There are no epiphanies, no demonic eruptions. Only a laying on of hands, an ineffable tenderness that ends in us, arms entwined, rocking one another to sleep. This letting go—small as it is—seems to be enough for Katie. And me? Sexually fragile as I am, it's as much as I can deal with. At least that's what I tell myself to pacify an occasional nag of doubt.

To celebrate my birthday, Katie and I had decided to dine at a

French café we ordinarily couldn't afford. Instead, she'd left a message for me saying there was a change of plans: I was to meet her at my place. When I got there—God, I hate being taken unawares—it was a surprise party, with the three of them leaping like fauns out of the bathroom, wreathed in radiant smiles, expecting me to melt at the cunning with which they had entrapped me. You would have to be a brute to trample on everyone's prodigious lovingness, so I graciously went along.

There were four of us—Katie, myself, Robbie and Daryl. We had met, the two men and myself, in the waning of the sixties and it was best friends at first sight. The three of us were impossibly different: Daryl, gangling goy from the Midwest; Robbie, the apostate son of an orthodox rabbi; and myself, twenty years older than they, drifting along no direction home toward middle age and beyond. Inseparable for all of this, we hung desperately around the cusp of rebellion, trying like the others to keep the light of dissent glowing in the gathering gloom of the seventies.

We even joined, long after it was stylish, a consciousness-raising group. Stretched out on the floor, a facilitator beside us, we tried depth-plumbing our racism, sexism, homophobia and whatever until it was clear there simply was no end to them. After that, Robbie and Daryl had a gradual falling out and now they are like fire and water together. Only in my presence—an ombudsman, so to speak—can they tolerate one another for long. I love them, dearly, nevertheless, and it was nice for Katie and me and them to be gathered at my house, mellowing out on reminiscences and sparkling burgundy.

Daryl was, of course, instantly ecstatic about the Kruger collage. "It's exactly the right finishing touch in your place," he enthused. "Aesthetically and content-wise, the perfect gift."

You could have predicted his seal of approval. Daryl is one of the small group who devote themselves to becoming "the new feminist men." After a catastrophic break-up with his wife, he set about remolding his whole masculine identity. "Her leaving me cold," he had explained to me, "was a shattering experience. After that, I wanted to strip myself of all forms of domination over women—my pornographic fantasies, misogyny, power needs, violence, fetishism . . . you name it."

There is something vulnerable—almost heart-rending—about Daryl when he is on one of his changing-men riffs. Toweringly tall, awkward and shambling, he grabs your shirt, his voice choked, and his eyes, huge and frog-like behind thick glasses, grow moist. Daryl works hard at his new role. He is a leading member of an Anti-Sexist

Workshop, where, Daryl says, "men like us can begin to deal honestly and openly with their sexism." Daryl has often invited me to one of his sessions. Up until now, I have resisted. The idea of a group of strangers spilling their erotic intimacies in public—whatever their good intentions—frankly appalls me.

Robbie, ah, he's a whole other cup of tea. He has, like an urban Thoreau, really shaved his life into a corner. A cheap room in Williamsburgh. Any part-time job—super, painter's assistant, newspaper distributor—that can sustain him minimally, yet leave him free for his existential existence. And what is this existence? To lose himself, for days at a time as he lies back on his couch, his brains on fire, evoking transcendental encounters of another kind. And when he's stirred, to compose wonderfully provocative manifestos and stories against personal and social corruptibility which appear occasionally in mimeoed magazines.

Robbie is constitutionally unable to become involved in any long-term relationship. He drifts seamlessly, or so it would appear, through a series of secretive, feverish love affairs that flare up like crises and die down after a few months. When I see Robbie and his current woman friend, who is invariably slim, oddly attractive and discombobulated, they seem to be clinging to one another as if this moment of togetherness is their last. Between affairs, Robbie lets it be known, if pressed, he is an active participant in a way-out sexually exploratory group. "Anything," he tells me, "erotically, emotionally, physically, that goes down between two consenting lovers is more than permissible . . . it's mind-blowing!"

After Daryl had delivered his whole-hearted approval of my gift, we sat in silence for a moment solemnly staring at it. "What do you think," Katie asked, looking at Robbie.

Robbie tilted his head back, a hand grasping his balding dome, rocking gently back and forth like a talmudist on the verge of disputation. "There are," he softly remarked, "gazes and gazes."

"What the hell is that supposed to mean?" asked Daryl.

"Don't push me," said Robbie, a very laid-back but excitable man. "I'm trying to say that not every glance at a woman is necessarily an eye-fuck. Sure, you can undress and possess a woman in your head when you look at her. But there are also other kinds of gazes—soft, not hard—of admiration, for example, of curiosity, of primal recognition. And yes, looks of desire that you know will never be fulfilled. So all you are saying is hello and, regretfully, goodbye to a passing stranger."

Daryl was on his feet, shaking. "What a crock of shit," he said grimly. "You know damn well, Robbie, what Barbara Kruger means. In this sick, sexist society, there are no neutral gazes. Men's eyes are pornographic: they penetrate like corkscrews, like pricks . . ."

Robbie too got up from his chair. "Talk about pornography," he said. "I went to your group once. A bunch of men, half-dressed, posing like nudes as if they were oppressed women. It's nothing but a visual jerkoff."

Daryl's face drained white. "That's a cheap shot," he said, moving closer to Robbie, "I want you to take it back."

The two non-violent men stood body to body, each trembling with rage.

Katie stepped between them and held them apart. "Okay, guys," she said, "that's enough. Cool it."

Of course the party was over. Daryl and Robbie made a pass at shaking hands, and each left at a different time to avoid walking home together. While we were cleaning up the room, Katie said to me: "What did you think of the argument?"

I shrugged my shoulders. "The last thing I need to do is to fight about sex."

"It wasn't about sex," Katie remarked, visibly annoyed. "It was about pornography . . . men dominating women through power and violence."

Now my dander was up too. "Maybe so," I said, "but I don't appreciate righteous people like Daryl being our judges—telling us what we can and cannot do or think."

"Then you agree with Robbie?"

"No, I didn't say that. Just that I can't bear Daryl's slogan-mongering, his politicization of intimate human relationships."

It was the first tiff on the subject of sex we'd ever had. For some reason, however, I was enormously uneasy, even threatened. Somehow, in an inchoate way, I was afraid it would open up the sluices about our own love-making. And what would pour out? . . . I had no idea.

Katie went to bed immediately that night. She had to leave early the next morning for a two-day feminist conference in Boston, where she was to deliver a paper at a panel on "Pornography and Male Force." Because I somehow couldn't bring myself to offer the first make-up gesture, I waited silently for Katie to fall asleep. Hearing her deep breathing, I fell into a depression so dark I had to read in the bathroom until the first light streaked the sky.

The next morning Katie seemed cheerful enough, as if nothing untoward had happened. During breakfast she kept advising me on how to avoid slipping into one of my severe psychic slumps when she leaves me alone for any period of time. "Why don't you visit your sister. You haven't seen her for months." "No?" "How about a movie you've been dying to see without me?" "Still no?" "Well, then . . ."

"I'll be fine," I assured her. "There's enough proofreading here for a week."

A moment before Katie left, she said: "Maybe this is a good time to see what Daryl's group is all about," and closed the door before I could respond.

Left alone, the two days stretched out before me like trackless wastes. In a few minutes I had already exceeded my loneliness quota. Lying back in bed, paralyzed, morosely staring at the Kruger woman, I felt myself begin to unravel like a damp, rotting rag-doll. Hours went by, with me locked into this intense inane. Then I got up and wandered aimlessly to the desk where Katie had prepared her Boston paper.

Wide open on the desk, with passages throughout that Katie had underlined in pencil, was Andrea Dworkin's opus *Pornography.* With Katie's urging I had tried reading it several times, but the brutal facts Dworkin had marshalled, and the prose style . . . the arguments driven like pistons before her . . . had discouraged me. This time, however, I found myself leafing through the pages that Katie had marked.

"In pornography," I read, "man's sense of raw phallic power and purpose are fully realized. She is the pinup, the poster, the dirty picture, naked, half-dressed, laid out, legs spread, breasts or ass protruding. She is the thing that makes him erect. . . She is taught to be that thing, raped, beaten, bound, used, until she recognizes her true nature and complies."

Then, further on: "Since men respond only to sexual fragments, bits and pieces, slivers of flesh costumed this way or that, this very incapacity is transformed into one of love's defining features."

And, finally, the horrendous sum-up: "The boys are betting that their penises and fists and fucks and rapes will turn us into what they say we are: the voracious cunts of pornography, the sluts who resist because they really want more. The boys are betting. The boys are wrong."

When I closed the book, I sat for a while stunned at the fury of her words. Then, instinctively, as I rose, I put my hand over my crotch, as if to ward off an arrow pointed directly at my cock. Surely, I played with the idea, I was not one of the boys.

After that, I left the house, and walked through the streets, letting my feet go wherever they wanted. They took me slowly west across to the river and north to Washington Place, to the meat warehouses where men in crimson-stained jackets haul carcasses for the market. I come here often, because the men who work here seem to me so rawly in touch with their lives.

It was lunchtime, and the men were sprawled on the warehouse steps, eating huge hero sandwiches. I stood there, near them, watching the women from the offices scurry—their thighs demurely drawn together—through the gauntlet of smokey, cunt-hungry glances. One of the men bit savagely into his meatballs, letting a line of bloody juice run down his cheeks. "Ssssss . . ." he hissed, sucking a breath of air inwardly through his teeth. "Could I eat her pussy!" An explosion of laughs, a round of mock jabs at each other, and the little confrontation was over.

I walked slowly to the subway and rode home. Once, lifting my eyes, I caught a miniglance, no longer than the flutter of an eyelid, of the young woman opposite me. When she stared back at me balefully, I closed my eyes tightly as if I were asleep. In my mind's eye, I could still see with amazing clarity the tight black blouse stretched taut over the nipples, the rounded belly, the short purple skirt that showed a flash of thigh, and the tall white boots. It startled me. I hadn't realized before how thoroughly I could absorb and retain all this visceral afterimage in a wink of time. When she got off the station before me, I noted, without meaning to, what long, provocative legs she had.

When was the day going to end? Already I was too removed to make any human contact. I played around with the pageproofs. I paced my room like a caged animal. I stuffed marshmallow cookies into my mouth until I was sick to the pit of the stomach. Lying before the muted TV, I saw the disembodied images cascading by—glazed faces, ghostly laughs, an army dumbly parading across the screen.

At midnight I opened the desk drawer and swept the last remnants of grass into a slim joint. The Dworkin book was on its back, so that I could see her picture. A mop of curly hair; pleasant, plumpish face; far-off, even melancholy expression; not a clue of vendetta in her eyes. I was horrifically aware of how she regarded us. How did I regard her?

I lit up the joint—the first in a long time. Katie didn't like my smoking them. Besides, I had had in the past a few bad trips that had landed me in the hospital. On the other hand, if I smoked only half a joint—maybe, ten, twelve drags—it sometimes gave me an erotic buzz, a hint of high, that tailed off into a deep sleep. This joint, however, bitter, stale, strong, didn't follow the scenario. I jolted up, heart chugging, palms wet, nauseous. Things had begun to break apart, run askew.

Hung on a hook from the color-crazed wall was a vaguely familiar figure, arms bound, head atilt. As the figure kaleidoscoped into focus, I saw that it was Andrea Dworkin. "Let me down," she said furiously. I must have been telepathic, because her lips weren't moving. Dworkin was wrapped in long flowing robes. Split-second pictures flew by, like a slide show gone berserk: Isis Dworkin . . . Medusa Dworkin . . . Madonna Dworkin . . . Medea Dworkin . . . St. Joan Dworkin. All with the same roundish face.

I climbed up the hill of pillows to the wall, where Dworkin's bare feet were visible below the robes. "I'm not like the others," I whimpered, "I'm a putty-boy, a sex negative, a soft marshmallow prick of a man. Believe me, I can't penetrate." With that, I kissed her dirt-streaked feet . . . licked the lint between her toes.

Dworkin yanked her foot away. "You are no fucking better," she said, without moving her lips, "than the rest of them."

"No, no," I protested. "Forgive me, I'm my mother's darling boy."

"Shit," she hissed, without moving her lips. "You boys are counting on it. You boys are betting on it. You boys are wrong." After that, the images dissolved, the wall was empty again and the flickering TV, its patterns weaving and reweaving, told me that dawn was at hand.

I don't clearly recall how I lost those first few hours the next day. I did what I often do when I feel abandoned—sat in a sweat near the phone waiting for a ring to rescue me. But no one rang. Finally, out of some obscure impulse, I mustered the willpower to call Daryl. "Katie suggested"—my voice was mucousy with anxiety—"that I look in on your group this afternoon."

Daryl was delighted. "Great," he said, "how about, say, two-thirty?"

The session was in someone's apartment nearby. There were ten or so earnest men present and one woman. We stood in a circle listening to Daryl describe the goals of his group. Inside the circle was a table spread with magazines like *Hustler, Playboy* and *Penthouse*. First he talked about pornography, the ways in which men "objectify and reduce women to body parts available to all men . . . We are all silent collaborators," he explained. "That's how society socializes us from childhood on."

Daryl picked up a *Playboy* and opened it to the centerfold. "What we do here," he told us, "is to encourage one another to look at pictures like these with new eyes, so that we can experience what pornography does to us. I want four of you," he continued, "to do a pose as close as you can to a photo in one of these mags. Meanwhile, the rest of us will help you make that pose as accurate as possible. Afterwards, we'll discuss what it feels like to experience the pose—and to observe it."

Daryl looked directly at me. "How about it," he asked, handing me the *Playboy.* "Will you be one of the four?"

The woman in the center spread was one of those dazzling beauties, impeccably curvaceous, invented as it were to measure up to exacting American specifications. She was leaning forward alluringly, a garter belt dangling from her waist, one hand on a knee, the other delicately parting her pubic hair to expose the moist pink inside. The odd thing was, though, she wasn't smiling like they are supposed to be. In fact, there was a distant, a troubled, even a hurt look on her face. Immediately, in that one instant, I felt simpatico . . . no, dismayed, confused, aroused? I'm not sure.

While I studied her, the other three men were already working on their impersonations. When I glanced up, I saw them struggling to assume lascivious positions and facial expressions. They were grotesque—clumsy imitations of transvestites, only without their charm or sexiness. I placed the magazine on the table and began to back away. All eyes were on me. There was a dense silence in the room. The three men, their poses suspended, were standing around slackly.

Daryl seemed crushed. "Give it a chance," he implored. "It takes time to get into the spirit."

"I'm sure it does," I said, "but I need to think about it." With that, I slunk out the door, certain I was breaking up a cherished friendship.

In the street again, relieved and distressed, I deliberately headed for a scene I had avoided for years. This was a disintegrative moment, I figured, ripe for plunging right into the eye of a storm. On St. Mark's and Lafayette, I stopped before a small table set up by FFP: Feminists Fighting Pornography. On the table was a board with a pinned photograph I had sometimes glimpsed in passing. It showed a bruised woman, her nipples stuck through with pins. I had to fight to keep my eyes riveted to the woman's dazed face. The FFP woman was expounding to a man, with the passion of a crusader, the barbarism of pornography. She was a tiny, wan woman with piercing eyes. When the man left, I took out my wallet and saw that I had several fives and singles and one ten-dollar bill. I slipped out the ten, folded it, and slid it into the contribution bottle.

"Thanks a lot," she said, warmly. "We can sure use it."

"Right on," I answered, "and keep up the good work." While I was walking back to my apartment, I realized, with a pang, how phony the words "right on" must have sounded. I hadn't ever used that expression before, even in the height of the sixties.

As I opened my door, the phone was ringing. It was Robbie, asking me how I was doing on my own. "A little shaky," I said.

"If you have no other plans," he suggested, "why don't we eat dinner together?"

We met in a cheap Greek joint, where Robbie chomped away at his falafel while I picked at my food. I decided not to mention the Daryl disaster—it would be like betraying a friend.

"Robbie," I said, "I believe I'm falling apart."

He laughed. "So what's new? It's my usual condition." Suddenly he brightened up. "I'm going to my ES group tonight. Be my guest."

Why not, I thought, ES couldn't be any more unnerving than Daryl's MAP or the St. Mark's women's FFP. The Exploratory Sex headquarters, a failed disco far west on 14th Street, was a cavernous room, painted black, with small round tables planted around what was once the dance floor. At one end was a raised stage, at the other the only brightly lit area.

There were seven of us—scattered at the tables—only two of them women. When we ordered beers, the waiter-host handed us an ES brochure. He had on a flaming-orange wig, heavily made-up face, a tight silk dress and spike heels. We sat around drinking glumly and glancing at the literature. From what I could make out, ES was dedicated, militantly and spiritually, as a matter of principle, to sexual libertarianism. "Nonsexist, open to straights, gays, lesbians, transvestites and others," the piece read, "ES believes that opening ourselves to every form of eroticism—fantasies, S and M and intra-gender experimentation—is a political as well as personal responsibility. In our opinion, sexual repression is simply another aspect of human oppression."

I had no comment to make. Robbie, sensing my unease, assured me, "Things will liven up later."

The host came over to our table. "This is an off night," he said apologetically. "If you're a member, you can come here for real action on week-ends—dominatrix and all."

A while later, a young woman walked into the room. She stood hesitant, near the lighted area, with her long, ratty fur coat flung open.

"Welcome in," said the host.

"I'm not sure if I care to," she said defiantly.

"It's a free country," the host shrugged.

The woman, in her twenties, let the coat drop to the floor. The overhead spots reflected off the red-spangled dress into a million dazzling fireflies. It lit up her young face, too, as vulnerable as it was lovely. Mesmerized, we gathered around her, the two women slightly hanging back. The young woman put her hands behind her back. "I want to be chained," she said; "even if I fight and say no, I need you to chain me."

The host caught her hands and, for all of her thrashing around, manacled her to a dead steam-pipe. "Let me go," she cried, but the fight was out of her. She stood there, panting like some bound animal. A curtain of stillness had descended over us. She had set up a magnetic vortex that was totally enveloping. She looked crazily from one face to another, as if for a reading. When she caught my eyes, like a hook, she called out. "Hey, you there, how old are you?"

"Fifty-nine," I answered, completely cowed.

"Same as my father, the damned bastard," she taunted. "Come on over here, grandpa."

I moved, in slow motion, as in a delirious dream, toward her. I was very close to her. Each time she turned her face, another woman looked back at me. Katie, in one profile, with her high cheekbones and strong chin. The *Playboy* model, with her wet rosebud of a mouth. And, in her other profile, another, unknown woman. No—the memory came flooding back—I knew who she was. I was ten years old then; one of the other kids had handed me a postcard. A young woman too, in her twenties, her hands bound behind her, her legs thrown wide open, a masked man, with a huge cock buried in her sex. It had stunned me, the desire and fear—which was it?—written on her face. For years after that, I would stare at that face, kiss and lick it while I masturbated. Until one day, the photo had disappeared, most likely discovered by my outraged mother and flushed down the drain.

I was so near now, I could see her lipstick-smeared teeth. "Do you want me?" she asked. She was heaving and breathing hard.

Did I want her? I was a sea of lava. A tongue of red fire was melting my guts. My cock was a bone of burning silver.

The young woman let herself hang toward me, the manacles supporting the weight of her body. "Do me," she whispered, "do me good."

I, who could only make love to a woman in the dark, was wholly oblivious of the lights . . . of the circle of eyes devouring the two of us. I was beside myself, and the imposter in me was beyond shame. I lifted her dress and, slipping it over her head, let it drop at my feet. She was altogether naked. I licked her eyes and her mouth and ran a swath of saliva under her neck. With my tongue I parted her swollen breasts, like the Red Sea, and travelled it down the slopes of her belly and thighs. Then, and only then, when I was on my knees, with my mouth moistening her triangle of hair, did I hear a collective moan, a keening, from those around me. And that sound broke the magic spell—the ritual was over, the sacrifice halted. I got up, and spinning around, saw in the mirror of their eyes what I was. An aging man, with a hard-on and the hots, about to eat a young woman who would never know my name.

"Don't stop now," someone sobbed.

"It was beautiful," Robbie said in a hushed voice.

At the shock of their voices, I bolted for the door, leaving my coat and scarf behind. "Wait," Robbie called out to me, but I was flying in the bitter cold, east across 14th Street and south down Avenue C, where I leaped up my front steps and unlocked the door to collapse on the bed.

For hours, it must have been, I lay there in a stupor. As I tossed and turned, waiting for Katie, wisps of dreams, slivers of nightmare, tore my sleep to shreds. Dimly I heard a key at the door and Katie came into the room. She saw me, in my dishevelled clothes, curled up like a foetus. In a moment of panic, she shook me awake and held my face in both hands.

"What's wrong, darling," she cried out, "what happened?"

I let out a great wracking sob that tore like a siren from my throat. "Nothing," I lied to her, "I just missed you terribly." I took both her hands and kissed them like a grateful leper. "Stay with me," I wept, "don't ever leave me again."

"I never will," she promised, "never again." She began to undress me. "Sweet love," she crooned, "my sweet, sweet love."

Naked, I waited for her to come back to me. She slipped under the blankets into the curl of my body. The heat of her, the smell of her armpits, the shame of what I had done, were making me dizzy. All at once it struck me that I had never before experienced a frenzy of want for Katie.

"Baby," she cried out softly, feeling my bigness near her. She had never before called me baby. I had never before been aggressive with her.

"Kate, baby," I echoed as I licked her eyes and her mouth. It was almost entirely dark. Nevertheless, in my mind's eye, I could see the rosebud of her lips, the swell of her breasts. I traveled my tongue down the slope of her belly. I parted her legs, like the Red Sea, and moistened her triangle of hair. I rose and wedged myself between her thighs, pinning her down with my weight. From behind me on the wall, I could feel the gaze of the poster woman . . . furious . . . unforgiving . . . phosphorescent . . . hitting the side of my head.

Only Thirty Feet Away

With his knees pulled up to his chest, he lies there broken, like a doll twisted out of shape. If I could rock him to sleep in my arms, as I used to when he was a small boy, I would. My arms want to but they won't, for the life of me, reach out.

Only thirty feet away—the length of our living room—my son Mike is lying on his mattress, most likely doped out of his mind, playing full blast one of his excruciating records . . . pop, punk, heavy metal, by a group, what is it called—Rat Droppings, Roach Motel, Scum Bags, or something even more repulsive. Some time around two a.m., he'll fall asleep with the hi-fi on repeat, so that the unbearable vibrations will go on and on in our heads as we try to fall asleep, like the buzz of a drill in your mouth when the dentist shoots you full of some pain-killer.

My wife Jean and I (we take turns) will have to go to his room to switch the record off. A smell of marijuana, thick as fog, will be hanging in the air. Mike will be on his back, nude as always, his body and face as pale as a fish's belly. Twenty-two years old, tall, burly and bushy bearded, he will be holding to his chest a toy robot which he mocks at but can't seem to sleep without. The dirty socks, the stained underwear . . . it's painful for me even to describe it . . . banana peels, empty soda cans, plates of dried-out spaghetti, some rotted gunk you can't possibly identify piled pell-mell in the corner.

On all four walls, my son has sprayed a day-glow purple, so that his room is with its one dim light an airless pit, a womb, a crypt, a black hole of Calcutta. What do other kids like him put up?—movie posters, psychodelic designs, blowups of rock stars? Not my Mike, oh no, on his walls he's pasted this big cloth swastika, and tacked in between the crossed arms photos of androgynes with plumed headdresses, naked girls spreading their sex apart with their own hands, blond boys stroking their organs as they look straight out at you with blank eyes. And the worst of it is, every one of these pictures Mike took with his own camera.

I'm not stupid. A high school teacher in social studies for twenty-five years, you think I don't keep up with kids . . . I'm not onto every trick they have up their sleeves? As I once told my wife, "I know that all this is a deliberate shocker on Mike's part to keep the distance between us. Yes, he *wants* his room to be a slap in the face of our values, a defiant statement that his space at least is off-limits to squares like you and me."

Still, I have to ask myself, does he have to be this extreme? I mean, the nihilism, the passivity, the filth he cultivates, the pills he keeps only half hidden under the pillow, the uppers and downers. And that disgusting Nazi emblem he flies like a flag on his walls. We are, after all, discussing a boy who when he was twelve, on his own discovered religion, insisted on studying Hebrew and, during that entire period did not so much as once allow a single piece of unkosher food to pass his lips. A kid who when we took him to see a documentary about the holocaust, practically vomited five minutes into the film when he saw the crematoria and that night had to be rocked to sleep by his mother, crying, "Mom, how come people do this to one another?"

It isn't as if he were traumatized by divorce, or pushed into a corner by ambitious parents. Whatever else you can say about us, we both have made practically no demands on him. He comes and goes when he wants, no questions asked. No one creeps into his bones to look for secrets. Jean and I, we have searched our deepest hearts and can honestly say we have no hidden agenda for his life. We never forced college on him—though I must say we were stunned half out of our minds when he dropped out on his own from high school without even getting a diploma . . . a boy of MENSA potential, who with an IQ of 140 plus could have gotten scholarships to the finest schools, could have been a scientist, a writer, an expert in whatever field he put his talents to.

What mystifies me even more, for all of Mike's being such an outsider, he is not . . . as far as I can see . . . any kind of a rebel. He's never belonged to any protest group, or expressed an interest in any worthwhile cause. Screw family values, moral issues, aims, purposes, dreams. Screw everything! That's about the sum of his beliefs.

Saturday and Sunday are for me—for Jean too, even though she won't admit it—the most difficult days of the week. She knocks herself out working as an art therapist with brain-damaged children. Me, after dealing with the little monsters at school five afternoons in a row, I am only too happy to collapse with her. My wife has a long-standing joke: "Bob, let's make this an invisible week-end. Phones off the hook, meals in, a good TV movie. What do you say, we're at home to nobody—totally dropped out of sight." Sure, let's drop out of sight. How?—with a twenty-two-year-old son locked behind his door incommunicado, twenty-four, forty-eight hours at a stretch, asleep or awake, the TV never off, him watching or not, the light shining on his face, comics, kiddy shows, news, sitcoms, junk movies, late show, late-late show, dawn sermonettes, the Star Spangled Banner, the tube dead for a couple of hours, and then the god-damned madness starting all over again.

Try as we may, it is impossible to ignore this constant presence in our midst. We cook, we laugh, we read, we knock at his door to ask, *Don't you want to share the food?* We say cheery things when he emerges for a few minutes, *There's some delicious fruit in the fridge. Why not take a stroll on this lovely day, go swimming, visit a friend, play ball, take a sunbath, sit in the park?* Meanwhile we are thinking, we would like to scream out, *When will you find a girl, some friends, a niche, a goal, a place, a life of your own?* By two in the afternoon we have drifted to our own bedroom, as he is in his, so that between us is a no-man's land of the living room, a vacuum that sucks up every drop of our energy until Jean and I have nothing left to say or give.

Occasionally I try to catch Mike offguard for a serious conversation. "Mike," I might say, as an opener, "long time no talk. How are things going with you?"

"Smooth as silk, Dad." A deadly silence, then he slips away.

If he's got himself one of his temporary jobs, I ask, "How's work?"

"Dull as shit." Another lead killed.

If he's unemployed—which is most of the time—"Any hot prospects lined up?"

"Nope. They're all lukewarm."

If I can't think of anything else. "Need any money, Mike?"

"Every little bit helps." He stands there, waiting.

I fumble in my wallet, crumple some bills, stuff them into his shirt pocket.

A "Thank you kindly, sir," and that's about it.

Sometimes I make a stab at cozying up. "Say, Mike, your mom and I are looking for a real good movie. Any suggestions?" A condescending answer: "If degradation turns you on, I strongly recommend 'The Last Home Left'. . ." or some equally unknown film.

In a more serious vein: "You used to play an awful pretty guitar. How come you packed it in?"

"Cause I'll never play as pretty as George Harrison."

Once it bothered me so much, I blurted out, "Why do you have to watch all that dumb television?"

A wicked smile. "I'm a McLuhan baby, Dad. I just love to drown myself in random images." Or words to that effect.

God forbid, also, I should let a word like "stoned" or "bugged" or "hip" come out of my mouth. Immediately a grimace crosses his face, his jaw tightens, as if the mere fact of a 58-year-old man using this precious vocabulary constitutes some kind of social disease. My impulse is to yell out, "Listen, little boy, you never earned your snotty superiority. These words, you did not invent them, they came with the sixties, before you were born." Luckily I manage to squelch any such displays of open hostility. If it ever got out of hand, there is no telling what might erupt.

What's even more aggravating, he has my number. With one remark he can make me feel so backward, so out of touch with the times, I will go to the most ridiculous lengths to prove that I'm not anywhere as straight as he thinks. Often, I jot down a way-out expression that Mike uses. In my classes I listen with close attention to my black kids, figuring a little of their street talk might rub off on me. Sometimes I rescue Mike's discarded music magazines and read them surreptitiously for clues to what young people are listening to these days. And why do I carry on so foolishly?: the hope that I might dazzle my son with a throwaway remark to show him how advanced his father is.

One day, I decide to take my son up on it and see "The Last Home Left" for myself. It's one of these midnight specials in a movie house way down in the Village. When I get there, I line up halfway around the block with several hundred noisy kids dressed for a masquerade ball—with masks on, faces painted, some with green hair or tomahawk cut, wearing tuxedos, corsets, high hats, black-net stockings.

In front of me, two giggling girls—lips painted black, wearing sequined black coats, rhinestone chokers and lace wedding dresses—look up at the midnight freak behind them. What they see is a gray-haired man wearing a black leather cap, blue denim jacket, old jeans and dirty white sneakers—the outfit he thinks appropriate for such an occasion. "What is the movie about?" I ask the young ladies. Both of them stop laughing. "Oh," one of them answers, "it's total camp . . . like, you know, rape, sodomy, the hero gets his cock bitten off, you know, the whole bit."

"If you got the stomach for it," the second girl adds, "it's really far-out . . . great."

An uproar of appreciation goes up around me. The entire line seems to be listening to me make a jerk of myself. I stand my ground, wondering how I can dissolve gracefully into the night. "Make up your mind, grandpa," a voice booms out. "You coming or going?" I mumble some excuse, ease my way out of the line and stride as quickly as I can down and across the street. It's seventy-odd blocks from St. Mark's Street to where I live, but I walk steadily, driving my legs like pistons until I reach home exhausted.

There's a crack of light showing through the bottom of Mike's door. He's playing one of his favorite records—the sound of whales singing to one another. Poor Mike . . . the midnight movie kids, they'll go back to their jobs or schools the next day, to love affairs, dates, intrigues with friends, to their normal lives as usual. For my son, with his prison of a room, his silences and loneliness, his pointless comings and goings, what's ahead—more of same?

That night I dream that Mike and I are together in a vast underwater cavern trying desperately to talk to one another in whale language neither of us can understand. When I wake at dawn with a start, gasping for breath, I can still hear the voices of the whales—so sad they can break your heart—rising and falling in Mike's room.

Shortly afterwards, an incident in our house between Mike and myself occurred from which I have not as yet recovered. He and two friends are watching a basketball game at night on the living room television.

So rarely does he invite anyone here, I can't resist coming out of my room to see what they're like. The lights are low, so I can't get a good look. They don't even realize I'm standing there, observing. Mike and his friends are having a great time, drinking beer, roaring their approval when someone makes a good play, passing joints. He knows we don't approve of his dope. Is he smoking it openly as a show of defiance? I suppose I should express my disapproval, but I can't. He's so rarely happy in my presence, I don't have the heart to interrupt. As I'm about to leave, without saying a word, one of his friends shouts out: "Wow, this here game has got itself an all-jigaboo cast."

"Let's face it," Mike says, "from here on in, whitey is going to be bucket-carrier and chief linament rubber for Mr. Black Superstar!"

"For sure," the second friend adds, "white athletes do not happen to have no natural nigger rhythm whatever."

You wouldn't believe how loud they laugh at their own jokes—Mike included—and bang their beer bottles on the table. Before I can stop myself, I hear my voice saying on its own: "Racism is not what I expect from Mike or his friends in our house." As soon as the words are out, I realize how foolish it is for me to put my two cents in, whether I am justified or not.

Mike looks in the direction of my voice, shuts off the TV, clicks on the lights. "Cool it, Dad," he says. "Do you have any idea how unreal you are, insulting my friends?" His jaw is twitching nervously, a sign he is trying to keep his murderous temper under control.

If I could do so gracefully, I would apologize and get out then and there. Instead, I continue mildly—almost meekly—"I'm sure it's all in fun, but it doesn't have to be at the expense of a whole race."

Mike is slumped over, catatonically, near the table. Suddenly, with one sweep of his hand, he scatters the popcorn, the beer bottles, onto the floor. "You phony," he says, "when the hell did you ever have a black friend? Or for that matter, when was the last time you related to any adult darker than dirty-gray? Racism? You have got to be kidding . . . teaching white bullshit to black kids before I was born. You live, breathe, you think, you dream lily white. Man, you are a subliminal racist—the innocent kind—and they are the worst . . ."

When his tirade ends, the silence is almost shocking. No one makes a move for quite a while. Then, one of Mike's friends remarks, very amiably, as if nothing at all has happened. "We're cutting out, Mike, thanks for the beer."

"Yea, man," says his other friend, "have got to do this scene again very soon." As they get up to leave and pull on their jackets, I note for the first time that both of his friends are black. One nods at me, the other waves a friendly good-bye.

We stand there awkwardly, Mike and I, averting each other's glances. "I'd better straighten up," I say. He nods, the fire gone out of him, and goes quickly to his room. The room is a total mess—popcorn strewn all over, pools of beer on the floor, stains on the chairs. If I don't wipe up, the smell will be vile by tomorrow. I fill a pail with soapy water and leave it in the sink. Then I switch the lights off and lie back on the couch in the dark. Waves of nausea rise from the pit of my stomach. I must calm myself—do what I was taught long ago by a yogi instructor—breathe myself into the center of nothingness, beyond the concerns of my petty ego. "Breathe in," I order myself, "breathe out . . . breathe in . . . breathe out." In the stillness, Mike's words—each one bitten off, humiliating, without mercy for his father—continue to echo from far away in my ears.

A really distressing phone call from Jean's smart-ass sister, a newly graduated therapist, no less. "I had lunch with Mike this afternoon," Helen says. "Can't you see he's in serious trouble?" The ones without children, I have noticed, those who have never once had to wipe up baby shit, they are the quickest to advise you how to deal with yours.

"No," I say, "I'm only his father. Tell me, what's wrong with him?"

"You must have noticed," she says. "His pupils are pinpoints, his talk is so thick, he's most likely losing thought connections. Whatever Mike's on, I'm sure he's zonked out most of the time."

What she says alarms me, I would rather she did not open that bag. "Maybe it's existential," I say, sarcastic, the way I am when under attack. "Maybe it's a phase he has to go through."

"Existential, balls," she answers. "Your son is lost. He's depressed to the point of being out of touch with reality. And the pity is, with your eyes open, you are letting him go down the drain."

There's a ball of fire in my belly. I'm beginning to tremble. In a second I'll scream into the phone. Jean, seeing me go pale, grabs the phone from me. My wife is calm, she turns away, she listens, she keeps saying uuuuuummm . . . uuuuuuhhhhummm . . . uuuuhhhmmmmmmmmmmm. It goes on without stop, her repeating uuuuuuhhhmmmmmm. . . "You think he might harm himself? . . . uuummmmhhhh . . ."He needs professional help?" ummmmhhhmmmm . . ."Okay, Helen," . . . uuummmhhhmmm . . . and hangs up.

The nerve of Helen, her unmitigated gall to tell us we are ignoring Mike—letting him go down the drain. Jean and I, who have memorized every hurt of his, knocked ourselves out dealing with every problem since he was a kid. Does she have any idea, the agony of living with a child who, for all intents and purposes, chooses to become a stranger in his own house. A fourteen-year-old normal, sunny, smart as a whip youngster takes it into his head, out of the blue, to cut out on the whole system. He stays away from school for days, weeks on end, tears up letters from his teacher, lies about where he spends mornings and afternoons, deliberately loses his books and report cards, refuses to take tests or do schoolwork. Meanwhile he has sold his rings, watch, camera—anything he can get his hands on—to buy grass by the ounce.

Oh, for sure we confront him, we have heavy talks, we understand, we forgive, we lay down rules, we wheedle, we threaten, we explode. And to what avail?—it's as if you were talking to a wall. Professional help? First we consult with his teachers, the school psychologist, then one shrink and then another. In the end it's always the same: Your son, they tell us, just sits there without saying a word, without communicating what is bothering him. Really, it's a waste of time—ours and his. And if we should ask Mike, "Why don't you let them help you?" he laughs, "Hell, they are the ones who need help."

He won't let on, my son, underneath all this bravado he is hurting badly. But they are right—there is nothing Jean or I can do. He will not allow himself to be touched! Like that night, years ago, when I hear from his room the sound of a sharp kick against the wall. Through the partially opened door I see that he is slumped back on a chair, a pencil stub in his hand, staring at a blank sheet.

"What's wrong, Mike?" I ask.

"I'm supposed to hand in my term paper," he says.

"So?"

"I can't think of anything to say."

"Well," I ask him, "what does she want you to write about?"

"Oh, what I enjoy doing best."

"That's fine," I say, "It should be a breeze. What do you enjoy most?" Mike shrugs his shoulders, puts his head down, doesn't answer. "Sports?" I suggest. He shakes his head no. "Reading?" "Riding a bike?" Silence. "Travel," I persist. "Stamps?" "Photography?" Still no answer. "Mountain-climbing?" I ask. "How about that for a subject?" He shuffles both his feet. "For chrissakes," I yell, "you used to be crazy about mountain-climbing. Didn't we buy you special picks, boots, gloves? Didn't we take you on a climbing trip to New Hampshire and when you got to the top you called down to Mom and me, 'Only God was here before me!' which is what I told you the first man ever to climb Mt. Everest said when he reached the summit?"

He's staring at me—I can't tell whether in resentment or what. "You once loved mountain-climbing, did you or didn't you? Dammit, then write about it! Tell how you couldn't wait to climb mountains . . ."

He lets the pencil fall from his fingers. He holds both arms out to me, palms outstretched, his shoulders shaking. A few tears roll down his cheeks. "It's not my thing any more," he says. "I wouldn't know what to put down."

My son's helplessness is making me crazy. I grab the pencil and paper. "Use your imagination," I spit out. "Whatever comes to mind, one word after the other, put it down on the paper!"

His whole body is trembling. He's trying to hold back his tears. "What do you want me to write?" he says.

"Nobody can think for you. Say something . . . say anything . . . I like mountain-climbing because it is a great challenge. I like mountain-climbing because it puts me in touch with nature. I like mountain-climbing because the wind feels wonderful in my face . . . because it lifts me to the top of the world... because I have to write a term paper, that's why!"

"I... like... mountain... climbing," he repeats each word as if he were a kindergarten child first learning to speak, "because... because..." a flood of tears pours out of his eyes. He buries his face in his hands and sprawls out on the bed. With his knees pulled up to his chest, he lies there, broken, like a doll twisted out of shape. If I could rock him to sleep in my arms, as I used to when he was a baby, I would. My arms want to, but they won't, for the life of me, reach out. I sit at the side of his bed until I hear him breathing deeply. Then I cover him with a blanket and tiptoe out.

For a long time I gnawed over these questions—how and why it could happen to our son—until they have become dry as bones. I would look at my students, most of them ghetto kids—and carry on this imaginary conversation: If you were like them, Mike, if you lived in a ghetto on welfare; if there were no culture at home; if you were raised dog eat dog on mean streets, with no hopes for a better life, it would be perfectly understandable—the passive lying around, the dropping out, the nothing means a shit, the anything goes attitude...

Twenty-five years, Mike, twenty-five wasted years teaching kids like this in slum schools. How many classes, five times a day, does that add up to, how many faces, black, plum, mahogany, yellow, brown, tan? How many senseless conferences, tests, lesson plans, units, final grades? And term papers... illegible, scrawled, illiterate scratchings, full of blots, food stains... for me to make a pass at marking. Social studies? If it weren't so tragic, it would be farcical. Me, lecturing like an asshole in front of a bored class about the Great American Conquest of the West, the Salt Treaty, the Ming Dynasties to a few kids who want to learn while the others trade joints, play cards, fight, sleep, throw erasers, look at comics, make faces at me, shout out dirty words, sneak out and don't come back. It's all right, though, par for the course, we do what our department head wants, scare them, distract them, placate them, anything at all to keep the animals out of sight, out of the halls, out of the principal's hair.

I don't recall too many of my kids—a few of the bright ones drop me a card now and then to say what they're doing. It's the mothers, though, I remember best... not as individuals but as group portraits. They poke their heads into my classroom after three o'clock, they sit in the rear patiently even though they've taken time off from their jobs, they wait without a word as I write a report or gather up my books. When I'm finished I ask them, whose mother are you, and they answer Joe Washington's or Jim White's or Raoul Sanchez's. They fold and unfold their soiled handkerchiefs, they daub their moist eyes and their dry mouths with the corners of the cloth.

I listen politely to their outpourings—the pregnant daughters, the stolen welfare checks, the kids' violent scenes at home, their run-ins with police. They put their hands on mine, they beg me, do what you have to do, you needn't ax me, if he need discipline, you be free to take matters in your own hands. I shake my head, yes, I assure them that whatever I can, I will do. They pump my hands up and down, they won't let go, they thank me, bless me, till I pull away and sprint for the stairs.

No, Mrs. Washington, I will not discipline your child any more than I do mine. I will not for too much longer—four years, to be exact, when I reach sixty-two—be your son's and daughter's white stand-up clown, nor spew out ridiculous misinformation, nor be their five-day-a week warden. Come sixty-two, I will retire on full pension, burn my lesson plans, dump my social studies texts, close the door over a mis-spent life as if it were a bad dream. I will learn how to make the most of my golden years . . . I will poke around bookstores, sit in the park on sunny afternoons, see only quality movies, dine with a few other retired friends. The fine art of growing old as painlessly as possible . . . there's a prospect that looms brighter and brighter as the days go by.

Out of nowhere there is a big to-do in the Singer household. Somehow, through a friend of Jean's who knows a hotshot in an art photography studio, Mike has an interview for an honest-to-goodness job. His first reaction is completely negative—in no way can he deal with a job that commodifies art.

My wife takes a surprisingly adamant stance. "Mike, we cannot let you lie around here wasting your life. You've handled cameras since you were a boy. You are not going to throw away this opportunity."

"Okay, okay," he mollifies, "it's a total waste for sure, but if it cools you out, I'll go."

"Not with that attitude," she says, "you make a real sincere try . . . or else . . ." As far as I can remember, these are the first threatening words she has ever used with Mike.

Jean and I have a critically important stake in this interview. Mike's job record since he quit school has been a complete disaster. Messenger boy, stock clerk, fast-food outlets, busboy, telephone sales, bagger at a check-out counter—you name it, he's run the gamut. And it ends inevitably, with his being fired after a few weeks, or else walking out on the job.

The worst experience of all—it makes me wince just to bring it up—was when he was caught stealing several records at a music shop where he was working as a salesman. The shame—you wouldn't believe it—security guards herding him through the store, crowds of shoppers watching, a gestapo questioning, threats of arrest, phone calls to us, a permanent record, so that he can't ever again work at a major music outlet. "Why did you do it?" I asked Mike. "If you needed money, I would have gladly given it to you."

He shrugs it off. "I was broke at the time, the record jacket was fantastic, and it was a great new group. I like their sound so much, I couldn't resist. That's about it."

After this incident, for all of his so-called cool, he withdrew for weeks, months. He would rarely leave his room or open his mouth to talk. He just lay around in bed in pajamas, a lot of the time in the dark, till we thought we would go out of our minds.

We don't want to get our hopes too high, but this interview could be a turning point. The way Jean's friend tells it, there is an assistant's job definitely open. She has praised Mike to the skies and it's mostly a matter of his making a good impression at the interview.

I give Mike money to buy a whole new set of clothes. "Please," I implore, "for a change, no weirdo outfit—just a white shirt, flannel pants, black leather shoes. Most of all, a solid tweed or corduroy jacket. The classic kinds—the ones that make a fine finishing touch."

He takes the money, goes out and comes back a few hours later with a pack of boxes. The afternoon of his interview, my wife and I take off early from work. We wait in the living room, practically beside ourselves with anxiety. At four, when he opens the door, he is wearing his new clothes—black shirt with pencil-thin white stripes, black chinos, a black zippered satin jacket. Pushed halfway down his brow is a dark-gray Fedora with a snap brim. Without so much as a hello, he marches into his room.

It's hard for me to place exactly what my son looks like: One of these new wave gangsters we used to see in French films of the sixties. Or maybe a punk mafioso in a cheap Hollywood movie. I lean back, stunned, on the couch. "Did you see what's he's wearing?" I ask. "He has gone and sabotaged the interview."

"Don't be so quick to judge," Jean says. "When Mike's ready, he'll tell us what happened."

It's not too clear how the rest of that day passed, except that by midnight I had just about bitten my fingernails down to the nub. Finally, we knock at his door and push it in. Mike is stretched out, reading, completely imperturbed. When he glances up he seems genuinely surprised. "How did it go?" Jean asks.

"An absolute ball," he says, "from one end to the other. First, they keep me waiting, not too long, only about an hour or so. Then this man comes out, real Yup type, slick suit, marcelled hair, Italian shoes, thin tie, the whole bit. He stares at me a minute, then he says:

"'You Mike Singer?'

"'As far as I know, yes,'" I answer.

"He puts his hands on his hips. 'You are not what we expected.' This dude, he never refers to himself as *I*—only *we*.

"'In what way?' I ask.

"'Oh,' he says, hesitating and backing away, like he wants to cut out then and there, 'you are not anywhere what we had in mind.'

"'I would be grateful,' I tell him, 'if you would spell that one out.'

"'Well,' he says, 'we are one of New York's top-flight studios. We can't afford to have employees who are . . .' a brief pause . . . 'flaky.'

"'Would you mind defining 'flaky,' I ask.

"'We're finding this discussion pointless,' he says.

"'No, no,' I say, 'this is most fascinating. In what sense do you use the term flaky?'

"'Let's not argue,' he says. 'let's say you don't fit into our image—and leave it at that.'

"'And just what the hell is your image?' I ask.

"By now he's halfway to his office. When I take a step forward to him, he says, 'Sorry, this position would never work out'—and holds both palms out to me as if to keep me off.

"'Know what I think of your job?' I say, 'it sucks, like you.' And he ducks, like a scared little rabbit, into his office.

"All this while the receptionist has been watching from her desk. She leans over to me and whispers: 'Don't take it so hard. He is one son of a bitch of a boss.' 'Lady,' I say, 'me, I'm home free. It's poor bastards like you who have got to deal with this shit.'"

Mike is smiling broadly, as if he were recounting a great big gag. Jean and I stand there listening—reproachful, disappointed . . . but beyond that, dislocated, in shock. Jean sucks in a deep breath—and hangs there with her mouth slightly open, strangely calm, as if she were in the eye of a storm. She's searching for the right words, but they come out in spurts: "Why did you . . . ?" "What could you have been thinking? . . ." "Dressed this way? . . ."

Mike jerks himself to his feet. "I am nobody's image," he rails. "I don't dress on consignment. I don't eat shit. Get that through your heads—I am my own man!" With that, he storms out of the house.

Just eight hours ago, we were a city of hope . . . now it's heartbreak house all over again. We are going to be stuck with one another forever, rerunning gruesome scenes like this over and over, unless we make some kind of a drastic move. And the thing is, Jean and I, we don't have the insight or the courage to do what needs to be done.

There's no point kidding ourselves any more. My sister-in-law's observation is right on the nose. Mike is no sometime pot-smoker; he's hooked on some kind of drug. Almost always now, when he comes home, he walks past us swaying from side to side, with a blank look as if we didn't exist. Somehow, though, in that damned room of his, he manages to sleep it off, pull himself together and disappear without even a mumbled good-bye until late that night. If I try to tousle his hair or put an arm around him, he slips away like a frightened fish. It's as if we were living with a fog, a phantom, a black hole in space.

Once, when she couldn't bear it, Jean begged him: "Mike, darling, maybe you need help—a doctor, a therapist, a drug program." "Fuck off, you guys," he spit out. "I'm no druggie . . . I can take it or leave it," and banged the door shut behind him. "Why didn't you put your two cents in?" Jean shouted at me bitterly. She's so right. I know I should have, but I didn't have the guts to push him to the point of confrontation.

A few days after Helen's call, I am at home, all by myself, too sick to work. As usual I'm obsessing about Mike, wondering why someone so far out has not once tried to find a place of his own. Given his tastes, he should by now be sharing a grubby lower East Side flat, a raw loft in Williamsburgh, maybe even an illegal factory in Astoria. How come Mr. Cool Cat has spent practically his entire life with his momma and papa in an eleven by thirteen foot space, once a maid's room in a West End apartment?

Usually I avoid Mike's room like a plague. On this afternoon, however, I find myself irresistibly drawn to his partially opened door. I push it wide open, lean forward and peer into the darkness. Somewhere in that overgrown jungle of junk, is there some key to my son waiting to be uncovered? Never since he was a teen-ager have I spent any time in Mike's room without his being present. What I am about to do is a gross violation of his privacy, a betrayal of trust. Every instinct in me says no, but I can't resist.

Painstakingly, as if I were wading through a tangle of underbrush,

I step inside. It's his unique universe, that's for certain . . . an animal's nest with his unmistakable spoor—exactly what is it: traces of sperm, incense, body oils? When I draw the curtain aside, it's even more depressing than by artificial light. With the sun pouring through the unwashed windows, I have to narrow my eyes into slits in order to soften the impact of the dishevelled bed, the closets jammed full of clothes, the drawers spewing out bric-a-brac, unravelled tapes, childhood games, pieces of broken equipment. In the shelves are records—hundreds of them carelessly stacked. On top of a small cabinet near his bed is a pile of books: Don Juan, Nietzsche, Allan Watts, The Book of the Tibetan Dead, Jung, Vonnegut and a few volumes of poetry, most of them by authors I do not recognize.

Why am I prying for revelations in this impenetrable welter? The shame of it if Mike should walk in and catch me red-handed. A noise at the front door—I freeze—is it him turning the key? No, it's quiet again—most likely a neighbor. It's clear that I must let myself quickly out the door. As I turn to go, I see from the corner of my eye an envelope jutting from the shelf. I reach out, take the envelope, note that it's from a photo studio, addressed to Mike. Inside are photos most likely taken by my son, newly developed, a grainy black and white. One by one I examine them—shots of penetration, men and women, men and men, into every orifice, taken from so close that each flaw is magnified . . . pimples on the faces, scars on bodies, pubic hair as thick as strands of wire, mouths contorted, organs distended, lips cracked and glossy. It makes me ill just looking at them, truncated, pieces of people, machineries for sex. I put the photos back into the envelope and slip it into the shelf. As I do, I see in a small hidden niche a red notebook tightly closed by a rubber band.

It's the rubber band that makes me pause; also the word *Journal* neatly printed on the cover. I draw the notebook out and hold it in my palm. Surrendering all will, I let my fingers do the work. They open the cover, turn the pages slowly. Inside are mostly brief quotations hastily scrawled, from one book or another . . . lists of record albums . . . comments about the music . . . pieces of magazine articles held down by scotch tape . . . crossed out writing . . . blank after blank page. And then, near the end of the journal, a bookmark opened to a clear, precisely written entry in black ink:

> Oh shit, next month is my parents' 25th wedding anniversary. Pathetic little Papa, bewildered Mom—what a combo of losers. It freaks me out to watch them grow old and gray down the

> pike to desperation row. Dad with his dentures and swollen prostate. Mom with her varicose veins and phony blonde hair. It used to be there were squeaky sex noises coming from the master—ha!—bedroom. I would have this image of them, belly to flabby belly, trying to work up a decent screw. Now nothing but silence: two altered pussycats curled up like slugs on opposite sides of the bed. Marry a nice Jewish girl and live straight till boredom kills us both? I'd slit my throat before it came to that...

At first, when the shock wave hits me, I tell myself: Keep a proper perspective. Don't make a big deal out of a half-assed kid pouring out his venom into a journal. How come, then, I stand there immobilized, studying the entry, word by word, line by line, until it is permanently branded into my brains? I close the pages, twist the rubber band around the cover and put the journal back where I found it. All that afternoon, until the numbness begins to wear off, I hear that refrain, pathetic little papa, pathetic little papa, pathetic little papa, repeating itself endlessly, like one of Mike's records, in my head.

Money, in the shape of small missing sums—has become a source of contention between Jean and myself. It's like this: every week we put our household money into a blue book—one of my textbooks—over the bed. Whenever we buy anything—groceries, toiletries, wine—both of us take what we need from the book and mark down the new total. Whatever is left at the end of the week—we call it our luxury fund—we slip into a red book—a novel—which we keep right next to the blue book. Sometimes there is as much as five hundred dollars in the luxury fund.

A few months back, small sums... ten, fifteen dollars, seemed to be missing each week. Jean and I are careless with figures, so we at first attribute the shortages to forgetfulness or poor addition. Pretty soon, Jean and I begin to ask each other, did you take out some money without marking it down?

Under the circumstances I suppose we should change the books in which we keep the money—or at least put them on different shelves. But we don't. To do this would be to admit that Mike is systematically ripping us off—and this is too painful to consider. For the following few weeks we leave the books in the same place, hoping against hope that the totals will magically add up right and we can let the losses of the past weeks slip out of mind.

Instead, the amount missing each week begins to climb—twenty-five, thirty, once even forty dollars. By now there is no mistaking it—the game of make-believe is over. Mike is the thief and the money leached out of the blue book each week is an evil portent—further poisoning the atmosphere between us.

The breaking point comes when fifty dollars are gone one week. "Speak to him," I urge Jean, "go in and ask, point blank, what he is doing with the stolen money."

"Why don't you ask him?" she answers. "He's your son too."

"You and Mike relate better," I say. "With me it would only end up in some kind of grotesque quarrel."

In the end—almost always she's the one who deals with him—my wife goes into Mike's room to talk about the money. When she returns, Jean is livid with rage. "Don't you ever again get me to do your dirty work," she shouts.

My heart sinking, I say, "Why, what happened?"

"Point blank," she says, "I asked Mike whether he'd been borrowing money from the black book above our bed."

" 'What book?' he asks.

" 'The black book,' I repeat. 'Social Studies for Secondary Schools.'

" 'I don't make a practice of borrowing my parents' money from black books,' he says.

"Right then and there," Jean says, "I would gladly forget about the money, but it's too late. I'm in over my head. 'More than five hundred dollars,' I tell him, 'has disappeared from the black book. Unless, of course, your dad and I are totally incapable of adding.'

" 'Either that,' he says, 'or else I'm a sneak thief. Right?'

" 'That's not what I meant . . .'

" 'Then what the fuck did you mean?'

" 'I don't know what I'm saying!' I yell out, and before I can stop myself, I begin to sob.

" 'Here's what I'll do, he says, 'You and dad want to conduct a search—I'm happy to oblige.' And he starts to empty his pockets, desk drawers, clothes, shelves, throwing everything onto the floor. 'Go ahead, be my guest,' he shouts, 'there's gold in that there shit.' Then he shoves my hand into his pants pocket. 'See for yourself! I'm loaded.' So I turn and run—and I warn you, Steve, don't you ever mention the missing money."

After this incident, the money in the black book stopped disappearing. Unfortunately, however, there is a postscript to the story. One day I go to the luxury fund to get money for concert tickets. This time the red book itself is gone. Before we panic, Jean suggests, could one of us, without thinking, have put the red book on another shelf? There is no point making accusations before we go through all of the books.

We do just that—we go thoroughly through every one of the bookshelves in our room, then the living room, looking for a red book that is nowhere to be found. There is not the slightest shadow of doubt. The four hundred or so dollars are gone—and we don't dare tackle Mike.

Jean and I, by mutual consent—understood if not discussed—have stopped talking about the missing book. The trouble is, the thought of Mike brazenly plundering and spending the house money week after week is always present—at our work, while we are eating, reading, trying to sleep. It's like a landmine planted in our house, waiting to detonate at the slightest jar.

Mike has been gone for two whole days and nights, leaving Jean and me with the premonition that something catastrophic has happened. Just when we have decided to call the police—at about 8:30 in the evening—we get an almost incoherent call from Mike. As far as we can make out, he's being held in arraignment at the night court, downtown, on charges of selling drugs in Washington Square. Does he need us to get him a lawyer? No, he wants to go all the way with the Legal Aid lawyer who's been assigned to him.

When we arrive at the night court, Mike is slumped forlornly behind the railing. From the front bench we can see purplish bruises around his eyes; several red welts are also visible on his chalk-white face. He barely acknowledges our frantic arm-waving to let him know we are here. In a while, the Legal Aid lawyer—a harassed woman in her thirties—comes over to fill us in on the details: for the last twenty-four hours, Mike has been detained—illegally of course—in the Raymond Street jail for scuffling violently with the two narcotics officers who caught him dealing drugs—in the bright daylight no less. He's been roughed up, spread-eagled on the ground, face down, searched for weapons and not allowed to communicate with the outside until tonight.

"Is there any way we can help?" I ask the Legal Aid woman. "Maybe," I add awkwardly, "another lawyer?"

"No," she says, "it won't be necessary. It's an open-and-shut case. He was caught with a hundred or so cocaine packets on his person, along with several hundred dollars in cash. "If we take him to trial," she adds, "there's a good chance he might get from two to four years."

What does she suggest? Well, the assistant DA is not too eager to press charges against a nice middle-class kid, first offender too. Besides, the judge is not a notorious punishment freak. Given all this, she feels, there's every likelihood she can plea-bargain a suspended sentence.

Before I can stop myself I ask: "Does this mean fingerprints—and a permanent record against his name?"

The lawyer breathes in hard, unbelieving. "Don't you think," she says, "that's small potatoes compared to a stretch in the penitentiary?" And clutching a batch of briefs in her hands, she goes off to rejoin her clients.

The court session is scheduled for nine-thirty, the clerk drones out, but the judge has been delayed. Meanwhile, no reading of books or magazines, no eating, no loud conversation or otherwise disturbing the peace. I sit there, in the gloomy cavern of a court, with the steam hissing, surrounded by families and friends—mostly black or Puerto Rican—who have come to commiserate with the arraigned. They sit back on the benches in tableaus of utter submissiveness, the mothers' arms around their babies, shushing the older brothers and sisters, who shuffle their feet and kick disconsolately at the benches in front of them.

As we wait, interminably, I slip in and out of uneasy dozings—as in a dream, only I'm fully awake, suspended and timeless. Up front, a circle of blinding lights gradually floods the faces of my son along with the other allegeds—the prostitutes, embezzlers and rapists, the arsonists, batterers and addicts, the muggers, shoplifters and con men. Around them, packs of lawyers crouch and weave, tearing at their papers, leaping like bird-retrievers onto their clients, to parade them in their mouths before the beaming judges. Now the lights are turned blindingly on us, seated body to body, like sardines in a can, packed together in the oil of our guilt. *Guilty of what,* I cry out to no one in particular. *Unnameable crimes,* a chorus of mocking voices booms out through the loudspeakers . . . *guilty of falling out of the safety net . . . of falling from white grace into the blackness of the night court . . . of fathering, harboring and abetting crime. No,* I shout, *not guilty . . . I am not one of these*—the word that wants to come out of my mouth is *jigaboos,* but I see Mike brandishing a fist at me and a circle of menacing black faces loop around me like a net.

Yes, Mike's lawyer is dead right about his sentence. When his turn comes, the judge—his eyes skimming over the papers—consults briefly with the lawyer and the assistant DA. He nods his head toward Mike and says in a barely audible voice: "I understand, son, that you plead guilty with extenuating circumstances—family trouble, long-term unemployment, severe emotional problems." He turns to the courtroom and barks out as if by rote: *One year in jail, suspended sentence under the recognizance of your mother and father, Jean and Robert Singer, a $500 fine for resisting arrest, and an order from the court to report to the Narcotics Legal Bureau once a month for the duration of the sentence.* When we walk toward his lawyer to thank her, she is wholly involved with a mother and son who can barely speak English. She waves a hand in our direction, flashes a perfunctory smile and returns her attention to the tearful woman.

All the way home in the cab, we sit back without a word, watching Mike stew in his despair. "We can thank our lucky stars," Jean tries to comfort him, "it could have been a disaster." When she reaches out to stroke his hair, he stiffens and pulls sharply away.

"The only reason I'm free," he says, "is because we're white and privileged. You better believe that!" If he's looking for an argument, he won't get one from us. "If I were black or brown," he presses on, "they'd have hauled my ass to Riker's Island. Know what I'd be doing right now? . . . waiting in a cell block along with the other poor bastards to be shipped out for three, four years."

I tell the cab-driver to pull up in front of a Chinese take-out place a few blocks from where we live. When we get home, Jean lights a candle to make things more festive. We spread the food on the kitchen table and eat, in deathly silence, right out of the plastic containers. Maybe this isn't the time or place, but I have to ask the question which has been bothering me since my son's phone call: "Why did you do it, Mike, on a sunny afternoon in the crowded park . . . You didn't have the ghost of a chance."

"No other exit," he answers. "I was crawling out of my skin."

"What were you going to do with the money?"

"Jump ship," he says, "take the money and run as far and as fast as I could."

"Living with us is that bad?"

"Nothing personal," he says, "but it sucks."

We pick at our food, watching the candlelight flicker. Jean takes the three fortune cookies out of a paper bag and puts them in the middle of the table. "It's fortune-telling time," she says.

"You go first," I tell her.

She breaks the cookie open, unrolls the little white slip and reads: "Very soon you will visit exotic lands and far-off places."

"If you had the chance, where would you go?" I ask.

She tears the slip in half. "I think I'll pass this one up."

"No, no, Jean," I insist, "I would like very much to know."

"Okay, then," she says, a wry smile on her face, "I'd sail off to the land of my lifelong dreams—the Sahara . . . better yet, the Gobi Desert."

"What the heck would you do there?" I ask.

"Oh, learn about the desert ways . . . maybe disappear with a caravan into the sand dunes." There's a strange lilt to her voice. She's breathing hard, off a million miles away on her own.

"How long would you stay away, Mom?" Mike asks.

Her son's words pull her back. "A few years," she says, "conceivably forever."

It frightens me, my wife's intensity, the sharpness with which she visualizes her going away—a woman who swears to me she has never, never had any fantasies.

"Now let's hear yours," she says, turning to me.

"Search your heart," I read out from the slip, "if you would discover where you truly belong."

"Well, well," says Jean, "start searching."

Funny how irritated I feel. "I'm a nowhere man," I snap. "My heart belongs wherever it's parked." What I'm saying doesn't make any sense, but I mean it to sound ominous.

"And just where is your heart parked?" Jean asks lightly.

For reasons beyond me, I can't find an answer. We sit, the both of us, staring at each other uneasily. It surprises me when Mike breaks the tension by reading his own cookie:

"If you gaze into the depths, you will see your own future."

"See anything in your crystal ball?" Jean asks.

He peers into an imaginary globe he holds in his hands. "It's all dark," he says. "Wait—I see a space suit, with a dead man inside, who answers to my description. Ah, the clouds are clearing up. . ." He brings the globe closer to his eyes. "He's alone in outer space, circling the galaxies from here to eternity . . . till the end of time. . ."

My wife shudders. She pulls her shoulders together and gets up from her chair. She puts her arms around his neck. He holds still while she hugs him as hard as she can. "The party's over," Jean says softly, turns on her heels and goes.

We sit for a few moments, Mike and I, across the table piled with empty food containers. His thin face looks lost in the bushy beard. I know I should conjure up some kind of move—some magical words I need to remember. The thing is, I have a dialogue rehearsed and polished a hundred times over for just such a once-in-a-lifetime situation. It is intended to be a heartfelt appeal for us to start from scratch . . . make our peace. But facing him here, it seems so phony, I can't get a word out. If I let this moment go, it will die forever between us.

"Mike," I say, "Mike"—it feels odd mouthing his name twice—"any time something bugs you, you say it sucks. Like you said a minute ago, living here sucks. What else sucks? No small things. I mean on a more fundamental—a philosophic level."

He pins me under his stare. "You really want an answer?"

"For sure," I say, "that's why I'm asking."

"Okay, then." Mike sways from side to side as if he's reciting a litany—in fact, the thought strikes me, this is the exact way he half-sang out his barmitzvah text—"First off," his voice is icy with irony, "heart to heart talks with your father suck . . . pretentious discussions like this one suck . . . Schools suck . . . teachers" . . . he repeats . . . "teachers suck . . . psychologists suck . . . the whole social work cabal like mom's sucks . . . history sucks . . . given wisdom sucks . . . everything most people cherish sucks . . . plastic, anything plastic sucks . . . armies, wars and rumors of wars—they all suck!"

He stops. "Had enough?"

"No," I wave him on, "let's have the whole kit and caboodle."

"Leaders suck . . . followers suck . . . crime and punishment sucks . . . clubs, handcuffs, prisons suck . . . locking people into genders sucks . . . and money . . ."—he hums the sounds *"mmmmm . . . . uuuuu . . . . neeeeee . . ."*—until they melt in his mouth . . . "the gestalt of money sucks . . . the accumulation of it . . . the hoarding of it . . . the counting of it . . . the love of it . . . money sucks!"

My son's eyes are burning into me. He's so into himself, the words are pouring out of his mouth like a chant:

"Marriage sucks . . . begetting children sucks . . . being a kid sucks . . . families suck . . . planning for tomorrow sucks . . . getting up in the morning sucks . . . trying to make it through the day sucks . . . waiting for nights to end sucks . . . growing older sucks . . . hanging around till you die sucks . . ."

"Enough," I say, "I've got the message," but he rides over me.

"Consult the bible—your book of vengeance: Israels' holy wars, Joshua's massacres, Elijah's bloodbaths—all in the name of Jehovah. Read about it in tomorrow's *Times.* Take a good look at yourself in the mirror, tonight, and make out your own list of a hundred favorite sucks."

Suddenly in the middle of the tirade, his voice falters, trails off into a whisper. He squints at me in surprise, as if I were all this time a blur and had only now come back into his focus. "I'm bushed," he says. "It's been a hard day's night."

I can't bear for us to part on this note. One of us has got to make a human gesture, however small. "There must be something sacred," I say, "something that doesn't suck. Like love . . . does that suck too?"

He glances up at me coolly. "I wouldn't know," is his answer.

"Your mother and father . . . they suck too?"

One shrug of his shoulders. "I hadn't really given it a thought."

There is nothing left to say. The party is most definitely over. Between us is a gulf of black space. He goes to his room, and I sit back stunned. We never even say good night.

As I lie on the couch, a reverie begins to assemble itself, against my will, image by image, on the screen of my closed eyelids . . . . a re-replay of a nightmare that I had a couple of years ago. I'm at school one day, I'm standing in the hall, I hear screams through the door, I step into my classroom to see a bunch of kids frantically holding onto a black boy—bigger, heavier than me—who is hanging by his hands from a window ledge six stories above the street. He has climbed out to show off to the class and can't haul himself back. I push my way through the kids, lean over the ledge and grab his wrists. As I lie there, my nails dug into his flesh, to keep from letting go, a lunatic thought crosses my mind:

What if it were Mike, not this boy, his weight twisting my arms, like a doll's, out of their sockets, six stories above his death? How long could I hang on? I can see his contorted face . . . his stricken eyes curved backward toward mine . . . I hear him shouting at me, "Don' let go, man, I ain't ready to die!" *Not too long, son,* I listen to me talking to myself, *I cannot hang on too much longer . . . No father, at least not this father, can keep you from plunging down to rock bottom if you have to fall . . .*

Help me, someone, my hands are slipping off his wrists. In a moment they will surrender, plummeting him (is he my son?) downward like a stone! With a crazed cry I dissolve the dream and sit up trembling on the couch. As if in prayer I rock slowly until the terror subsides.

It's going to be a long night . . . I can tell from my dry mouth, the thin asthmatic wheeze, the gasping for air. I can't cope any more. I want sleep to rescue me, Jean and I wrapped in each other's arms. As I think of my wife, Mike's ugly words leap into mind—*bewildered Mom, pathetic little Dad. Two altered pussycats on opposite sides of the bed.*

I pull myself up and walk unsteadily to our bedroom. If I know Jean, she will be curled up in bed like a sad child, maybe even quietly sobbing. Instead when I open the door she stands before the full-length mirror, combing her hair. "Did you hear Mike ranting?" I ask.

"Every word," she says, without looking at me.

"Well, what do you think?"

"It's too late to discuss it," she says. The tone of her voice hovers between a simple statement and an accusation. What does she mean, too late? Too late at night? Too late for Mike? Too late for the two of us?

I lay my hand gently on her shoulder. She pulls away with a sharp twist of her body. My heart is hammering like a piston out of control. "About wanting to leave me," I ask, "you were only kidding, no?"

"I don't want to discuss that either," she says sharply.

"Please, Jean—" I can hear myself cravenly pleading, "talk to me now." Without answering, she puts the comb away and slides into bed.

A blue flame is burning in my belly. I can't stand the thought of Jean wrapped in her solitude beyond my reach. It's too painful this way, our rigid bodies side by side. I know that sleep won't come, even with the morning sun.

As soon as I grope my way in the darkness of the living room, I hear, wafting through the door of Mike's room, the sound of Bob Dylan: *How does it feel, to be all alone* . . . Oh, that nostalgic rasp—one of my few good memories left over from the sixties. *No direction home . . . like a great unknown . . . like a rolling stone.* I gave this record to Mike on his sixteenth birthday. Know what he said?: "God, he's so old hat, fake folksy." He never even bothered, out of politeness, to play the record for me.

The bluish-white crack through the bottom of the door tells me that the light in Mike's room is still on. I can visualize him lying on his mattress wide awake. The record ends, the needle hisses along the empty grooves, a pause, and then the twang of Dylan's guitar begins again. Since Mike can't bear Dylan, how come he's listening to him over and over? Is it because he knows how much I love Dylan? Could this be some kind of subliminal signal, a telepathic synapse he's beaming at me? Does he want me to make the first move? Knock at the door? Let myself in? For Christ's sake, will somebody tell me?

Tiptoeing to his room, I stand at the door without breathing. I press forward, one hand clenched, the other poised on the knob. Alert as a nerve, mind tuned in like an antenna, body atremble, I listen in the intense stillness for a directive.

Black Is the Color

Violet, the cleaning woman, is on her hands and knees, scrubbing the clay tiles until they take on a burnished glow. The ammonia fumes drift to the couch where Lionel lies in the sunlight. Propped on the pillows he hears her hum one of the songs—"His Eye Is on the Sparrow"—she learned as a child in Jamaica. Blues, Gospel, Caribbean, the low lush voice fuses into one outpouring so moving, he can imagine her dark-bronze face radiant with belief as the music pours forth from her in a small backwoods church.

As she works the mop over the floor in a slow, steady rhythm, Violet interrupts her song to relate a favorite story. "Sunday mornings," she says, "we young-'uns, no more'n thirteen, come marching uphill to church in our white blouse—Mama wash mine till it dazzle—and shiny leather shoes." After all these years, Lionel has given up trying to master the Jamaican dialect. To converse with him, Violet has to pick her way laboriously through an English that is largely alien to her. He regrets the small but sad rift of tongues between them. It has robbed her lilting speech, he feels, of much of its bite and imagination.

Lionel leans back languidly, savoring the same tale he has heard so many times. "And the boys, Violet," he goads, "did they flirt?"

"Oh my God," she laughs and wrings out the dirty mop, "Did they ever? They jus' stand there showing off—poking each other in the ribs, pulling our pleat hair till they see the old peoples comin' up the steps."

"And then what?" he asks.

"One of them, the tallest, good-looking too, leans over and whisper, 'Hey, girl, you the pretty one, you be my steady, what you say?' "

"What do you say, Violet?"

"I tell him, 'Not if you was the last boy on the Island.' Then we scream, the girls, how we do scream!" She leans forward for a moment, both hands on the floor. "Not long after that, we start going together and he become my husband."

Here it comes, the part of the story Lionel doesn't want to hear, but Violet is too deep in her memories to stop. "They was the best of it, them young years. I give him three childrens—two pass away, only my Jenny is left." A long sigh. "After that, it was hell. Him out of work, starting to drink, playing around with the other girls."

Lionel gets up and pulls a sweater over his head to cut her off as gently as possible. "St. Louis, Detroit, Chicago, Erie, Pennsylvania." She reworks the itinerary in her head. "Buffalo, and then Harlem, New York." Violet is staring ahead, no longer talking to him. "Two of my children sick all the time, me having to leave them with my sister. And my husband, there wasn't much left of him by this time."

"I have to run," Lionel says brusquely. "I left the money on the table. And something too for your birthday."

She glances across the room and sees a brightly wrapped gift with a small envelope on it. "Oh," Violet says, "that awful nice of you, Mr. Zeller." All these years and she will not call him Lionel. When he leaves she will laboriously read on the card: "To Violet, who helps make my aging days worth living. Love, Lionel."

Sometimes, when he should be reading or marking papers, he secretly watches Violet through his open bedroom door. Humming softly, she seems to withdraw completely into her housecleaning as if in the grip of an internal ritual. Without a wasted movement, she serenely choreographs her chores through the entire apartment until, by late afternoon, when the house is spotlessly clean and the air is clorox-fresh, Lionel has black cups of coffee ready for them at the kitchen table.

He glances up at her as they sip, this handsome big-bosomed woman with jet black hair, almond eyes and full rose-mauve lips that open slightly to show her white teeth. Though she is his age—sixty-one—he has long since fallen into the role of errant younger man. Lionel, who cannot remember his own mother too well, deviously plays up his boyishness. She has fallen in comfortably with his bad-boy posturings. He has often thought, with a melting ache, how easily he could sink, sobbing on his knees, into her honey-black motherliness.

How long ago was it that Violet had come into his life? Nineteen, twenty years ago? Long before his wife had died. The kids had just begun their college studies away from home. His wife Bea and he were alone, giddy with freedom, for the first time since the children were born. If it were possible, they both agreed, they wouldn't lift a finger to do housework as long as they lived.

Lionel doesn't like to recall how it was that Violet had become their steady woman. Someone had called to recommend her own domestic. "She needs work bad," the woman had said, "and you can't get a better girl. Talk about being honest, you could trust her with your diamonds. And does she clean, I mean, my girl works like a beaver."

Bea had been quick to say: "Look, we need a reliable woman, not a slave girl."

"Okay, okay," the woman had apologized. "All I'm trying to tell you is, Violet is terrific."

From day one, three times a week, Violet was a take-over woman . . . shopping for food, doing the laundry, whirlwinding through the house with supreme good nature and an efficiency that was awesome.

At times, looking at the shiny-clean apartment with a small stab of guilt, Bea and Lionel would discuss Violet's cleaning up after white people like themselves. Once, in the middle of the night, Bea had blurted out: "Honest, Lionel, I'd rather turn tricks than mess with other people's shit, like Violet." If his wife had expected a comment, it wasn't forthcoming. He just kept on breathing heavily as if he were asleep.

Before long, they couldn't imagine what it had been like without Violet. Bea, who worked all day, gratefully let the household reins slip from her hands. Lionel, a part-time college teacher, was often home when Violet arrived. Sitting at his desk, he could hear her key turning, the door opening and her soft voice: "You home, Mr. Zeller?"

"No," he would shout back, "I'm out to lunch."

She'd throw her head back and let out a peal of laughter. The joke was always fresh. Each time she would shake her head, exhale and say, "I swear, next time I'm not going to ask."

Earlier, Lionel would have already done the preliminaries. The cleaning items were lined up in the kitchen—powder, wax, glass cleaner, detergents, mop, pail, rags, rubber gloves. The vacuum cleaner was plugged in, fresh bag and all, the wastepaper baskets were empty, a new plastic neatly tucked into the trashcan. In the bathroom sink, there wasn't a trace of hair left for her to wipe away.

Violet would look around, put her hand on her waist and say: "You ought not do this, Mr. Zeller, that's what I paid for."

"I'm practicing, Violet," Lionel would answer, mimicking her Island singsong. "If I lose my job, I'm gonna have to be your assistant."

"Don't know," she would sigh, her eyes flashing, "what I'm gone do with you."

•

In a few months, Violet, simply by the majesty of her presence, had insinuated herself wholly into the ambience of their lives. But what was she, Lionel would puzzle, this black woman who three times weekly flashed across their firmament and after erasing the accumulation of their daily dirt disappeared into her own existence? An extended family member? Substitute mother image? The perfect domestic they could graciously condescend to? Bea and Lionel—perhaps out of a nagging guilt—didn't discuss it ever, but it preyed on Lionel's mind.

Once, observing her at work, there had flashed into Lionel's mind a slave narrative, *Incidents in the Life of a Slave Girl,* he had assigned his class. Its harrowing story of a "house nigger" on a plantation had evoked in him images of Violet cleaning their own household. Annoyed by the palpable unfairness of the comparison, he had argued with himself: What nonsense. Violet is a proud woman, free to leave if she wants. One of these days—you know how these things go—they could get a call from her saying she'd found a better situation. Still, he fervently hoped that, no matter what, she would never choose to leave him.

Violet revealed herself slowly, in layers or petals, like an unfolding bud. Take, for one, her spiritual proclivities. She was, Lionel and Bea had discovered, a diviner, a reader of horoscopes, of handwriting, tea leaves and palms. She had even hinted at her leading seances—if there were dead to be reached—and using voodoo powers—if an occasion warranted it.

Though he told himself, it was all an amusing game, Lionel was amazed at how seriously he took her advice. "Your higher and lower planes," she had warned him once, "are in a terrible war for your soul." Another time, she had read his horoscope. "You are one of them stubborn Leos," she had told him, "who have got to tame their lions." She had held him firmly by his hand. "Fight the Satan in you, Mr. Zeller. With God's help you can wrest him from your mind."

It was stunning, her insight into the turmoil he was passing through. Only that week, after a cruel argument where Bea had threatened to leave him, Lionel had resolved to soften his dogmatism, open himself to reason.

His wife, who scoffed at anything spiritualist ("occultist crap," she would sneer) had only once allowed herself to be urged into a reading. Staring into Bea's palm, Violet had said: "You have got a very long lifeline, Mrs. Zeller. But then"—she had traced the crease with a finger—"see how it splits and fades toward the end?"

Picking up on Violet's odd tone of voice, Bea had sharply asked: "What does that signify, Violet?"

Violet had shrugged it off: "Don't pay it no attention. You most likely going to live a hundred years."

That first year, Violet had set a pattern by inviting Bea and Lionel to a Christmas celebration at her tenement building on 147th Street. They had walked along in the early evening, uneasily, through a neighborhood they hadn't visited since they were young. Inside Violet's tiny railroad flat, a group of her relatives and friends were waiting for them stiffly. From the first, the politeness on both sides had been killing. There were handshakes, introductions, overenthusiastic hellos to people whose names they would never remember. Violet had walked them over to an easy chair where her husband, face frozen by a stroke, had mumbled something incomprehensible to them.

Throughout the night, everyone had danced gingerly around their solo whiteness in an all-black surround. The talk was small and safe—children, young people today, the weather, the high price of food, the terrible state of the A train. To get over an uncomfortable lull in the conversation, Violet had suddenly bragged: "Mr. Zeller, he's a big professor at the University. And his wife"—she had awkwardly pulled Bea toward her—"she runs a whole department."

Smiles of approval on all sides, even a little round of applause. "What do you teach?" a young woman had asked.

He had hesitated, trying to think of something not too pompous. "Oh, American literature—the contemporary period. That is," he had hastily added, "stuff that's being written currently."

"Now ain't that nice," a very old woman wrapped in an antique lace shawl had said.

Violet had prepared a feast of Island fare—goat-stew, an okra and rice dish, yam pie. "You folks ready for a special treat?" the woman who heaped their plates had asked.

Lionel watched Bea, a vegetarian, desperately spearing bits of green from the dish of meat. There was a frenzy of lip-smacking and appreciation. "Ain't it heavenly?" the woman had said.

"They forgot how to make it this way," the old woman had confirmed.

After the food, they had all gathered around the tree for the singing of hymns. Violet had led the group, her voice trembling with ardor. It had struck Lionel, for the first time, that in her natural habitat Violet was fervently religious:

"I love to tell the story,
the great old Bible story,

the story of His glory,
of Jesus and His love."

When the voices had faded, they had all sat back quietly . . . the first moment, Lionel had thought, of genuinely shared feeling.

Afterwards a man had leaned over to ask: "You a Catholic, Mr. Zeller, or Episcopalian?"

Violet had leaped in to answer. "Oh, no, they of the Hebrew persuasion." For some reason, she could never bring herself to say the naked word "Jew."

"Oh, well," the man had affably said, "we are all children of God."

There was a murmur of general assent, a shaking of heads yes, a chorus of amens.

When it was time to leave, Violet had taken Bea and Lionel to her bedroom to show off a photo of her daughter Jenny. "She was only fourteen then," Violet had said, proudly holding out the photo. In it, a sullen young woman defiantly looked out, her oval face, huge eyes and close crop of ringleted hair already foreshadowing the beautiful woman to be. "Jenny's with my sister," Violet had explained. "She ain't easy for me. I can't deal with her in the city."

On the way home in the cab, Lionel had tried to blot out the image of Jenny's striking face that had fixed itself in his head . . . her old-young knowingness, the point-blank stare, the ironic tilt of her lips. Turning to his wife, he had felt a rush of affection and put his hand gently on her face.

"What is it, Lionel?" she had asked.

"Nothing . . . except that I love you."

The next time Violet had come to clean, she had been glowing with praise for them. "Goodness," she had gushed, "everybody loved the two of you. They said I was lucky to have such a wonderful boss."

Lionel had winced at the word. "We had a wonderful time too," Bea had quickly said.

After that, the social exchanges between Violet, Bea and Lionel had multiplied, it seemed, on their own—holidays like Passover at their home, their daughters' birthday parties, other really special events. Vivacious, sociable, brimming with joy, Violet fit in like a glove with any company. Besides that, the leavening of a working class black woman at a white middle-class gathering was—though it pained Lionel to admit it—a social asset he really appreciated.

Lionel's first meeting with Jenny was at her father's funeral. Sixteen now, she was even more lovely than the photo of her had promised. Standing at the graveside, Violet and her daughter, they had watched dry-eyed as the coffin was lowered. Later, in the limousine with Bea and Lionel, Violet had bitterly complained: "My sister tell me, Jenny quit school, do nothing but hang around the house and go out half the night. You go to Mr. Zeller for advice, Jenny. He's a professor, he tell you what you have to do with yourself."

In a rage, Jenny had half-opened the door and shouted. "You keep on like this, Mama, I'm getting off this second. And I'm not coming back!" From there on in, it had been a silent, disconcerting drive.

Only a few months later, they had driven Violet to a New England law school for their younger daughter's graduation. When Marsha, cap-and-gowned, had stepped forward to receive her degree, Lionel had noted Violet bent over, handkerchief in hand, weeping quietly. Driving back, Violet was in a darker mood—morose, uncommunicative—than they had ever seen. "Is something wrong?" Bea had gently asked.

Violet had stiffened at the question. "No, Mrs. Zeller," she had answered, rocking from side to side as in prayer, "ain't nothing you or anybody can do for my Jenny. Girl like her pissing her young God-given days away." It had shocked them, hearing Violet spitting out an unseemly word. "The bad mens she's been with . . . the mean things she has had to do . . ."

"Violet," Lionel had said, reaching back to touch her from the driver's seat, "it isn't that late. Jenny is a young woman."

Violet had flung his hand aside. "Oh no," she had cried out, "your daughter and all those white girls in their fine gowns. You ain't gonna catch them cleaning house, or some other shit jobs and tripling up with their folks in some dirty slum . . ."

They had continued in cold silence, Bea and Lionel, not able to find words of comfort. Violet had barely mumbled a good-bye when they had left her in front of her house. Their last sight of her, she was dragging herself, one hand clinging to the rail, laboriously up the long flight of stairs.

Two years later, Bea fell into a long illness. Her doctor called Lionel to say: "It's a malignant tumor, Mr. Zeller, that's metastacized through her colon. Frankly, we all think it's too late for surgery. Or radiation, for that matter." After a brief hospital stay, Bea had come home to die.

Violet moved in with them, taking over the girls' room. They clung to one another, day and night, Violet her only comfort, her black angel of mercy.

Lionel slept on the living room couch, doing his schoolwork on the table. Listening to them behind the closed door, he could hear them chatting cozily, their voices feather soft. Nothing else but Violet seemed to exist for her. If she inquired after the children, it was in a distant manner, as if she had already dispensed with them for her coming death. As for Lionel, even when he sat for hours beside her bed, trying to cheer her, he too seemed to be growing distant in her mind. It was as if their long marriage together—the complex web of their intimacies—was dissolving in the mist of her pain.

Violet, indomitable as ever, fed her, washed the wrecked machinery of her body, lay her strong hands on Bea to draw out with lovingness the terrible hurt. Often, when Violet came out of Bea's room, she would say: "You have got yourself a real brave wife."

Toward the end, when the doctors no longer came for their routine examination, Violet resorted to her own magic. "An African friend of mine taught me this, incantations and special healing herbs," she explained to Lionel. "Of course, it's supposed to be for believers only," her voice trailed off.

Even when the healing rituals failed, Violet didn't give up. One night he saw a glass of water on the dresser, covered with a gold and red cloth. "What's it for?" he had asked Violet.

"With God's will," she had answered, "your wife won't pass away until the water is all dried out." The glass was still full the night Bea died.

At the funeral Violet, weeping uncontrollably, had told him: "I knowed all along the healing wouldn't help. It was your wife's lifeline, Mr. Zeller. Like I told her once, it drifted away and faded off her palm."

After his wife's death, Lionel moves to another place just large enough for himself and an occasional visit from his daughters. At first Violet tells him. "Mr. Zeller, you alone now. It don't make sense my coming here more than once every two weeks."

Lionel overrules her. "Forget it, Violet. I want everything like it was before. Same three times, same afternoons."

"It wouldn't be right," she insists, "throwing good money away."

Lionel has carefully gone over his budget. With his part-time salary, and his income from a fair-sized nest-egg, there will be enough. "Please," he tells her, "allow me to spend my good money on a good woman."

And that was that. Things are the way they were before, except that Violet suffers from severe arthritis in her knees. The pain has slowed her down to a walk. Instead of whizzing through the house, she goes through the slow motion of painstakingly polishing up a small apartment that barely gathers dust between her visits.

Whenever he sees her favoring her aching knee, Lionel urges Violet to rest on the couch with him and chat. Living by themselves, the two of them, they can speak more freely than ever, leaping from subject to subject, whatever crosses their minds.

They talk once about her hidden dreams. "If you had the chance again," he asks, "what would you do, Violet?"

"Oh," she answers, surprising him, "be a famous gospel singer, like Mahalia Jackson. Or maybe, if I was young, like Aretha Franklin." She looks at him with fierce eyes. "I would raise my voice," she says, "me in my white gown, so's the peoples in the last seats would hear me loud and clear praising the works of the Lord."

Violet settles back into the couch, a faraway smile on her lips. When she has come back, Lionel says: "Me, I would never marry, never have kids or settle down. I would be a world traveler, live in a cave in India, join a caravan in Africa, bum my way from Texas down to the tip of South America."

Once he asks her: "How come you stayed so long with a man who treated you real bad."

Violet clasps her hands together. "When you choose your own burden," she says sternly, "the Lord expects you to carry it forever, no matter how heavy it is."

"Funny," he muses—the words maliciously slip out of his mouth—"Though I loved Bea, it wasn't a very happy marriage."

"The Lord," she says, "brought us on earth to be righteous, not happy."

While he is pondering her answer, Violet brightens up. "Good news," she tells him, "my daughter Jenny coming home to stay with me a while. She leave her little girl with my sister."

Lionel feels his heart leaping at her words. Hiding his excitement, he makes a show of being calm. "Oh, that's great. When will she be here?"

"In a few days," she answers, "soon as she gets my ticket money."

One afternoon, shortly after this conversation, Violet unexpectedly asks: "Ain't none of my business, Mr. Zeller, but do you mind if I ask you a question?"

"Try me," he says.

"How come you taking up with these young women. It ain't right."

Lionel reddens. He had no idea Violet was aware of the little affairs he's been drifting in and out of since Bea's death. It had astonished him—a man who has never had another woman in his long marriage—how being open to women set up a field of mutual attraction. There were women, he discovered, half his age or younger, who in a chaotic or transitional moment welcomed a man like Lionel for a quick, uninvolving fling. Possibly it was his seriousness, his intense interest in them, even his fatherliness, that unconsciously set the trap. In any event, they came to him on their own, without his flirting. One was a student of his, asking advice on her term paper, another a college secretary recently split from her husband. The latest was a bank executive who had been appalled at the mess of his financial records.

"You need a woman to take care of you," she had said.

An imp had driven him, ordinarily a shy man, to answer: "Well, then, why don't you take care of me?"

It had lasted only a few weeks, the thing between them, flaring up and dying down to nothing, with a little sadness but no regret on both sides.

Confronted by Violet, Lionel doesn't deny the accusation. "How did you know?" he asks her.

"They leave hints around, your girls," she tells him, "like they want someone to find out."

"Hints?"

"Yes," she says, "young girls' hairs in the shower, powder case, bobby pin, lipstick on the cigarette near your bed. Even the perfume tell me you been with them."

"You think that's very bad, don't you?"

"Buying young girls, an older man like you. What you think?"

Stung, he says, "I don't buy them. They come to me on their own, and they leave when they want."

"Don't make no difference," she argues, "it's the devil's work. If I caught my Jenny . . ." She doesn't finish the sentence.

Days pass without a mention of Jenny. Lionel has the sense he must not ask questions about her—let Violet speak first of her daughter if she wishes. On a Monday morning Violet, beaming when she arrives, tells Lionel that Jenny is home. Lionel will never forget the sequence of events that began on that Monday and abruptly ended that same week on a Saturday afternoon.

It begins when, while Violet is dressing to go home, someone knocks at his door. She comes in and whirls around, taking in the room. "I'm Jenny," she says, "coming to see where my Mama gave you the best days of her life."

Shyly, Lionel lets himself look at her face. Her skin is a glowing golden-umber. He hadn't remembered the full bow of her heart-shaped lips. It would be easy, it occurs to him, to drown in her hazel-green eyes.

"So you are *the* Lionel," she says, hands on hips, coolly appraising him. "All these years, shining up your house, she has been singing your praises. Lionel this, and Lionel that. Or didn't you know?"

Before he can formulate a protest, he thinks the better of it. Lionel can't deal with her needling—she's too street-wise, out of his league. He shrugs his shoulders and grins amiably. Jenny glances at one of the bookshelves that line the wall. "These books," she asks, "you read em all?"

"Not necessarily," he answers. "Some completely. Others in part, or lightly over."

"That don't leave you too much time to live, do it?" She stops at one of the shelves to kneel. "Hey," she says, "so many books about black folks. You must have a thing about us Neegrows." She prolongs the vowels with wicked relish.

She is playing with him. Lionel feels faint and elated at the same time, a boy on his first date. "No," he protests, "I do not have a thing about black people. These books are part of my studies . . . my curriculum."

Jenny will be gone soon. He must make a quick move, without maneuvering, without thinking. He must let himself swim on the tide of his instinct. "Jenny," he whispers, "I have known you would be here—in my house—talking to me like this, from the first moment Violet showed me your photo, I can't recall how many years ago, on a Christmas eve."

She shakes her head, as if in disbelief. How callow his words must have sounded to her, how inauthentic, out of a bad movie. "Will you have dinner with me?" he presses on.

Jenny stares at him. "Well, now," she says. "What for? Why should I have dinner with you?"

"I can't think," he says, "of a reason in the world why you should."

She waits for a moment. "You want two of us on your string, don't you, Mama and me?"

Violet walks toward them, holding her arms out to her daughter. "What do you think of my girl?" she asks.

"Almost as beautiful as her mother," he says.

Jenny and he shake hands soberly. "I hope we have the opportunity," he says in his most formal voice, "of seeing each other again."

When they have left, Lionel slumps onto the couch. "What an old fool," he tells himself, "she must think I am."

That evening Jenny calls. "I haven't had a great meal in ages," she says. "When do you want to see me . . . and where?"

They meet in a Thai restaurant. Waiting for her, he worries: Is this place elegant enough? Or too showy? What if I make a false move? Say something insensitive? He tries to figure out a strategy for dissolving her suspicion, her cool. There is however no need for his studied charm. As if his ties with her mother all these years have paved the way, the attraction between them is quicksilver—almost hypnotic. They float, barely noticing the food, through the meal. In the cab, their first kiss is for him a press of fire. In his bedroom he fumbles as he undresses her in the dark. He does not want Jenny to see his slack body. Terrified that he will be an inept lover, he clumsily strokes, kisses and enters her body. He makes love with violent sobs; she lies back passively, her only sounds a rhythmic breathing. Afterwards he hasn't the slightest idea whether he has pleased her. When they lie side by side, smoking, he asks, "How old are you, Jenny?"

"Thirty-four," she answers. "Why do you want to know?"

"I'm twice your age," he says. "As old as your father would have been."

"Older," she says sternly, as if it were an accusation.

When they are dressing he asks her: "How does it feel to be young, black and beautiful?"

"How does it feel," she counters, "to be old, white and tryin' so hard?"

They laugh sadly. Outside the first light is showing. In the street he hails a cab and presses a bill into her palm. When he tries to kiss her mouth, she turns away. "I'll call," she says, "real soon."

Violet, feverish with an Island malady that keeps recurring, can hardly drag her body around. He helps her to the couch and puts a cold pad to her head. He has prepared her favorite lunch—sardines and beer. She eats wordlessly, then pushes the food aside. Glancing at her, he observes an old portly woman, her eyes veined, her hair limp and thinning. She should be at home with her daughter or sunning herself. Instead, she lies on his couch, filled with anxiety.

"What's wrong, Violet?" he asks.

"Jenny ain't changed a bit," Violet says. "Still sleeping away the day, disappearing nights, snapping at me if I so much as open my mouth." There are tears in her eyes. "We ain't meant, my daughter and me, to be living in the same house."

Lionel fights off a surge of guilt. All day long he has been feverishly evoking a convoluted yet what seems to him wholly plausible scenario. He has to resist this crazed impulse to cry out to Violet: "I'll take care of your daughter, Violet. She'll bring her little girl back from Chicago.

We'll settle down, the three of us, in my place. You'll come here often, Violet. We'll be a real family, loving, happy." Suddenly the mawkishness of his fantasy stuns him. Is he really prepared to marry Jenny? Be a father to her child? Support them while she finds some kind of career? A flood of self-abasement rises in him like bile. He breathes heavily and bites down hard on his lips.

"I don't feel good," Violet says. "I'm gonna have to go home."

"Go, go," he urges. "Take care of yourself. And call if you need me."

At the door she tells him: "Jenny likes you, Mr. Zeller. Talk to her. Help her make something of herself."

Violet and he hug. He has an intuition that their spring is overwound. That it will snap soon, scattering broken pieces as it does.

Night after night, that week, Jenny stays at his apartment as long as she can. Knowing how much Violet worries, he insists that Jenny go home no later than midnight. They eat take-in food and drink wine until they are both giddy. Each time she goes through his dated dance records Jenny shakes her head. "My God, you're hopelessly square." Humming a bluesy tune, she tries to lead his awkward body over the floor. Shyly he pulls away and watches her move beautifully by herself. Later, one knee on the floor, she selects from his line of bookcases the works of black women writers he admires—Toni Bambara, June Jordan, Paule Marshall, Gwendolyn Brooks, Audre Lorde. Turning the pages slowly, she drinks in the writing, oohing and ahhing when she comes across a paragraph or line that touches her.

Once, when she reads aloud from Lorde, "But I have peeled away your anger, down to the core of love, and look, Mother, I am a dark temple where your true spirit rises," she buries her face in her hands and weeps. Comforting her, his compassion turns into desire and they make gentle love. Buried in her, he drinks her life force, consumes her anatomy. "I am resurrected," he tells himself, "improbably happy, impossibly young."

Later, as they lie entwined, she whispers in his ear, "Disappointed, I bet. Thought I was going to be a wild animal in bed, like us black women are all supposed to act?"

"No, Jenny," he says. "you're perfect the way you are."

On a sudden impulse he pulls aside the blanket so that they can see each other naked in the full light. He sinks a fist into the flaccid flesh of his belly. "How long, Jenny, before you wake up thinking, what am I doing with this tired, ridiculous old man?" She doesn't answer. They hold hands, surrounded by their solitude. They sleep uneasily till the alarm clock tells them it is time for Jenny to go.

•

On Saturday morning, one of Violet's no-work days, Jenny and Lionel are in bed. Earlier, they had tried to make love but Lionel had gone completely soft. They hold hands and stare ahead without speaking. It's evident that they have slaked each other for the last time. The waning, he thinks, is even more melancholy than the waxing is full of joy.

"I'm sorry," he says, "don't know why it happened."

She touches his sex tenderly with her hand. "It's telling us something we both know," she says.

"What will you do in New York?" he asks.

"There's nothing for me here," Jenny answers. "I gotta get back to my kid."

"Can I help? In any way? Money, for one?"

"No," she says, "I'll manage somehow."

As they lie back, Lionel senses in the sudden void another presence in the house. Sitting up with a start, he hears in the sickening silence a key turning softly in the front door. Now he recognizes the footsteps—he knows it is Violet—limping on her bad knee across the living room floor. He tries to rise but falls back, frozen on the bed. Violet flings open the bedroom door. She tears the blanket away from her naked daughter. Lionel tumbles to the floor, manages to pull on his pants. Jenny leans against the wall, the bedsheet held against her breast.

Violet, sobbing, slaps her daughter, backhand, with the full force of her anger. She catches the side of her mouth. The ring on Violet's finger rips Jenny's lip. A rose of blood gushes out of the wound. Jenny presses a wad of tissue to her mouth.

"I knew you were here," Violet says between sobs. "All those whisperings on my phone. The gold earring I found in this bed—the earrings I give you. The smell of you on his sheets. Did you think I didn't know the smell of my own daughter?"

"Violet," he says, reaching out toward her, "it was all my fault." Without turning, she savagely sweeps his hand aside.

"Dress yourself," she says to Jenny, "and go on home." With that, she walks out of the room. As they pull their clothes on, they hear the water in the bathroom running at full force. A swish of liquid being poured sounds out from the living room. Lionel flings the door open to see that Violet in a rage has emptied a pailful of soapy water across the floor and over the couch. She stands there trembling in the gray flood at her feet. In a moment, her anger drained, Violet sinks to her knees. "Get out, both of you," she says in a dead voice. "I'll clean the mess up by myself."

In the street Lionel begs Jenny to talk things over in a bar. "Really" —her voice is weary, distant—"what's left to say?" While he tries to think of an answer, she wheels and without a goodbye strides quickly away. Before he can shout, "Keep in touch," she has disappeared into the crowd.

Lionel is in a pit of depression. Taking stock of his life, he cannot find a bright spot. A recently retired teacher, he no longer has a sustaining center. A scholar, he hardly opens a book. His friends have died or drifted away. He has mercilessly exposed to himself his shallowness, vanity and womanizing. Worst of all, Violet is irretrievably gone.

Lionel won't give up though. He waits a few days before he phones her. "You don't exist for me, Mr. Zeller," she says, her voice steely cold. "I don't want to hear from you again." When he calls a day later, she bangs the phone down at once. "She can't ignore me forever," he comforts himself. "With her Social Security pittance, she can't afford to."

When the meanspiritedness of his reasoning strikes him, Lionel writes her a note: "Dear Violet. I'm not asking you to forgive me—or trying to explain what happened with Jenny—or why I did it. Call it, if you want, an old man's folly. Enclosed is a check for your week's wages. I will be sending you a check each month. After all these years with me, Violet, you have more than earned a pension."

A few days later the check comes back, neatly torn in two. The curt note says: "I'm doing fine without your money. And, mind you, don't ever try to reach me again. You hear me, Mister?"

By now, Lionel's apathy is bottomless. He has reduced his necessities to the barest minimum. He no longer goes out, except for food and the *New York Times*. He sits glazed over the unmarked crossword puzzle. Falls asleep before the TV, watching, in the late movies, ghosts of actors who were alive when he was a boy.

His older daughter, who lives in Providence, calls him in alarm. "Marsha and I are worried sick about you. Violet says she doesn't work for you any longer. You never write or call. What's wrong, Dad, are you sick?" When he holds the phone without answering, his daughter shouts: "Tell me the truth, Pa, did something happen between Violet and you?"

Before he can think, the words spill out: "I did a terrible thing, Eve, I slept with her daughter."

A shocked pause. "My God, Dad, and she found out?"

"Found out? She caught us in bed, naked."

"Oh Dad," Eve groans, "Dad, Dad, Dad."

"I have no excuses," he says, "and she will not talk to me."

"What do you want?" Eve asks, "She's your domestic, not your wife!"

What does he want from her? Violet, he pleads, without moving his lips: No, I don't want you, ever again, to swab my floor with Murphy's oil soap, or Spic and Span, or Pine Sol or Mr. Clean. I don't want you to bring up the lustrous waxed shine of my furniture with Pledge. I don't want you to make my windows shiny bright with Windex, or my dishes squeaky clean with Cascade. No, Violet, never again the foaming cleanser for the tiles, the Fantastik to whisk away the soiled spots from my walls, the Endust for my shelves, the Drano for my plugged sinks, the Woolite for my washables, the Vel for my stubborn laundry dirt. And Violet, I swear to you, I don't want you steelwooling away my greasy linoleum, or on your knees scrubbing the fine spray of excrement from the inside rim of the bowl, or the circle of scum from the bathtub, or the dried toothpaste from the faucets. I beg you, Violet, no more folding the linen in your warm hands, or gliding with your soft touch the electric iron over my shirtcollars. . . .

"Papa," his daughter's voice cuts through his reveries, "you still there?"

"Yes, yes, I'm still here. Please, leave me alone, I'll get back to you soon."

"You promise?"

"I promise."

"Papa . . ."

Lionel slowly hangs up the phone. He leans against a bookcase and runs his fingers over the thick dust that covers the tops of his books. "Violet," he sings out aloud, "lunch is ready," imagining her seated, her hurting knees on the coffee table, thanking him as he brings in a tray . . . "Oh, Mr. Zeller, you shouldn't have bothered," she says as he sets down a tuna plate, or pepper sausages, or sardines. Violet, all I want is for you and me to chat quietly about ourselves or whatever it is that old people reminisce about, with the wide bands of sunlight falling on the lemon walls, and you smiling fondly when I say something outlandish and time suspended, we two at this moment the only people in the world, nothing existing but the delicate joy between us, and finally you saying, "My goodness, it's late," and me, "No, no, stay awhile, it's still early . . ."

Dusk has come, the sky through the window a fading robin's-egg-blue before the sun sinks, the bluest hour of the day for him, the nothing hours before he can lose himself in the old TV movies.

He wonders dimly, should I try making a last-minute date with an acquaintance? A poetry reading maybe? Or a string quartet? Or a lecture? Or even a meal out? Didn't he once love doing these things?

Lionel lies back on the couch—the exact spot where Violet loves to sink into the cushions. If I go out, he thinks, maybe I'll miss her phone call. You never can tell, she could be as lonely as me and dial this very second, saying, "Is that you, Mr. Zeller?"

His head nodding forward and rising, nodding forward and rising, Lionel wakes with a start from a dream in which Violet, dressed in a billowy white wedding gown, is pushing a mop over a vast church floor. Then suddenly the dream fragments, his mind gone blank as he struggles up to his elbows and remembers with a sharp-as-needle pang that he is waiting for a telephone call he knows in his heart will never come.

A Fling Later in Life

A week ago tonight my father, in a worn robe, walked out his door, down the block and onto the Brighton Beach boardwalk, where he fell into a coma on a bench above a stretch of sand no more than fifty feet from the water. The police officer who found him records the incident quite succinctly:

> Wednesday, 12. A.M., Nov. 30, 1982. I was driving along the boardwalk on 3rd Street, when I observed an unconscious man on a bench, his head slumped over the rail. The man, about 80 years old, was not adequately dressed for the 15 degree weather. I lifted him into my car and drove him to the Emergency Ward, Coney Island Hospital.

It's the medical report, however, that's more telling:

> The patient, Sol Klein, suffered a massive aortic rupture in the region of the lower abdomen. There was some blood in the mouth, as well as a considerable amount of freshly spilled semen on the penis, the inner thighs, and the scrotum.

Over and over again I imagine him looking out toward the ocean, on one of the very same benches where he and I sat together so many times in the past. His hands on the rail, my father stares at the white-edged breakers that boom onto the shore and hiss their way back to the ocean. In the bright moonlight, the sand that stretches before him has turned luminescent, like a vast expanse of radioactive bone.

I will never know, of course, whether my father is still conscious. With the wind seeping through the thin flannel, does he feel the cold? If he's touching himself, does he moan when he ejaculates? Does he hear the rush of blood when the aorta in his guts tears open? Is anything left of him but the bloody sperm-smeared container bluing itself numb in the bitter frost?

I don't dare tell my sister Lily about the sperm on the sex of her darling father. As far as she is concerned, an eighty-year-old man in extreme distress, maybe even senile or temporarily deranged, returned out of sheer habit to our own home beach, our own little Jewish ocean front for so many years. "It's as if he were a wounded animal," is the way she put it, "who wanted to crawl back and die in the comfort of a familiar place."

Of course Lily can't help getting in a slap at Vanka Slavinov, the young woman friend of Papa's whom he met a year ago under bizarre circumstances. Speaking to me about Vanka, Lily begins to rant. "That awful woman"—her voice is at a near-hysterical pitch, so unlike her—"that vulgar slut. Believe me, Aaron, those last few months, she must have driven him crazy."

I can't in the least agree. Without the slightest taste, yes, but she's not a slut. Whatever else I think about her, she has transformed my father's life. A lonely man with a bad heart, more than ready to die, he gratefully surrendered his melancholy from the moment he met her. In spite of myself, I found his utterly childish joyfulness in her presence quite moving.

I remember my father's telling me how he had stumbled, by chance, into his relationship with Vanka. Walking up the stairs one evening, he had heard, from behind a closed door, the wild cries of a woman being beaten with thudding blows. Without thinking, he had pushed the door open to see a thick-set man holding Vanka down by her knees while he battered her with the side of his fist. When the man turned his way, my father recognized him as the super of his house.

"*Es is a shanda.* Such a shame!" my father had cried out, pushing beyond his fear. For Dad, shandas come in varying degrees. A filthy home is a minor shanda. Lying is a medium shanda. Not giving to the poor is a serious shanda. Beating a woman is an unforgivable shanda.

Mr. Slavinov, the Hungarian super, had spun around astonished. Composing his face into a beneficent smile, he had slowly flung both of his hands outward toward my father. "You want my wife, Mr. Klein," he had sung out. "Then take her, she's yours."

Each time my dad relates this story, which he never tires of doing, I stop him precisely at this point. "Are you saying," I ask him, "that a man offered you his wife and just like that . . . you took her?"

"No, no," he says impatiently, "I didn't just like that take her. We sat for a while—the super, Vanka and me—around a table. He had a sweetheart, he said, a young crippled girl who lives nearby. 'I don't want Vanka, but if she pleases you, be with her whatever you like—her father, her lover, her friend. As long as you both leave me alone, you understand, I give her to you with my blessing.'"

"And Vanka?" I ask, stunned. "What did she say to all this?"

"Nothing," my dad answers. "She looked at me with her big eyes. She folded her hands together like she was praying. And she nodded a yes."

"And that was that?"

"Uh-huh, that was that."

If it were anyone but Papa, I would not in a million years believe this story. But my father has never been a weaver of tall tales. Besides, the arrangement between them is so patently off-the-wall, it can't be anything but true. In any event, as we soon discover, my father is not exaggerating a whit.

When Lily and I visit him, a few days later, he is not at all shy about declaring their involvement. "Children," he announces proudly, "this is my chomming new girl friend Vanka." Her cheeks aflame with excitement, she glows at us like a mail-order bride about to be unveiled before her husband's family. It may be, though I'm not certain of this, that she bends her knees in a slight curtsy.

As soon as we shake hands, I'm overwhelmed by the reek of cheap perfume in which she must bathe her body. The mop of wild ringlets—which frames a chubby and childlike face—is tangerine dyed. The kewpie doll mouth is a circle of fluorescent-red lipstick. On her right cheek, I note, she has penciled a gross beauty mark my father so volubly adores. Her blouse, nylon shiny and too tight, is low cut, so that her heavy breasts swell visibly into half melons separated by the deep line of cleavage. At first impression, at least, as my sister will bitterly tell me later, "She's so sleazy, it hurts just to look."

Vanka holds her hand out shyly to Lily. "Is so gret"—she turns imploringly to my father—"how you say? for to haf mit you." It will always be this way when she tries to communicate with us. She will spit out fragments of Hungarian and Polish, with a scattering of weirdly mispronounced English. My father speaks enough Russian to make the necessary connections with her. He will in fact be delighted to serve as her word-by-word translator even when we understand her.

My father pats Vanka's hair fondly. "She wants you to know," he says, "she's happy to make your acquaintance." The two beam at each other ecstatically, with broad winks from my father meant to underline his delight in her very existence.

By now Lily has had more than she can bear. "I have to go, Papa," she explains, "my daughter is waiting."

"No, no," he objects, "stay, please, a while. I made a little something for lunch. Chicken liver, home-made, pea soup, salad, tea. And for you, Aaron, raisin cookies, the kind you like."

There's no way we can escape. Papa seats us around the wooden table which my mother chose because she hated plastic tops. Across from us sits Vanka, a bewildered smile on her over-rouged face. A waiter before his heart attack, my father serves—for effect, to be sure—with a white napkin draped over his arm. Gray hair swept back, wide cheekbones, nose gently broken like John Barrymore's, his lips full and chin cleft, Papa is still a very handsome man. "Ladies and gentlemen," he says, his face aglow, "no tips, please, in this house."

At his little joke, Vanka lets go a raucous squeal. "Him vonderful mon," she whispers, her eyes bright with admiration. She reaches across the table and strokes the back of my hand. "You nice man too," she says. We see clearly, Lily and I, that she's wearing my mother's engagement ring . . . the one she'd left for her granddaughter.

Afterwards, when Lily has managed to get my father alone for a moment in the spare room, I find myself directly facing Vanka at the kitchen table. She gazes at me expectantly, as if she were waiting for a revelation to come forth. Her eyes, I observe, are violet-green and quite soulful. For the life of me, I can't dredge up a thing to say.

A moment later, Lil and my father reappear, her face porcelain-white, his flushed pink. All of his flamboyance is gone. "Come, soon, children," he placates. "Vanka will cook a meal"—he sucks noisily at his fingertips—"like you never ate before." I nod at Vanka and make a show of hugging my father. Lil's good-bye is barely decent.

As soon as we are alone in my car, Lily breaks into a flurry of sobs. "You saw what she was wearing, Aaron. On her left index finger. The ring Mama never took off, the one she slept with till the day she died."

"Don't aggravate yourself," I say. "Sure, he was insensitive. We both know that. But he's only trying to make a good impression."

"The old fool," she rants. "Mama wanted to leave something of herself . . . to pass along a piece of her life to my daughter."

I have no idea how to comfort her. The rest of the ride she sits, as she did when she was unhappy as a child, frozen and unreachable behind closed eyelids. Just before I drop her off, she says: "Okay, so he needed a woman. Couldn't she at least have been someone remotely like Mama."

Later, driving by myself, it occurs to me: Why am I so sure Vanka is Dad's terminal fling of infatuation? What if she proves to be the best, the most sustaining, love of his life? In that event, wouldn't we have to be eternally grateful to this grotesque woman? The thought is so disconcerting, I turn the radio on full blast to blot it out.

Early that evening, my father catches me on the phone before I have decided how to deal with the sticky new situation. I make up my mind, for the time being, to be polite and distant. "So," he begins, "such a lovely girl with an eighty-year-old like me. If you didn't see with your own eyes, you wouldn't believe, ha, son?"

I understand what he needs—my wholehearted approval. Well, why not? Instead, my words are edged with venom. "How old is Vanka, Papa?"

My father picks up on the dig in my question. "Two people like each other," he says, flustered, "they get along fine. So what difference does the age make?"

"Nothing, Dad, I was just curious."

There's a long-drawn-out silence. I can feel my father, on the other end, trying to take a new tack in the wind. "I fixed Vanka a bed in the storage room," he says. "Anytime she's tired, she can rest there."

"Where," I ask, "did you get the extra bed?"

"Where you buy beds"—his voice is defiant—"in a furniture store."

"I see." My dad is drawing me in deeper than I intended. "Aren't you maybe pushing things a little too fast?"

"I'm not sweet sixteen, you know." There's an irritated edge to his voice. "So how long should I wait?"

"I'm only expressing my opinion, Papa."

Another awkward pause. I don't recall us ever being this sharp with each other. "Lily spoke to you about Mama's ring?" he asks.

"Yes," I say, "it hurt her a lot."

"What's to hurt?" he blurts out. "In the bank, there's three thousand dollars. I'll buy a new ring for my granddaughter."

"That's not the point, Dad." I can hear someone else . . . a stranger in me . . . being malicious. "Mama wanted her ring to be a memento. A personal gift for Susan's wedding."

"You think maybe"—he's too rattled now to fight back—"I should take the ring back?"

"*You* think about it, Dad. Then do what you have to."

"It's too late." I hear a heavy sigh. In one second he'll break out into tears. "I would never in a million years hurt my Vanka."

For a moment I have an impulse to shout: *Follow your heart, Dad. Love who you want. Shower her with gifts if it pleases you.* Instead, I say abruptly, "I've got these papers to grade. Let me say goodnight."

"Wait, wait," he pleads. "Maybe I shouldn't say this. Whatever Lily thinks, she always was and will be my favorite. Tell her that for me, will you, sonny boy?" After I sink the receiver into its cradle, I have this surge of remorse. Couldn't I have been more gracious?

For weeks after my father's call, I find excuse after excuse for not visiting the two of them. Finally he phones to ask me over that Sunday noon. "Aaron, I need you to help me write a legal letter."

"I'm a teacher, Dad," I say, "not a lawyer."

"No, no, it's a simple letter. It'll take only a few minutes." He can sense me weakening. "Please, son, I don't ask much for favors. The letter is very important. So you'll come? You will! Oh, thanks."

When I arrive at his house, a whole raft of changes have taken place. The apartment is painted a light peach. There's a thick blue carpet in the living room. A glossy linoleum livens up the kitchen. The old couch and chairs have been reupholstered and the windows hung with flowered drapery. It strikes me that, when Mama was alive, my dad let the place go gray and shabby, its tin ceiling flaked with rust, the walls soot-streaked. At this rate there won't be much left of the money that was to be dad's legacy to his two grandchildren.

It's Dad, though, even more than the apartment, who's made a leap into high fashion. Before Vanka, he had taken to wearing ill-assorted sweaters, shirts and oversized jackets. When I asked him why he wore old ties instead of a belt around his baggy pants, he answered: "Who in this whole world but my children notices what's holding up an old man's pants?"

Well, these days Vanka's noticing, and my father will go to any length to impress her. "You like how it fits me?" he asks, twisting and preening to show off his natty new double-breasted suit.

"Fine," I say curtly.

"You notice something else, son?"

"Yes, the house."

"Vanka," he says, "she picked everything. The drapes, the colors, the rugs. How you like such taste? For an immigrant girl too!"

I cut him off again. "So what's this about a legal paper."

"Yea, yea, I have it here."

We sit around the table, trying to decipher his handwriting:

> I Sol Klein and Vanka Slavinov sware to God to be good friends and noting but good friends on a vacashun we are going togedder to Kutsher's hotel for a week from Jan 13 to Jan 20, 1981. The husband Rudolf Slavinov agrees to the vacashun only if his wife and Klein should sleep in single beds even in the same rume. Also he agrees he will not sue Klein for escoting his wife, so help him God.

"Tell me, Aaron, it's legal okay? I mean, with a judge in court, Slavinov can't take against me financial action?"

I resist the temptation to explain why the letter is absurd. Besides, I want to get away before Vanka returns. "Yes, Dad, it's legal okay. I'll rewrite it now in ink." It takes me ten minutes to redo the letter. "Here," I instruct him, "you, Vanka and Mr. Slavinov sign it. Then get it notarized and give everyone a copy. Understand?"

When he has the new letter in his hands, Dad can't stop thanking me. "Wait for Vanka," he pleads, "I want to show off my brilliant son."

"Sorry, Dad," I say, "too busy." But as I back off to leave, Vanka opens the door and catches sight of me. Immediately her face breaks out into a smile that's nothing less than beatific.

"Aaroon . . . how you say? . . . Aahrahn?" This is the first time she has ever spoken my name. "I so glod you come."

Taking her hand, my father escorts her to the center of the living room. "Show him, Vanka," he urges her, "show my son how stunning you look."

"No, Sol," she says, trying to pull out of his grip. "Is not nice."

"Go ahead. What's not nice, to see a stylish woman like you?"

Vanka stands on the soft rug, uneasy under my gaze. I see that she's wearing my mother's blue wool coat, only with a new muskrat collar and fur trim lining the bottom. My father slips her coat off and throws it on the couch. She's wearing a new dress, much too short, tight and revealing around the bosom. Guiding her under the arm, he walks her slowly around in a circle. "A regular model, my Vanka, no?" he asks.

A blush suffuses Vanka's face. Is it possible she senses that I'm furious at her parading around in my mother's coat? As for my dad, he embraces her suddenly and plants a long kiss on her lips. When he turns to me, his mouth is a smudge of wet lipstick. Vanka wets a handkerchief with her tongue. She reaches toward his lips and wipes the red away. As she does, she scolds him softly in a stream of Polish.

"I really have to go," I say, and back off to the door. As I do, Vanka stammers out some incomprehensible words. My father laughs. "She doesn't like," he says, "I should kiss her in public. Some girl, ha!"

Vanka hesitantly offers me her hand. Pinned to her collar is the silver and turquoise brooch I gave my mother on her sixtieth birthday. Brushing past her hand, I stomp down the stairs without a good-bye.

That evening, when I tell Lil about the brooch, she asks, "Why can't he see what a violation it is?" A little voice in me wants to answer, "Papa doesn't think it's shanda in the least. Maybe it's his way, misguided of course, of honoring his love for our mother." The trouble is, I'm still so furious with my father—and Vanka too—I won't grant either of them the slightest benefit of the doubt.

Soon after this, Lil informs me that my dad and Vanka are in the Catskills for a week's vacation. A day or so later, I come down with a flu that reduces me to a shivery and aching bundle of malaise. At night I float much of the time in a void between sleep and wake. In this state, dreams shameful and wanton form, then completely dissolve before I can fix them in mind. One dream, though, remains so vivid, I have only to close my eyes to evoke the exact details:

I'm hiding in a room—or maybe I'm invisible—empty except for a double bed with a lumpy mattress. It's a room I recognize, in a Catskill hotel, like the ones my dad took us to summertimes, when we were kids. And the double bed? Of course, it's been my parents' bed at home for as long as I can remember.

Vanka mysteriously materializes, wholly naked, in the middle of the bed. Her arms are wide open, so that the mounds of hair, flaming orange, bristle out of her armpits. Her legs too have fallen wide apart, but I can glimpse only the curled edges of her pubic hair. Now my dad, naked too, is lying beside her, on his back.

Slowly my father turns and lifts himself onto her torso. Vanka cups her ripe breasts in her hands and, pulling her legs together, forces him back onto the bed. Though he screams, his face contorted like a Greek tragic mask, no sounds come from his mouth. He beats at her with his frail fists until she lets her thighs fall open. He mounts her ungiving body, his arms pinning her down. As he pumps feebly, Vanka lets her head fall to one side, rolling her eyeballs backward. "No, Sol," she wails, "keep your hands off. I don't want you to touch me." Curiously, her voice is my mother's. When my father's body continues to rise and fall into hers, she puts both hands over her eyes and begins to sob, softly but bitterly, until the dream fragments.

By the week's end, the horror of this dream has almost entirely faded away. I have, however, a niggling sense that sometime in my past I've heard a woman screaming, "No, no, keep your hands off!" And it comes to me clearly when I wake up in a sweat one dawn:

The woman is my mother, behind the bedroom door which she has bolted herself. The man is my father, kicking and beating at the door while I lie aghast at the other end of our flat. "*Luz mir arein, du malchemovize!* Let me in, you angel of death!" he shouts. I'm only a small boy listening in my bed to our gentle world falling apart. I put a finger into each ear, huddle under the blanket and wait for sleep to erase the pain.

When I call Lily, she is far too indignant to deal with my conjecture seriously. "Are you out of your mind?" she snaps. "Mama and Dad loved and respected each other till the day she died. Nothing, you hear, nothing like your dream could have even remotely happened."

"An invention of mine?" I ask. "That's how you see it . . . manufactured out of the whole cloth?"

"Yes," she snaps, "a whole *dirty* cloth!"

I sigh a retreat. "Could be, Lil. I'm always pretty weird when I get sick. Let's forget I mentioned it, right?"

"Sure, Aaron. And please, take care of yourself."

I'm still not recovered when my father comes, unannounced, to visit me. Even before he takes his coat off, he pours out the good tidings of their week of single-bedded bliss at Kutschers:

"Ah, what a hotel! Five meals a day, a midnight snack. An indoor swimming pool a block long. Such a night club, with the biggest comics, a girl singer. A whole orchestra, you hear? I danced, for the first time in so many years. My Vanka, you should see how she fox-trots."

Only after the outburst is over does he realize I'm sick in bed. "Aaron, what's wrong? So much weight you lost. Did you see a doctor?"

"I'm fine, Dad. A little cold, that's all."

"You're sure, son? Vanka could take care of you. You didn't know she was a nurse, ha? In Poland. In America too."

"No, Dad. I had no idea she was so talented."

He pushes right through the irony. "There's a lot you don't know about her. In 1972, a young girl, she was an aide here in a mental hospital. She took care of a very sick boy, Rudolf Slavinov's son, that's who. He was—I'm not sure how they say—a shkitz. He laughed crazy. Sometimes he talked all mixed up to himself."

"Schizo, Dad, a schizophrenic."

"Yes, that's it. Anyway, soon she married Slavinov. A greenhorn, how should Vanka know what a son of a bitch he is. He beat her, all over her body, Aaron. You should see the black and blue marks. Such a brave woman, a woman with real character."

Why is he telling me all this? The last thing I want is to hear him sing her praises.

"Son"—he reaches over to tousle my hair, the way he did when I was a little boy—"an old man like me, I need a person in my life."

"Fine," I say, "you already have such a woman."

"No, no, Aaron." His voice has dropped to a whisper, cozy and conspiratorial. "I mean a woman in my house, permanent, like, like a wife."

I have this revolting image of Vanka, her overpainted face, her Harpo Marx mop of orange hair, her heavy bosom and gross thighs. My mother was so refined, so self-effacing. Never with more than a trace of lipstick. Her clothes always in the best of taste. I'm beginning to feel ill again. If only I could cut off the conversation, here and now. Taking a deep breath, I make an effort to speak reasonably:

"Papa, you're an eighty-year-old-man with a very bad heart. You're lonely, you want companionship? Okay, so you have Vanka, no? You see her when you want; you're alone when you want. If she moves in, wedding or no wedding, it's a marriage. The financial support, the commitment, the disagreements, the psychological pressure. Then there is"—I say this as delicately as possible—"you understand . . . the marital obligations."

My father listens intently, a frown souring his face. Then he makes a leap in logic I'm not prepared for. "From the first day I could see how you didn't like her. She wasn't a fancy lady like Mama. Lily and you, you couldn't bear I should slip a ring on her finger . . . And the beautiful blue coat. Better it should hang in the closet for the moths? Did you once speak to her on your own? Say a kind word to her? Ask her what was in her head?"

His voice has risen to a frantic pitch. His face is turning red. In a minute, the anginal pains could begin to run down his arm. "Please, Papa," I plead, "calm down, it isn't worth arguing about."

No, my father is beyond appeasement. Bad heart or not, he is going to pour out all the fury he's been bottling up these months. He stands up, his hands clenched, his body all atremble. "You know how many times that woman cried from how you treated her? 'What did I do to them,' she used to ask me, 'that they should shame me?' "

"Honest, Dad. Whatever you do is fine with me. You want her in the house; you want to marry her? I couldn't be more delighted."

It's too late to stop him. His mind is leapfrogging into forbidden places I never knew existed. "You think maybe"—he points a ramrod arm at me like a spear—"the fifty years I lived with her, your mama was an angel? Believe me, it wasn't peaches and cream." Without realizing it, he has lapsed into half-Yiddish. "She was *ungeshpart*—stubborn, hard-core, bitter as gall. Three times I left her when you were kids. Three times the family brought us together."

I lie back, hardly breathing, on the pillow. "What's happened," I say, "is past history. Let it be."

"Bad chemistry," he shouts, "that's what it was. For years, in bed, I didn't touch her. Quietly, so you kids wouldn't hear, we tore each other's hearts apart... Tell him, Celia"—he wheels toward my mother's room—"I'm not lying..." His eyes, though fixed on me, are clouded, unseeing, as if he's still there somewhere back in time with my mother. In a little while, he comes back into focus. "I'm so tired," he says, "all I want is to go home."

I reach out and draw him to me on the bed. "Things will work out," I console. "You'll see."

"Sure, son." He closes his hand over mine. "You don't remember"—a wisp of a smile—"what good times we had when you were a kid? How you loved the rides. Steeplechase. The Iron Horses. The Big Slide. The Double Whip. And the Cyclone. My God, how you screamed when it came down like a shot! But then, each time, you begged me to let you go again."

"Of course I remember, Dad."

"Ah," he sighs. "Brighton Beach. The baths. Coney Island. Geller's knishes...Nathan's frankfurters. It's all *ausgeshpilt.* Played out, finished for the Jews." He leans over and embraces me, so close I can feel his heart fluttering against my chest. When he sits up, he puts two fingers to his temple. "Wait, wait," he says, "I was going to ask you something. Oh yes...how's your wonderful wife Betty?"

He's drifting again. My wife has been dead for nine years. "She's fine," I say.

Abruptly, my father gets up to leave. "Stay for the night," I urge him. "You haven't slept in my house for ages."

"No, no," he says. "Vanka will be worried."

He slips into his coat. "So long, boychick," he says. He opens the door, hesitates a moment, then closes it, as it turns out, for the last time between us.

On a chilly night, some time later, I receive a phone call from my father just as I'm falling asleep. "Hello, son, did I wake you?"

"No, no," I lie. "I was just reading."

"Guess where I'm calling from."

"No games, Dad. Where?"

"From a street phone, outside the Apollo movies, near Times Square."

The Apollo! When I was a teen-ager, Papa would take me there Saturday afternoons to see French and Russian classics. He had never gone past public school. I don't think he'd ever read through a book in his life. Yet, for some reason, he would speak of Dostoevski or Zola or Tolstoi with the passion of one who knew and loved their works at first hand.

Oh, those long Saturday afternoons in the movies. "Crime and Punishment," "The Idiot," "Grand Illusion," "Germinal." The wonder of it, my hand in his, waiting in that vast, nearly empty cavern for the films to begin. Finally, the lights fade, the music comes up, the credits flow across the screen, and the first scene draws us into its life.

Leaning back, we sit enthralled as Sonia weeps and Raskolnikov finally confesses to the Inspector. As for our dull everyday existence, how can it compare with Prince Myshkin gazing up at the sun, his eyeballs rolling wildly backward into an epileptic haze?

After the double feature is over, we emerge suddenly into the blinding sunlight. "You see," my dad says, pumping my hand that's still snugly fitted into his, "this is what you call movies. Not that Hollywood drek. For that whole shtick, I wouldn't give a nickel." And then, all the way home by train, his arm around my shoulders, we're still so deep into the films, we can hardly speak.

"Papa," I ask, "what are you doing twelve o'clock at night in the Apollo?" Is he aware that the Apollo has been strictly porno for the last twelve years? Is this the first tell-tale sign of senility? Or, has he taken the train and let his feet wander over to an old haunt in a moment of nostalgia?

"I just saw a movie," my father explains, "with my own eyes, Aaron, a movie you wouldn't believe."

"What, Dad, what did you see?"

"The name I can't remember. Wait, wait. 'I am Furious Yellow.'"

"*Curious* Yellow, Dad."

"Furious, Curious, what's the difference? You saw it maybe?"

"No," I answer, "I don't go to dirty movies." As a matter of fact, I did see "I Am Curious Yellow." The last thing I want is to let him know.

"Well, there's this young girl, Aaron, from Sweden. A blonde, beautiful girl like an angel. And she comes to a big city with her camera, looking for work. So they bring her to a studio where they lock her up—you hear, Aaron . . . and what happens to that girl I almost can't look."

Not a sound from me. I will not let him drag me into his fantasies.

"Hello, son, are you there"—I can't escape—"you still listening?"

"Yes, I hear you, Papa."

"This sweet girl, like sugar, Aaron, this innocent, they tear her clothes off, they chain her down. She begs them not to. She cries out, 'Mama, help me.' She prays to God. Then the things they do to her. Aaron, are you still there? You are? Okay. But here's the craziest thing of all. In the end, her whole body naked, she lets them do anything, everything they want. And she enjoys it, son, she enjoys every second of it!"

Is this possible, my octogenarian father, Lily's darling, blowing his mind over a third-rate skin flick? This is a man so modest, we never in our lives saw him entirely without clothes. Once, he told Lily and me when we were kids: "The Bible writes it's a sin for parents to stand naked before their children. Remember, that's for your kids too!"

"Go home, Dad," I urge him. "It's freezing outside. You'll catch a terrible cold."

"No, son," he answers, "talk to me now"—there's no stopping him. He is going to ride right over my objections. "Tell me, Aaron, how is it in eighty years an intelligent man like me, a person with deep feelings, is like a clumsy boy in bed. He doesn't know what's right or wrong between a man and his woman. He's ashamed of the strange thoughts he carries around like a secret in his head."

"Please, Dad, this isn't the time or place to discuss such things."

"So when is the right time and place, ha? Speak to me now—this minute!" I hear his voice beating at me across the void. "Explain to me, Aaron, the facts of life, the ones every boy knows. Otherwise I'll go to my grave with a dead thing still between my legs."

I move the phone away from my ear. Oh yes, Papa, you were right, there are secrets too naked for a parent to reveal. "Please, dad"—I hear him breathing heavily. "Take a cab home. I'll pay the fare."

"Shit on the fare, Aaron!" He has never cursed at me before. "Who needs it? Who needs you?" His phone comes crashing down, leaving me with a castrated receiver in my hand.

I spend half the night puzzling over the Apollo episode. A naive old man, I decide, feels an unexpected itch of lust for a younger woman. A domestic twist on the story of Susanna and the Elders, with Vanka as the beautiful temptress. What a sad farce! Hopefully it will blow over.

I don't hear from my father for quite a long time. I don't try to reach him either, thinking, maybe it's a good idea to let his anger at me cool down. But one afternoon, when I'm in the middle of marking term papers, Vanka flabbergasts me with a call: "Aarohn, this is Vanka."

A spurt of fear . . . "My dad, is he okay?"

"Yes, him fine. I need talk with you. Is all right?"

"What about?" I ask uneasily. Is this going to be a heavy conversation with a woman to whom I haven't spoken a dozen words?

"Your papa," she says, "vant marry me. Is very bad."

"Well, why not, Vanka? Don't you love him?"

"Like my father, yes. Like good friend, yes. Not like"—she searches for the word—"how you call, like real man."

She's drawing me into a sticky, confusing mess. I feel sorry for her. But I don't want my father to be hurt. Still, I have to take some stance. "Well, why don't you explain to him exactly how you feel?"

"I try tell him, Aarohn. He beg me to marry. He begin to cry."

"Look, Vanka," I say. "I know how hard it is for you. But there's nothing I can do about it."

"Please"—I can hear her stifling a sob—"you a kind man. You tell your papa marry me is not good for an old man like him."

"You're a mature woman, Vanka. If you say no, and you really mean it, he'll understand."

"I say no, no, no, no. Ten times a day. He not listen."

"For God's sake, Vanka, then leave him. Go back to your husband."

"How I move back?" she implores. "He live in his house with his cripple girl friend."

"I'm sorry, Vanka, I really am. It's between you and dad."

"Thenk you," she says, almost contritely. "I'm sorry to bodder you." I can imagine her staring hopelessly at the phone till she hangs up.

Going over the conversation afterwards, it strikes me that my dad is, most probably, about to be abandoned. Like it or not, I'm already whirling around in his maelstrom.

A week or so later, on my father's eighty-first birthday, I invite the two of them for lunch to an Italian restaurant in Coney Island. The party is meant to cheer them up, but it never takes off. Instead, a pall hangs over us from beginning to end.

As soon as we're seated, I note how he surreptitiously slips a small pill under his tongue. Nitroglycerin, of course. "What's wrong, Dad," I ask, "don't you feel well?"

"It's nothing," he assures me. "I can't breathe too good when it's so cold."

Under the garish lights, his skin is pasty white, puffed deeply under the eyes and into the cheeks, as if his face were shrinking into the skull. The ends of his gray hair, usually so neatly trimmed, are straggly and dirty yellow. Looking at him fade away, a terrible thought assails me—am I not, below all this compassion, waiting for his death to finally free me from his ever-present weight?

The three of us pick at our food in listless silence. I try to spark things up with a toast of wine: "To the youngest and best eighty-one-year-old father I'll ever have." No one even cracks a smile.

When we raise our glasses, Vanka turns anxiously toward him. "Vot," she wants to know, "your son say?"

Ignoring her, he puts down his glass and rises abruptly from his chair. "Excuse me," he says, "I have to go to the bathroom."

While we're alone, I ask Vanka, out of politeness, how things are between them. She lifts her shoulders in a shrug of resignation. Still clutching the wine glass, she spaces her words out, slowly, "No gut. I look for odder house to move."

"Why, what's happened?"

Her face is masked, like a wary stranger's. "I don' vant talk."

After lunch we stroll along Stillwell Avenue, where Papa and I had had so many thrilling times together. He'd never cared much for nature —parks, mountains, country. For him the pleasure was in the beach and sunning. And afterwards, he would take me to Coney Island—alive with games, rides and hustling carnies. Instead, before us is a wasteland of rotting structures. And there—oh no—my beloved Cyclone—looming over the street like the skeleton of a decaying monster.

My father seems entirely lost. "Vanka," he asks, pulling on her arm, "where are we? . ." When we pull up at his house, I don't even make a pretense of wanting to visit.

"Good-bye, Dad, Vanka," I say, "we'll be in touch." As the taxi pulls out, I see her leading him by the arm, step by step to the stairs, lovingly, like a daughter with an old man who's suffered a stroke.

•

The ring, ring, ring from Coney Island Hospital pulls me violently out of sleep in the middle of the night. "Aaron Klein?" a woman asks.

"Yes, what is it?" I hear my heart thudding madly.

"I'm sorry," she says, "but your father is in critical condition. I think you'd better come right over."

At the hospital I'm ushered into a cubicle of an office. The intern, younger than my son, is grave and professional as he hands me the police and medical reports. I have to read them twice, three times before they make sense. My father, in a thin robe, lying unconcious on the boardwalk on a freezing night . . . a massive aortic break . . . semen present on the scrotum. It's unreal!

An operation was necessary, the intern explains, to close his aorta. He's close to death now, probably won't live through the night. They have him on a respirator, in the intensive care unit.

My father is lying, eyes closed, tubes running from his mouth and nose, in a room with three other sleeping patients. Above his head is a cardiac monitor. Its white bleeps are floating, like tiny tennis balls, across the screen. Each signal, so small, so feeble—it seems to me—could be his last.

A nurse's aide, curly-haired like Vanka, is wearing dirty sneakers, one of which has become untied. Aren't nurses supposed to be antiseptically clean? As I turn to my dad, the thought occurs I should have called Vanka to be with him these last few hours. "He can't speak," the aide says, "but the doctor thinks he can hear."

Standing at his bedside, I watch his motionless face in the yellowish light. His robe has crept open, exposing an ugly purple weave of stitches on his belly. I lean over until my mouth is only inches away from his ear. "Papa," I whisper, "can you hear me?" His head nods a slow yes.

"I'm your son Aaron. Do you recognize my voice?" Once more, the head bobs yes.

"Are you in pain, Papa?" A steady up and down movement of his head.

"It hurts a lot?"

He stirs uneasily. His eyelids flutter but remain closed. His head keeps moving yes, yes, yes, until I stop it with my hand.

"I love you very much, Dad. Do you know that?" A sad smile forms on his face—at least, I think it does—as he keeps on nodding his head yes.

"I hope you love me just as much." Yes, yes, yes, yes, yes, his head keeps telling me.

"One more question, Dad. You want me to stay with you?"

Now his head is turning no, no, no, from side to side.

"You shouldn't tire him," the aide says. "It's bad for his heart."

"I'm going to say good-bye, Papa. Is that what you want?"

The yes, yes nod commences again, then slowly, gradually, stops altogether.

"He's asleep," the aide says. "It's a good time to go."

"Keep an eye on him," I tell her as I go.

All the way home through the deserted streets, the cab purrs along, disembodied, as if in slow motion. At home, I take two sleeping pills, slip into bed, my clothes still on, and sleep without stirring until the sky outside is barely gray. At nine someone calls from the hospital to say: "Mr. Klein, sorry to inform you, your father died a few minutes ago." A bellow of air, as much a sigh of relief as a cry of anguish, breaks out of my throat. I'll have to call my sister at work, I think. And yes, of course, Vanka too.

My father's funeral is modest, even as small funerals go. A few cousins, second cousins, old friends of his, Lily, Vanka and me. A total stranger, the rabbi delivers an overwrought and unctuous eulogy just this side of embarrassing. Weeping before the open casket, Lily is in a state of collapse. After a few seconds, I have to close my eyes on the piece of painted waxworks the embalmer has primped up in white satin. As for Vanka, she stands before my father for a long while, shaking from side to side and mumbling a prayer, like an old woman in the balcony of an orthodox synagogue. Perched on her head is a pillbox covered with a veil. She is wearing—it dismays me to see this—a shabby old black coat, much too thin for the bad weather.

At the cemetery, in the depths of Queens, they bury my father in a small plot next to his wife. The empty space behind the two graves is reserved for Lily and me. The wind and sleet are so fierce, the rabbi has to cut his prayer short. Before everyone leaves, I whisper to my sister: "Shouldn't we have a bite to eat with Vanka. Maybe drive her home?"

"Take her home yourself, if you want to," Lil answers. "I wouldn't give her the satisfaction."

"Wait for me at the car," I tell Lily. "I'll be right back."

Vanka, drenched by the sleet, is watching the gravediggers shovel the spadesful of brown clay over the casket. "Where will you be living now?" I ask her.

"I haf new place, not too far from papa." She speaks to me without lifting her veil.

"Do you need any money?"

"Sol gif me enough till I find job."

I would like to offer her a few words of solace, maybe even embrace her. Instead, I say, "I'm so sorry things didn't work out better." Even as they leave my mouth, my words seem hollow. I hold my hand out toward her. She barely touches it with her palm before she withdraws. "Have a good life," is the only thing I can think to say.

Without a word, Vanka turns to my father's grave. Sinking to her knees, she scatters a handful of earth into the still-open gash. It strikes me, with a pang, that this tableau could be my last glimpse of Vanka. For the first time since my father's death, a cloud of tears mists my eyes.

A few days later, Lily and I drive to my dad's house to collect a few keepsakes. We also have instructions from him on giving away the furniture and clothes to needy neighbors.

In one of the drawers we find an envelope marked "*Special:* To mine Children. Dear Lily and Aaron. I know I put this money away for mine dere grandchildren. But I tink Vanka needs it more. Can you find it in your hartz to give it better to her. Luv, your Papa."

On the table in the kitchen is my mother's blue coat, neatly folded. In a cup are the engagement ring and silver brooch.

"Lily," I say, "I'm going to give my son's share of the money to Vanka. How about you?"

She slips the ring onto her finger. "I'll think about it."

Weeks pass before I hear from Vanka. "Aarohn," she says in a choked voice, "I haf big trouble. Could you come, please, to my house?"

"What's wrong?" I ask.

"It's about Papa. I need speak to you. Very, very important."

Vanka's new place is one of a row of old stucco buildings leading down to the beach. Like most of the others, it was owned by Jews, who have long ago left Brighton Beach to Puerto Ricans and Orientals. Vanka greets me in a dank basement room sunken halfway below sidewalk level. A sour smell hangs in the air, as if sand and salt water have rotted the floorboards . . .

She looks softer, much different. She's washed the dye out of her hair and is letting it grow brown. The rouge and beauty mark are gone. Only the perfectly bow-shaped lips, painted a glossy scarlet, are the same. We sit on the couch together, twisted awkwardly, knees touching, so that we can face each other. She nervously clasps and unclasps her hands. "Aarohn," she says, "I haf things to tell about your papa. Terrible, sad story."

In the stillness that has suddenly grown immense, I can hear the different parts of my body—temple, neck, heart, wrists—beating to their own erratic rhythms. *No, no, Vanka, no terrible tales. I want only to lean back and gently float away into unclouded sleep.*

"One night, when I go sleep, Sol come into my room, and sit with me on bed. 'I vant you like wife,' he say. 'I friend,' I tell him, 'not you wife.' 'Vanka,' he say, 'you girl friend, just like wife.' "

I breathe deeply, in, out, in, out, to stop the panic that's washing over me. "Enough, Vanka," I beg her. "I don't want to hear this."

"Listen, Aarohn, is not a long story." She lays her hand softly on my knee. "Your papa, he come in bed and put his hand inside nightdress. 'Please, Sol,' I cry, 'what you do is bad.' I push him away. I slap him, not hard, in face. He tear open dress. He climb on top me. I so sick, I lay quiet. You papa take me, one, two, tree. Is all over. Noting else to tell."

"Noting else to tell..." Her last words, like music heard in a half-sleep, dissolve into nowhere. The only noise in the room now is the low hum of an electric heater. If I let myself block out everything but that hum, I might easily fall into a dense forgetfulness.

"After he do this"—Vanka's voice brings me sharply back—"he sit on bed and say: 'Vanka, I no feel so good' and he go out of room. Is last time I see him alife."

Closing my eyes, with my hands held tightly over them to shut out the light, I can see my father clearly. Already a ghost, he stumbles along Brighton Beach Avenue in his slippers and bathrobe.

Vanka gently shakes my knee. "I haf to let you know," she says, "what papa done. Is not good I should keep in myself."

"Yes," I say, "but why me?" I mean only to ask, not scold.

"I haf nobody else."

We sit in the gloom for a long while without speaking. I have, in these few moments, to recast my father in a wholly other light. The idea of him raping her—yes, isn't that what it was—is still too grotesque for me to absorb.

"I'm so sorry," I finally manage to say. "Believe me, I wish with all my heart it hadn't turned out this way."

"He sick old man"—God, she's actually trying to console me—"not understand what he doing."

I stare up at the bare, hanging bulb. "You shouldn't be living here," I say. "It's dark, it's cold and it stinks. Can't you move?"

"I work in laundry, few hours a day. Not enough pay for rent."

I take, from my jacket pocket, a neat roll of six hundred dollars—

my father's legacy to his grandson. "Here," I say, holding the roll of bills out to her. "No vant," she protests and pushes the money away. A few tears meander down her cheeks, smudging her face with mascara tracks. "Help me, Aarohn," she sobs. "I a sick woman. Alone by myself all time. You be my good friend?" Suddenly the demands upon me of her being, her hopelessness, the weight of her misery are intolerable. What I want most now is to go home to my own life, with its small routines. "I'll help you," I hear myself saying. "Whatever you need, money, advice, you name it, just give me a call." The sound of my voice is metallic, distant—entirely without conviction. Rising, I place the six hundred dollars on the couch beside her. Vanka leans back and stares at the money. "Take care," I say as I back off. She never once lifts her eyes. I think of touching her. Kissing her on the cheek, or the head, or the hand is almost impossible. But I look at my watch and just slip out of the room. Without further goodbye.

Months later, going through my father's few belongings, preparing to clean out my closet, in a shoebox stamped with the store name, *Regal Shoes,* containing my father's and mother's marriage license, my understated birth certificate, my father's parchment naturalization diploma, I come across a small gold plastic brocade handbag I know at once is Vanka's. It could not belong to my mother, who always dressed modestly, her only jewelry a wedding ring and a string of imitation pearls with its 18-karat gold clasp. Feeling a little guilt, I open Vanka's mysterious handbag: I find two torn ticket stubs for a Hudson River Night Boat to Albany, a change-purse, eight dollars, and a Roosevelt dime. Inside one of the side pouches, there is also a photograph, apparently taken on the deck of the Hudson liner. It shows them holding hands, looking at each other joyously, lovingly. Vanka's face, younger, is adazzle with adoration and something like sweetness. My father is luminous.

At first I study the photo without a reaction—disoriented. Who are these happy strangers? Gradually, however, I'm flooded with feelings of guilt, remorse, pity and yes, a sense of my own smallness. And what can I do, I ask myself, with her eight dollars? I try to reach Vanka by telephone, she has disappeared, her old telephone number reassigned to a Puerto Rican accent. I am pleased with myself when I get the thought: with these dollars—and only with them, no more, no less—I'll buy Vanka and Papa a commemorative gift, a little memorial. I think of the candle of remembrance I burn each year for my mother, that costs a dollar or two. But that's out of the question. In the days and weeks that follow, I wander through discount department stores, variety shops and special outlets for a fitting memento. With an eight-dollar top, what an array of plastic, sleaze and kitch I try out in my mind! Once, in desperation, I almost settle for a pair of black china mugs, one inscribed in gold letters with the word *his,* the other with *hers.* New, they already seem old and dirty. And oh, the other appalling items that momentarily attract me: A second-hand music box that plays "Let Me Call You Sweetheart" off-key before it runs out of song. A model of the Statue of Liberty in bronze plastic. A crystal ball that snows on the enclosed garden when you shake it. A porcelain figure of a shepherd and his flock. An embroidered square that reads: "A house without love is not a home." I could of course spend my own money for a tasteful memento. But that would only undercut the symbolism of my gesture. By this time my enthusiasm is waning and my quest seems childish, the matter almost disappears in the clutter of everyday events. Finally, the question of my searching for a gift comes to an abrupt end on its own. Opening my wallet, I notice that the eight singles, once in their own compartment, have been accidentally merged, somehow released by me into the sea of my own money. In effect they no longer exist.

That leaves me of course with the two excursion stubs and the photo. The torn tickets I file back carefully into the Regal shoebox. The photo, in its plastic frame, I place on the bookshelf above my desk. At first, I keep glancing up again and again at the two lovebirds. After a few days, however, I remove the snapshot and put it away in the box along with the stubs, things not meant for my eyes—this photograph resurrecting something in my father's soul I never knew and cannot imagine. Is it possible, I smile to myself, that I do not understand the world? And then, "now, don't exaggerate."

The Blues Bed

My God, Lancelot Stevens, of all people! I had forgotten—or maybe blocked out—that bizarre encounter in an Army hospital more than forty years ago. But there was his notation, when I was leafing through some old books, on the inside cover of Kafka's *Journals:*

> To my friend Samuel, who still believes you can come out of it alive.
>
> Lance Stevens

And when I saw that scrawl again, oh what a procession of painful memories came drifting back, one by one . . .

I was twenty-two, a draftee fresh out of college, with no future in sight except for a war that might drag on forever. They were supposed to send me to a basic training camp down South. Instead I found myself inexplicably transferred to the medical corps as a night orderly in a psychiatric hospital off Governor's Island, a short ferry ride away from Manhattan. Across the dark waters, a swirling confluence of two rivers, I can see the tiny triangle of land which is to be my Army home. To the left is Hart Crane's Brooklyn Bridge: *telepathy of wires, sigh of stars, white choiring wings.* And rising dimly at the far end of the harbor, the barely visible Statue of Liberty.

After all these decades, I can still re-create my first sight of Ward E: two rows of Army beds; barred windows; bedlights shining eerily down on the patients, who followed my every step down the aisle. And there, fifteen feet or so ahead, a three-sided room with an observation window looming ominously into the ward, like the prow of a lost ship.

Inside the room, a corporal—empty whiskey bottle in hand—is sprawled face down across the desk. He's supposed to share time with me, three hours on, three hours off, overseeing the patients. It's clear, however, that he's plastered out of his senses. This is the way it will be—me in the ward twelve hours each night; the corporal sleeping off a drunk inside the office—for as long as I'm here.

•

It's nerve-wracking the first night, walking as if I've been stripped naked between the double row of eyes. I move from bed to bed with a fixed smile, dropping whatever inanities come to mind. "Watcha reading, soldier?" I ask a patient. He spits out in disbelief and turns away. "My name is Levy," I say to another. "What's yours?"

"Levy, trevy, blevy, nevy," he chants back until he's run out of rhymes.

A few patients burrow their heads into the pillows. Someone behind me aims a mocking laugh in my direction. Clearly, I'm an opening night flop. My face flushed, I walk toward a blond soldier, hair clipped brillo short, who sleeps in a straitjacket. Across from him a black soldier—hands over his face—is swaying from side to side. A voice, sandpaper and honey over a ripple of piano notes, is coming from a radio on the soldier's bed. It's Jelly Roll Morton:

> Lord, Lord, Lord, won't you look at sis',
> she's down on the levee doin' the goddam' twis'.
> O my winein' boy, won't you look at sis . . .

Out of some bottomless pit the soldier pulls a sob. "What's wrong?" I ask. He looks up, sees me and draws the blanket over his head. His sobbing has stopped. The ward is hushed. Through the window, the skyscrapers of lower Manhattan are lit up with rows of fading fireflies. I've never been so faraway and lost in my life. Seated that night opposite the soldier, I rename his cot "the blues bed."

In the darkness I sometimes hear a cry, as from a haunted flute, escaping from his mouth. Down the ward, voices thick with dreams swarm around the sleepers' heads. Later, through eyes droopy with fatigue, I see the sun striped with iron window-bars rising from the bay. By eight, corporal—shaved, shoes polished, uniform GI sharp—is on his way out. He stops when he sees me wiping away dribble as I feed the blond soldier his breakfast. "Gold brick," he says with a knowing smirk and disappears until evening.

Saturday—my only day shift—two guards bring in a new patient named Lance Stevens. "Watch out for this weirdo," a guard warns me. "He's suicidal." I make up the blues bed, which has been empty for a few days. That's how it goes here. Patients flow in and out on a conveyor belt. They stay for several days to several months and abruptly disappear. Except for the long-term ones, like Boertz in the straitjacket, they will leave behind in me not the slightest memory trace.

I can tell, from my first glance, that with Stevens it will be different. It's not only his improbable name, or his chiseled Wasp face, like an ad for elegant clothes. Mostly it's the books he unpacks from his duffle-bag and lines up neatly on the windowsill. I recall wondering, how come someone suicidal carries a little library along with him in the Army? Stevens tosses one of his books onto the bed. As I mop the nearby aisle, trying to catch a glimpse of the title, he turns toward me. "No games, soldier," he says. "All you have to do is ask." He holds the book out for me to see.

I read the title aloud. "The Meaning of Death."

"Read it," he says. "It might do you some good."

"Some other time," I say. "Mind if I look at the others?"

"Be my guest," he says.

I read off the authors one by one. "Hemingway, Virginia Woolf, Faulkner, Kafka, Heidegger, Camus . . . Kafka, Heidegger? Not exactly a barrel of laughs." I say this lightly, as a warm-up between us.

He regards me with baleful eyes. "Neither are you, Levy," he drawls acidly and turns away. Yes, I'm being summarily dismissed. Lying back, he lights a cigarette, sucks in and swallows the air, puff by puff, until his breath gives out. Through the corner of my eye, I see him finally whooshing a stream of smoke through his nostrils, his stare riveted stonily on the ceiling.

As far as I can see, Stevens stays up most of the night, tossing from side to side. Around dawn, still chain-smoking, the closed book on his lap, he watches me sweep the floor. His face is extraordinarily handsome—perhaps even . . . beautiful. Ash blond hair, a cleft chin, fine cheekbones, aquiline nose without a hint of dip or flare. Altogether it should add up—at least to my jaundiced view—to an all-American prototype . . . a flawless, nonethnic, characterless vacuity. It's his eyes, however, that save him. Deep-set, implacable, luminously blue, the whites crisscrossed in pink with ruptured veins. As I look up, our eyes meet. He stares me down with an intensity that's almost hypnotic.

"How come," he asks, "they got a nice Jewish boy like you doing the shitwork?" I wince at the small malice. "You gotta be one of these smart New York college kids," he continues. "Wait, let me guess. City College, right?"

"And you," I answer, "wait, let *me* guess . . . Swarthmore, no. Dartmouth, no. Haaa'vard, of course, right?"

"Touché, buddy boy," he says, and lowers his voice into a mock whisper. "Know why I'm here, Levy?" Without waiting for an answer, he goes on: "Self-destruction. I have a penchant for it. No, let me rephrase that. A positive obsession!" He searches my face for a reaction. I try not to move a muscle. "Any bright thoughts on the subject?"

"Not really," I answer lamely. He's way over my head. "I guess I haven't lived long enough to be fascinated with dying."

"Ah," he says, "isn't that a pity. Given this absurd world, it's the one thing that makes sense. Don't you think, Levy?" He reaches for a book from the sill behind him. "Let me read you what Camus says: 'There is but one truly philosophical question—and that is suicide.' "

"How is it," I counter, "that Camus never killed himself."

"Who knows? Cowardice, life instinct, being a rebel maybe. Luckily I don't suffer from any of these flaws. Matter of fact, soldier boy, I find the prospect of death irresistible."

Is he playing with me or serious? I sweep up the dirt and continue down the ward. There's an odd smile on his face. I can't make out—in fact, I never will be able to—whether it's contemptuous or amused.

Saturday morning, three doctors—one a psychiatrist—are making their rounds. Records in hand, they speed through the patients, stopping at each bed to ask a few routine questions. When they're ready to leave, I get up the nerve to ask the psychiatrist: "Major, sir, there's this new patient, Stevens. I've been told he's suicidal."

"Yes," says the major. He eyes me expectantly.

"Well, no one has instructed me on how to deal with him."

"That's our job, private," the major says sternly, "not yours."

"I understand, sir, but Stevens keeps talking about killing himself. Shouldn't he have some form of treatment?"

I've stung the major. "What the hell do you think we're here for?" he barks out.

"Of course," I press on, "but meanwhile, what do I do about him?"

"Not a damn thing," he half shouts. "Just keep an eye on him. Is that clear?" I step back, properly chastened. Before he goes, the major relents. "I wouldn't worry, soldier. Corporal says you're doing fine."

A few nights later, Boertz' howl shatters the silence. Aroused from sleep, the patients leap up, caterwauling in unison. Cats'-eyes pass their glow from bed to bed. Whispers, a scuffle, someone shouts, "Fuck off, Whitey!"

Two soldiers—we call them the Schizo Twins—sit at the edge of their beds, improvising each other's words. "Listen, Boertz," twin one intones, "you'd better keep your dirty hands off her." "Hands off the edge of the world," echoes the second. "He twisted the knife," says one. "Into my wife, life, strife," twin two answers.

One light goes on, then another. The tension is contagious . . . it flows across the ward in waves. “Cut it out, guys,” I shout. “I want those damned lights off.” At my words, every bedlight in the ward goes on. It strikes me as I race frantically down the aisle, I’m a prisoner of the patients.

Thrashing violently from side to side, Boertz won’t let up on his roars. The ward is an echo chamber, bouncing the noise from wall to wall. “Call a nurse,” someone yells. I race toward the phone in the sleeping corporal’s office. As I do, I see that Stevens is standing near Boertz’ bed. He leans down, with his hands on Boertz’ shoulders and sways in rhythm to the soldier’s twisting.

“Steady, boy,” Stevens croons, “steady,” as if he were calming a horse gone berserk. In a few minutes, Boertz’ movements stop. His sounds dwindle to a low moan. Almost at once, the patients’ noises die down in empathy. Once again, thankfully, the ward is serene.

Stevens stands over the sleeping Boertz, a hand on his arm. “Peace,” he smiles at me—“it’s wonderful.”

“You’ve got magic hands,” I say. “It’s a real gift.”

“For you, Levy Samuel”—his voice has taken on a sing-song Yiddish inflection—“any old time at all.”

I let the slur pass. “Get some sleep,” I say.

“Ah, sleep,” he recites. “ ‘To die, to sleep no more. . . ’Tis a consummation devoutly to be wished.’ Shakespeare incarnate, don’t you agree?”

“Under the circumstances,” I say, “it’s not my favorite Bard.”

“Chacun à son gout,” he says glumly. He walks to the window near his bed. Resting his arms on the windowsill, he stares out at the tiny diamonds spangling the darkened skyline.

The next night, as I fight to keep my eyes open, Stevens calls out softly: “How the hell do you stand this dreary, unintelligible grind?”

“It’s a living,” I answer.

“Really?” he asks. “It’s more like a living death.” He motions me over with his finger. “Listen, Levy,” he whispers. “It’s intolerably dull talking to myself in the dark. Can I persuade you to let me read in the toilet?”

For one instant, I toy with the idea. “I wish I could, Stevens. We have strict orders to keep you in sight.”

“Christ,” he says, “if I wanted to slit my throat, do you think you or anyone in this fucking Army could stop me?”

I hold my hands out toward him in a gesture of empathy. “Let me think about it,” I say. “Maybe I’ll come up with something.”

He suddenly uncoils, slides across the bed and puts his hand gently to my face. "If it's any solace," he says, "you, Levy, are my last frail reason for existing."

Stevens' presence has begun to transform the whole tenor of my work. It used to be that my free time would stretch out like a wasteland. I would take the long ride to my old neighborhood, where my mother was waiting to die. She would tell stories that all began with, "Remember when Papa . . ." until we both fell into a state of catatonic gloom. I would return more forlorn than ever. Now, without asking myself why, I phone home only to appease my poor mother. The patients, with their squabbles and idiosyncrasies, have faded into the background. Time, which crawled like mucilage, moves swiftly through the night.

Stevens has become my project. Piece by piece, I try to fill in his background. From his medical records, I learn that he is twenty-six, from Chevy Chase, Maryland, and an Army publicist with Special Services. Under "Remarks," I cull the following: "Chronic depressive, manic tendency, several suicide attempts (two by sleeping pills), insomnia. Below there is a pencilled note: "Patient's father—Colonel Stevens—requests that his son be released from the Army at the earliest possible date."

When I ask Quinn, the day orderly, about Stevens, he isn't very flattering. "Oh, that little prick with the fancy books. I'd watch him like a hawk." He shrugs. "It's okay by me if he wants to kill himself, as long as I'm not around to clean up the mess. Another thing," he adds. "No visitors. He doesn't want to see anyone—not even his mother."

Surprisingly, it's Stevens himself who supplies some vital information. Out of the blue, one evening, he calls me over. "After long deliberation, I've decided that you are the only person in the ward even remotely worth talking to. We ought therefore to be in constant communication."

He offers this with a straight face, but as usual I can't tell if he means to be complimentary or condescending. "I'm highly flattered," I say. "On what basis do you consider me compatible?"

"Oh, on a number of levels," he answers.

"How so?"

"For one"—Stevens gestures at the books, "shared literary interests. For another, the opposites-attract factor: You Jew, me gentile; you, up from the ghetto, me, down from the Maryland bluebloods. And third"—he hesitates—"believe this, Samuel, I like you a hellava lot. You are one of the Chosen People, no? Well, then, I've chosen you as my constant companion until I get the guts to do myself in."

This is supposed to be amusing, but somehow I find his heavy-handed flipness chilling. "Forget it, Stevens," I say. "I don't intend to be a soul-mate for your suicide."

"My solemn oath"—Stevens raises his hand—"and a Mayflower Stevens' word is sacred—that I won't kill myself without fair warning. Rest assured, Levy, you'll be the first to know."

"Thanks for nothing," I say.

Stevens waves off my remark. "Are we friends?" he asks, extending a hand. "I sincerely want us to be."

"Friends," I answer and lock my palm firmly in his.

Big, blood-roiling excitement in the ward. Of course it doesn't take much for the patients to work themselves into instant delirium. This time, it's of my doing. I've persuaded an odd-ball Army friend—a chef in the hospital kitchen—to send us officers' food for Sunday breakfasts. Instead of the usual glop, an aluminum truck will bring us fresh omelets, bacon, real coffee, warm rolls and cinnamon buns. What's more, I announce, "I want us all to eat at one table. We can put together our bedstands in the aisle."

Cheers and bed-thumping greet the news. One dissent only. From his end of the ward, Stevens shouts: "How about Boertz, does he eat with us?"

"Not with knives and forks around," I demur. "The last time his hands were free, he almost choked Corporal to death."

"Chickenshit," says Stevens. "He has the same rights as us."

"Well," I say, mollifying, "Boertz gets to eat officers' mess same as we do."

"Count me out, then," he says. "Boertz and I eat by ourselves."

All week long I've been imagining the patients, with me at the head of a long table, like my father at Passover. If it works, we'll commune weekly at this festive meal, each of us joyful and mutually healing. Stevens' adamacy is a wet blanket. Still, things go smoothly on Sunday morning. The breakfast arrives, hot and copious, on a chill but sunny March day. Crowded around the tables, laughing and kidding, we devour the food along with mugs of coffee. Only Stevens, feeding Boertz spoonfuls of omelet, is missing.

Afterwards we sit around, blowing cigarette smoke at the barred windows. In the clear air outside, Manhattan looms ahead, picture perfect, like a postcard of itself. Small boats drift by slowly, as if they're cut-outs drawn by invisible strings. Gulls—laundered white—soar, dip and bob on the greasy swells. Gradually a stillness descends. Not, I find myself hoping, in sadness, but of separate memories sorting themselves out. On this morning, at least, no one here is out of his mind. We could be any old bunch at a reunion, sated with food and drink, each of us privately reminiscing how it was when we were young and together once.

While we clear the tables, I note that Stevens has come over to pour himself some coffee. "Any volunteers for the garbage detail?" I ask. Eighteen hands shoot up, including Stevens'.

"I haven't been out for months," he pleads. "Can I volunteer?"

His request stuns me. The garbage dump is near the sea wall, a few feet above the water. A short spurt, an easy climb and he could disappear forever into the rocks that rise like sharks' teeth out of the water. I stand there, searching for an excuse to dismiss Stevens' request.

"Trust me, Levy," he urges. "I gave you my word of honor."

Before I can stop myself—and appalled by my decision—I blurt out, "Okay, it's Stevens and you—Flynn"—I choose one of the sanest patients in the ward—"but no games, get it?"

"Scout's word," Stevens says, smiling.

With me in tow, the two of them carry the refuse to the dump. They untie the bags, empty them and let the garbage slide into the container. Stevens and Flynn tamp down the lid and the three of us start back for the ward. Suddenly, Stevens twists around and races for the sea wall. In what seems to be slow motion, I start after him, as if I'm wading through a sea of gelatin. In one stride he scales the rough stones and stands erect on the wall. He bends at the knees, arms held backward and up, and balances himself on his toes.

"No, Stevens," I manage to get out, "you promised."

He leans forward, like a grounded bird coiled with energy, about to take off. He sways, poised on the brink, and hangs there, motionless above the water. Then, astonishingly, he turns and leaps gracefully back onto the ground. When I reach him, he opens a smile dazzling with even white teeth.

"Sorry, Levy," he says, "I couldn't resist the impulse."

"Fucking showboat," I rage.

"Not at all, Samuel. I was only trying it on for size. Nothing serious, I assure you. Slimy, snot-green ice water—uuuch—it's definitely not my thing."

As we walk silently back to the ward, I jam my fist, furiously twisting it around his belt, into the small of his back. I can't make out what I feel most—relief or betrayal.

•

Since his suicide charade, even though Stevens has made several overtures, I can't let go of my resentment. To me, it's the end of trust. But why? Except for his intelligence—and amused self-awareness of his suicidal impulse—Stevens is as mentally ill as the others. A fine, borderline madness, maybe—but no less crazed. By what logic can I blame someone like him for not keeping his word? As I walk by his bed and sense him lying morosely awake in the dark, I imagine what it would be like to pour out with absolute candor what is running through my mind:

The truth is, Lance (have you any idea how farcically gentile your name comes over to me?), I'm floundering with our relationship, or whatever that fragile web between us can be. As for the so-called sophistication I display when I'm with you, I'm sure you know it's only paper thin. I have, actually, very little experience with deep male friendships. And here I am, all flustered, confused, even unhinged. Not only when I'm speaking to you, but in whatever I think and do nowadays. It's sheer foolishness, Lance, but there it is: I've never felt more alive—yes, expectant—with the possibility of a connection between us for which I've been starved for as long as I remember. In the three weeks you've been here, with a few random exchanges—words, eye contact, small gestures—you've wormed your way into my consciousness to the point where your smile or frown can make or spoil my day.

What's even worse, I have this outrageous notion—one of my Jewish traits, no doubt—that I can possibly save you from yourself through the sheer force of a kind and loving heart. It's my mother in me, I guess. But then, what am I to you, Stevens, Tolstoi's peasant bringing Ivan Illyich the life force he needs to shore him up in his hour of dying? Bullshit, soldier! Any time at all, when my back is turned, and you feel ready to kill yourself, you'll do it anyway. When I'm on duty too, you bastard, so that I have to clean up the mess. I want out, Lance, I refuse to play, even subliminally, your guardian angel. And yet . . . and yet . . .

For several days now, I've completely ignored Stevens, cutting him off sharply when he tries to engage me. Finally, one night, he puts his arms through the bed posts to block me. "Oh, Levy," he says, "why hast thou forsaken me?"

Right off, he's dissolved my anger. It's the knack he has for disarming me. "The name," I say, "is Samuel, the son of Levy, not of Joseph."

"For my sake, then"—his voice is harsh, urgent—"relate to me. I can't bear your silence. It reminds me of my father."

"What shall we talk about?" I ask.

He cups his hands around his mouth, pulls me toward him and speaks into my ear: "About my coming death," he says. "The one thing I've wanted so much for such a long, long time."

"You need help," I say. "I'll arrange for you to see the psychiatrist."

"Spare me, Samuel, will you?" he says. "I have to do my deed quietly, quickly—no fuss. There's no other way to go."

Stevens is sucking me down with him. I don't want to swirl in his maelstrom, his blackness. Some instinct tells me to play it nonplussed. "Those who really intend to do it," I say, "they don't read Camus. They don't discuss it. They go ahead and get it done with."

"Levy, Samuel," he sings out my name, "I would have long ago—if I weren't so chicken . . . like the guy on the sea wall."

"You had three chances," I point out. "Two by pills—one by water. Why don't you quit while you're ahead?"

"Shut up, you guys," someone shouts from a nearby bed. "We're trying to get some shut-eye."

"Shhh," I say to Lance, but he's beyond listening.

"Try to understand, Levy, there's nothing ahead but the question of how and when. Have you any idea the different ways I rehearse dying. By drowning. By leaping. A handful of pills. My throat slit. My wrists razored. I call my shots, Samuel. I am my own assassin. My private undertaker."

I put my hand over his mouth. He gulps down a choking sob. His anguish is so palpable I can almost touch it. We're so close, I could embrace him . . . comfort him into oblivion. "Maybe it would be better," I suggest, "if you went home."

"Home," he intones, "is where you hang"—a mocking pause—"yourself."

Stevens has stripped me of words. "Hang in," I whisper, "something will turn you around."

"It's all shit, my friend," he hisses. "Me . . . and you too, Levy."

Stevens rolls over and buries his head in the pillow. When I reach out to touch him, he closes his fist around mine. "Rock me, Samuel," he cries. "Put me to sleep."

I move my hand feather-soft across his shoulders until the even rise and fall of his breathing tell me he is no longer awake.

The morning after our harrowing exchange, I lie exhausted in my barracks bed, mulling over the options. I could overnight grow a thick skin—distance myself from Stevens. Or else, I might be able to get myself transferred to another Army post. Instead, I walk to the supply depot, where I bribe a soldier for a flashlight and a dozen batteries. Later that night, when the ward is asleep, I hold out my gift to Stevens.

"What are you offering me?" he asks. "Salvation?" He unwraps the package.

"No," I answer. "Only a guiding light."

Stevens presses the button and shines the flashlight in my face. "Well, whaddya know," he says, "a Jew with blue eyes. Now we have still another bond to join us . . . till death do us part."

He sees my distressed look. "A little light humor," he jokes.

As we both laugh, he turns the beam on his own face. In the dark, the glow paints phosphorescent shadows on the sides of his skull, under his eyes. I imagine this is how his death mask would look. "From here on in," I say, "you can read under the blanket whenever you want."

He exhales a deep sigh. "My God," he says, "the soldier really cares. He actually believes he can deliver me from myself."

Though his words are derisive, I know that he's moved. There's an awkward silence between us. I can feel the two of us trembling, under the cover of night, like nested birds.

"Give it a try, Stevens," I urge. "What have you got to lose?"

"This much I can assure you, Levy," he says. "I'll stay alive at least as long as the batteries last."

"They're the long-life kind," I say, "and I can always buy a new batch."

The flashlight—or maybe the concern that prompted my gift—has had a tonic effect. These nights he can hardly wait for the witching hour when the ward lights go off. I've invented a whole new routine to keep things moving neatly until ten. I go from bed to bed to chat with the old patients and to say hello to the newer ones. On some nights I even look in on the corporal and listen to his boozy advice before he mumbles off to sleep.

Stevens himself has come out of his shell. He banters with the others, argues about the war, sometimes laughs with them at their favorite radio shows. While I wash down the ward toilets, he diligently scrubs the sink and shines the mirror. All that's left is for me to fill out a few minimal records. Meanwhile, Stevens rolls himself into a tight ball on his bed and dozes off for an hour or two.

At about midnight, our friendship flowers underneath the blue Army blankets. At first, Stevens makes a cozy woolen tent and reads by himself for a while. As I rest, leaning back on the chair, the flashlight beneath the blanket shows through like a dim luminescent cocoon wrapped around Stevens and his book.

When he emerges, the flashlight off, we sit wordlessly in the delicious dark. Then Stevens motions me toward the tent, where I duck my head under to read the pages he has finished. At first, our twin readings—the idea that we are covering the same literary tracks—is enough to sustain us till morning. After a few nights, however, he pulls me toward him.

"Get under," he commands, "we'll read together." Before I can object he draws me completely under the blanket. Head to head, faintly alarmed at the closeness of our bodies, I fight off the impulse to move away. I have to read swiftly to keep up with his pace as he turns the pages. Occasionally, when something piques him, he whispers a comment in my ear.

I lie there with him, willingly trapped, transported back to my childhood, when my friends and I would make tents out of torn sheets in the fields that bordered the railroad tracks. Smoking our fathers' cigarettes, we would tell each other stories so ineffably secret, it would make me faint with happiness. I was one of them and at one with them—pledged by friendship, closer than kin. And oh the warmth of us huddled under the tent, the world not real, only us . . . forever inner, forever safe. *Be with me, Stevens, the way it was then, the way I wish it were again . . .*

Our ongoing liaison has already made small waves. "How's your pretty boy friend?" Flynn calls out maliciously when I pass his bed. Quinn, too, has been told about my lavish interest in Stevens. No doubt the other patients hear our nightly whisperings. All this should bother me, yet curiously, it doesn't. What I wait for most is the moment I walk toward him in the evening and see his sad face light up at the sight of me . . . then rearrange itself into a smile.

Since our under-the-blanket reading sessions began, we've swept through a good part of Stevens' library. We argue a good deal on the choice of books. When I object to Heidegger, for one—"He's too morbid for night reading"—Stevens answers, "Levy, your City College taste is up your ass." In the end, though, we agree on what comes next. *The Sun Also Rises, Light in August, The Lighthouse, The Lonely Hearts*—we go through these first. Then some stories by Chekhov, a few essays by Emerson.

Emerson precipitates a hot quarrel. When we come across the line, "Nothing is lost," Stevens comments, "Fantastic, isn't he?"

"Oh, I say airily, "more of his transcendental windiness. Sounds profound, but exactly what does it mean?"

"It's obvious as the nose on your face," he says angrily. "Everything in the universe is renewable—systole and diastole—a cycle of living, dying and renewal. Nothing—including my life or even your irrelevant existence—is ever lost. Get it, dumb-dumb!"

Yes, I get it. You'll twist any philosophical prop into a vindication for suicide. That may be grist for your mill, Stevens, but not mine. I wait for his temper to cool, so we can push ahead into safer terrain.

After all this intimacy, it's strange how little we know of each other. Once, in a hiatus between readings, Stevens unexpectedly asks: "What were you like as a kid?" He's so guarded about his private life, the question startles me.

"Let's see," I answer. "Oh, yes, I was a mess. Lonely, very few friends, afraid of violent sports, shy yet obsessed with sex. I played girl games with my sisters. Mostly to stay off the streets. How about you?"

"Suspicious, distant, difficult, snobbish, ungiving, unforgiving. Same as I am now." His iciness warns me against further probing.

In spite of his reluctance, some of the gaps begin to fill in. It comes out obliquely—as when we discuss characters in Hemingway, Faulkner or Fitzgerald. I know that he is an only child, that he will never speak of his mother, and that his father—an ill and retired Colonel—comes from the distinguished line of Maryland Stevens. Only once, in an offhand remark, he makes a personal reference to his father. "Pitiful bastard," he says, "he's one of the last of the big believers in iron discipline." Another time, in reading Faulkner, he mentions the overpowering closeness of Southern mothers and sons.

"Is your mother anything like that?" I ask innocently.

"Not in the way you think," he answers. "She's a pure, bitchy cold-blooded Dixie charmer." His venom is so intense, we both fall into a pained silence. "Be grateful," he adds after a pause, "for a nice little devouring Jewish mama like yours."

The heat arrives, full blast, early that June. Our friendship has mellowed the two of us. In my own confused way—if I recall right after all these years—I've never been more content. As for Stevens, he isn't anywhere as mordant as before. The undercurrent of suicide is no longer apparent, as well. We don't speak as much or as animatedly as we did. That's okay, too, since we've learned to savor the silences. In our reading we've gone as far as we could. When we try now, it's like plowing an exhausted field. Somehow, too, I don't see the point of bringing in any new books. Nothing is wrong, really, except that a cycle seems to be nearing its end. We can sense it in our bones. Any day now, according to Quinn, Stevens will be discharged and sent to a veterans' hospital nearer his home. Inexorably, an ambience of melancholy is ebbing our spirits. Neither of us wants to admit it, but the sense of time running out is pervasive.

One night, when Stevens can't sleep, he asks me about my plans. "I'm not sure," I say. "After you leave, I'll put in for a transfer. Hopefully, a whole new change of scene." When he puts both hands over his face, I quickly add: "You know what? Once the war ends, why don't we get together? Go to graduate school maybe. Find something to do in New York. Whatever . . . our hearts desire."

"How sporting of you," Stevens says. "But do a pal a favor, Levy. shovel me no horse manure. Tell me no tales."

When I try to protest, he reaches over to the windowsill and runs his hands over the books. "Here, Levy, I won't be needing them. I hereby bequeath the selected madhouse library to you. Just a little something to remember me by."

His voice is so definitive, I don't even try for a topper.

Out of nowhere, I receive a letter from Stevens' mother:

> Dear Mr. Levy: I know of you through Private Quinn, whom I have spoken to by phone several times. He tells me that you are my son's only friend. So you must know that Lance won't see me or even read my letters. I'm sure he's told you we're monsters, but this isn't the time to defend his father or myself. I want only to beg you, Mr. Levy, to tell Lance that his father has suffered a severe heart attack and stroke. He's been left practically paralyzed.
>
> Please, please, ask Lance if he can find it in his heart to call his father as soon as he hears about him. It would be a tragedy for us all if Mr. Stevens died without a word from his son. With thanks and gratitude for your help at this terrible moment.

What am I supposed to do with this letter? The irony is, it comes when Stevens has begun to unravel again for no compelling reason I can understand. He seems to have shut the door on himself again. Often he looks through me as if I were transparent. If I speak to him, he mostly turns away or keeps his eyes glued to the ceiling.

I have to remind myself that Stevens' mood fluctuations are part of his illness. Maybe if I wait for an upward swing, he'll take the letter in stride. On the other hand, what if it triggers a catastrophic reaction? I've held Stevens' hand too long. I need somebody to hold mine.

When I report to the ward the next evening, I grab Quinn in the hallway and show him the letter. "You've got lots of experience with depressives," I say. "Do I tell Stevens about his father?"

"How the hell do I know?" he answers, not unkindly. "Anything could happen to a screwball like him." As he starts to leave, he says: "If you give Stevens a sleeping pill, make sure he swallows it. Some of them stash it under their tongues. In a couple of days, they have enough for a suicide try."

He walks away, then suddenly turns. "About the letter, play it by ear. And for Chrissakes, you ain't his mother. Stop being a bleeding heart."

It's the twilight hour before dawn. I've given him two sleeping pills—I can't understand why—without following Quinn's instructions. He lies, curled up, dead asleep. His mother's letter is with me, burning my back pocket. I've picked at the pros and cons of reading the letter to him, like a dog at a bone. I haven't a clue what it means to play it by ear. Would I want—under any circumstances—not to be told that my father is dying? Of course not. I'm my own jury. There is no doubt whatever. I vote yes, with my guts.

When I hear Stevens stirring, I lean over him. "We have to talk." He opens his eyes by degrees. His head twists on and off the pillow, violently, as if he's climbing out of a bad dream.

"Is that you, Levy?" he asks.

"Yes," I say. "I have a letter for you. From your mother." I take the letter from my pocket.

"Shove it," he says. "I don't get letters. You damn well know that."

I throw the flashlight beam on the open letter. "Just this one line," I plead, "it's about your father."

Stevens tears the letter from my hands. In a quick motion he rips it into shreds and showers them overhead. The pieces float down like snow onto the two of us and then to the floor.

Almost numb at what I'm about to do, I'm in the grip of some kind of madness. "Hear me out, Stevens. Your father's had a bad stroke. He may be dying. Give him a call."

"Screw the bastard," his voice is shrill, "and my cunt of a mother and you too, Levy . . . you pimp, you cry-baby mummie's boy, you little ass-licking Jew!"

One by one the bedlamps go on. The ward is in a turmoil. At the observation window, shocked out of his drunken sleep, the corporal is shouting. "What the hell goes on out there?"

"Shhhh," I keen into Stevens' ear and fall back with him into bed. His rigid body doesn't offer the slightest resistance. We lie there, locked together. I hold him even after his shuddering stops. Vaguely it occurs to me, what must the patients be thinking? After a while, the ward goes back to sleep. Only I, my heart thudding like a pump, am awake when the first gulls begin to caw.

The morning after, asleep in my barracks, I dream about my father for the first time since his death. My bed is sinking toward three graves on the bottom of the sea. A configuration of three gravestones is strangely familiar. Of course, they are the plots my father bought for his family to rest in forever. Papa is seated on a mound beneath which his coffin is supposed to be buried. "How is it, my son, you never visit. You don't call either. Or write me a letter?" Staring at him—his eyes feverish with love . . . or is it rage? . . . I can't think of a lie to invent. With a wrench that sends the bed rushing upward, I catapult myself through my eyelids into wakefulness.

When I enter the ward that evening, still oppressed with the dream, Quinn stuns me with the news. "Your pal, Stevens," he says, pointing to the blues bed, "he almost pulled it off."

When I reach Stevens, he's lying on his back, drugged, a retaining sheet around his chest. His face, porcelain white under the bedlamp, is stubbled with fine golden hair. It crosses my mind that the two bound soldiers—Boertz and Stevens—are directly in line of each other's vision. "How did it happen?" I ask.

Quinn frees Stevens' arm. A thick strip of tape holds the bandage in place. "He was in the toilet," Quinn explains, "three, four minutes before I got suspicious. 'That's it,' I yelled, 'time's up!' When he didn't come out, I tried pushing in the door. It didn't give way, so I kicked through the panel—and there he was . . . wedged in between the wall and the door. Talk about a mess. He had this razor blade in his hand, and both wrists—they were spurting blood like faucets."

I fight off the spasm in my belly. If Quinn goes on, I'm going to puke. "How is he?" I say, cutting him off.

"The weirdest thing is"—Quinn pushes past my question—"he had this message to you spelled out in blood on the mirror. 'Nothing is lost, Levy.' What the hell does that mean, nothing is lost?"

"Beats me," I say. "Must be his private joke."

Before he leaves, Quinn warns me, "Don't let him out of your sight—not for a second. Most likely, they'll transfer him in a coupla days."

I watch Stevens sleeping, his head thrown back, mouth twisted, as in a coma. When I train the light on him, his eyes flutter open. He looks at me foggily, without a sign of recognition. Yet I'm convinced he's aware of me hovering over him, my gaze fixed on his face.

I rehearse the tone I will assume when he awakens. *Chiding:* Isn't it about time you gave up this kid's stuff? *Apologetic:* About that letter—I had no other choice. *Amused:* You sure don't take no for an answer. *Rueful:* I thought we had something special going for us.

Instead, when he barely manages to whisper, "Stick around, Samuel, I miss you," I say, "Why did you do it, fucker. You promised to tip me off first."

"I had no choice," he says. "It's existential."

"Cut that crap out," I insist. "I want a real answer."

"Ripeness is all," he says. "It's as simple as that. I'm a rotten fruit, ready to fall."

"Shit," I blurt out, "shit on your phony philosophy. Listen . . . they're sending you out of this suicide trap. To a real hospital, with trained personnel. I'll visit you, Stevens. I'll get a pass and stay until you're well."

"Samuel, Samuel," he says. "You don't know when you're licked, do you? Okay, then, I'm hereby giving you fair warning."

Stevens rolls his head fitfully onto his pillow. His eyelids are shuttered, his brows furrowed; he's slipping away into sleep.

"Stay up awhile," I beg. "I'll read to you."

"If it makes you happy," he says.

I take a book that's at the edge of the windowsill and open it to the page where Stevens has inserted a scrap of paper. It's Kafka's diary for the year 1913. The first entry I see (it's circled in red) is for December 4:

> Viewed from the outside, it is terrible for a young person to die, or worse to kill himself. To die would mean nothing else than to surrender, nothing to a nothing, but that would be impossible to conceive, for how could such a person, even only as a nothing, consciously surrender himself to the nothing, and not merely to an empty nothing but rather to a roaring nothing whose nothingness consists only in its incomprehensibility . . .

As I scan the ghastly message, I see that Stevens is slipping off, far out of reach, into a nothingness entirely of his own. Before he goes under, I hear him faintly saying, "Whatever happens, Samuel, you get an A for effort."

Sitting on the bed beside him, I keep watch through the dragged-out minutes, trying to imagine some transcendent affirmation I can present Stevens with in the morning. If the night has any magic words, I'm too frozen, too tired fighting off sleep, to hear them.

At dawn, when a shaft of sunlight falls on Stevens' bed, I note that he is lying on his side, in a fetal position, knees against his chest, arms hidden by the blanket. One corner of the bedsheet, folded over, is visible. And there, splotched on the white, is a circle of dark-red blood. In a panic, I tear the blanket off and see that Stevens' pajamas are blood-soaked too. Oh Christ, he did it . . . while I sat, half-glazed beside him, he has shredded his bandages open against the sharp coils of the bedsprings underneath the blanket. Slowly working the steel edges into his wrists, he has emptied his gashed veins into a purple pool under the bed. And all this ingenious machinery of dying with me no more than an arm's length away!

It astonishes me, this aura of alert calm in which I seem to be floating. I feel neither shock, nor loss, nor defeat. Not even resentment that he chose me as his accomplice in death. Only, though it shames me, a surge of lightheadedness, as if an immense stone has been dislodged from my being. I remember consoling myself: finally, it's all over, a period at the end of an impossibly long and convoluted sentence.

I turn Stevens onto his back. His face is doll-peach and waxen, without a glimmer of expression. Through his wide-open eyes, the half-circles of white are cross-hatched with ugly red blotches. Before this, I've been present at only two death-beds—my grandmother's and my father's. Now Stevens is my third. I rearrange the blankets neatly, with his hands covered, so that the torn veins are out of sight.

I sit at his side, wondering what kind of goodbye he would have appreciated. Out of some obscure instinct, I close one of his eyes, then the other, with my thumb. Leaning down, I wrap my arms around him and press my lips into his. "A for effort," I whisper, "but F for execution. Right, Lancelot?" The sound of his name, the thought comes to me, is as ridiculous now as when I first heard it.

Immediately afterwards, I phone emergency: "Hello, this is Private Levy. One of our patients—Stevens—just killed himself." While I wait, I carefully mop up the pool of blood under the bed.

That Saturday—my first free day since Stevens' death—I receive word that my request for overseas duty has been approved. Before I leave for embarkation camp, I visit Ward E to collect the books that Stevens had wanted me to have. When the day orderly—a new man—lets me in, I see that big changes have taken place. Of the old patients, only Boertz and the schizo twins still remain. The twins wave at me feebly as I pass. The others are mostly dozing on this hot afternoon.

It's unnerving, this mixed sense of dèjá vu and estrangement as I look down the aisle. Nothing is different, only more so—the loonies marooned in their beds even more solitary, the waxed floor almost garish in its glossiness, the ward claustrophobic behind its prison bars.

From the windowsill behind Stevens' bed, I take only those books we had both liked best. The others I leave behind, except for *The Meaning of Death,* which I toss into the wastebasket. There's nothing left to keep me now . . . I should leave then and there. But something draws me to Boertz, a vague sense of business unfinished. Sitting on his bed, I think, with a pang of regret, that my one human contact with Boertz has been my feeding him his daily meals. Outside of that, I have not made the slightest effort to reach him.

He's stretched out rigidly, head propped against the pillow, his zombie stare aimed through the window at some private void beyond. I try to imagine what it must be like, shut into the darkened cell of one's self, as with a cloth over a bird in a cage, beyond nostalgia, dreams, anticipation, the passage of time.

"Boertz," I ask softly, "are you thinking about anything—a face, a special room, the way the dust is dancing in the window?" No response. "Jesus," I say, "give me a sign . . . smile at me . . . move your lips." A blank face. Not a wisp of recognition.

On a sudden impulse, noting that the orderly has stepped into the office, I loosen the restrainer and slip my hand into his. "Hold my hand, Boertz," I tell him. "If you do, I'll know you mean goodbye." Then I push my hand into his huge and clammy fist. It lies there inert. I press my nails into his flesh, waiting for a quaver, a twitch. It's no use—nothing is getting through. I draw my hand out and retie the straitjacket.

"So long, Boertzie," I say. "Try to keep out of trouble." I run my finger lightly across the livid scratches on his cheeks and let them linger there like a caress. For one brief moment—though I couldn't swear on it—I see his eyes flicker faintly. Then, almost imperceptibly—or is it an illusion?—he lifts the corner of his mouth into a smile. And his head, is it turning slightly?—at least I hope it is—in my direction. Why not, why shouldn't I believe it? I've touched him. He's signalling across the abyss. With that, a chain of associations leaps clear out of my head: "Nothing is lost," I hear myself saying, "You read me, buddy? Absolutely nothing at all!"

In the silence of the ward, my brave little epiphany dissolves with barely an echo. Has Boertz heard me? I search his face intently for a reaction. When I waggle my hand before his ice-blue eyes, they never even waver. If anything, they are even more remorselessly unseeing than before. And all at once it strikes me how pathetic my imaginary exchange has been. For my own good, I warn myself, I must stop inventing these happy endings.

I rise quickly from Boertz' bedside... Carrying Stevens' books in my arms, I stride down the length of the ward and, for the last time, let myself out the double doors. It amazes me, the bitter elation I feel in not having once looked back at the blues bed.

Kissing Stalin

Here I am incarcerated in a decaying mental institution on the Upper West Side, and my half-assed psychiatric aide (I'm sure she doesn't even have an MSW) keeps pestering me about the basic factors underlying my delusional seizures—which is how they describe them—that have brought me to this pass in the first place.

No, Miss Snyder, I am not suffering from an acute depression that emanates from loneliness, fear of death or any other geriatric syndrome. And no, my so-called hallucinations are not—overtly or covertly—sexual in nature. It appalls me to hear a young woman like you pursue this line of inquiry with an eighty-year-old man who has not put a hand on a woman, much less had sex with her, since his wife left him, let's see—I can't even remember how many years ago.

As I have tried to explain, my dilemma, far from being of psychological origin, is purely political. Let the psychiatrist in charge—it is his professional privilege to do so—classify me as paranoiac with schizoid tendencies. Yes, that's what I read on the yellow card when you left your desk. In order, however, to grasp the chain of circumstances that entangled me in the affairs of Svetlana Alliluyeva, the daughter of Joseph Stalin, you would have to possess virtually an encyclopedic familiarity with my life.

Project yourself if you can, in this me-first day and age, into my background. A Depression boy in the thirties. Slum-bred at a time of mass layoffs, Hoovervilles, breadlines, evictions in the streets. A Young Pioneer at sixteen. Three years at City College. A non-stop Party member from then on. And, for a livelihood—in order to be close to the working class—a job as a mink-stripper in one of the prime shops on Twenty-seventh Street.

Beyond that, you would have to be conversant with the ins and outs of radical politics and have a reading acquaintance—if not of *Das Kapital* and other Marxist classics—then at the very least the Little Lenin Library. Above all, though—this is a rock-bottom essential—a profound insight into my unquenchable love for the heroic leader of the Soviet Union . . . Joseph Vissarionovich Stalin.

Lacking these, can you make an effort to understand the ambiance of my first encounter with Comrade Stalin, and the consequent events that drew me irresistibly into his orbit? It was a winter day in 1933. A young woman handed me a leaflet announcing a protest meeting of the Young Pioneers on Rivington Street. "Don't forget to be there," she ordered. That evening, my pulse fluttering wildly, I climbed the steep flight of stairs to a bile-green-painted hall, with wooden chairs and a table for socialist reading material.

Hung on the wall were three giant photos. On the left, Lenin, with his massive dome of a head. In the center, Marx, his beard all bushy and tangled like a bird's-nest. And there, on the right, in a gray tunic, his crippled hand curled into a sleeve, someone I did not recognize.

As I stared at his elongated face, over which a halo seemed to be playing, the young woman with the stern voice came over to ask: "You know who he is, of course?"

When I hesitated, ashamed of my ignorance, she said: "Wait here a minute" in that no-nonsense tone which she was to assume throughout the thirty-two years of our marriage. *"Foundations of Leninism,"* she said, handing me a yellow pamphlet. "It's by the man you are looking at. Read it and tell me what you think."

"When?" I asked, already captivated by the two of them.

"Tomorrow," she answered, "same time, same place."

It isn't possible, you say, for a slim booklet to change someone's life in one sitting? Don't be too sure. As I read Stalin's words—so blunt, simple, clear as water—I felt, how can I describe it?—a flame illuminating my whole being. Till then, if I thought of history at all, it seemed to me a senseless mess. Now, studying Stalin's booklet, I began to see that there was meaning behind this chaos—a movement towards a world without oppression. Dialectics, that's how Stalin explained it. Contradictions, negations, unity of opposites. Words I barely understood but knew in my heart were true. Can you appreciate this magical moment when an ordinary man like me—afraid, confused, alone—glimpses that it is possible to help bring about a beautiful future?

The next day, when I saw Sophie, I was too shy to reveal this—how would one call it?—this conversion. "I need to read more," I told her, "to study more." Ah, she answered, "then join my socialist study group."

I did just that and in a few months we were married. After that, we became one of those burning radical couples for whom the Party was a haven, a close-knit family, a vessel filling their lives with joy and meaning.

To be sure, the existence we led was not everyone's cup of tea. Endless meetings, cranking out leaflets, marches, clashes with the police, picket lines and hawking literature. Also, the pain of being marginal, of talking mostly to ourselves, to be ignored by passersby and heckled by red-baiters. Meanwhile, all around us, the glitter of money and ambition, the fantasy of success. And capitalism itself, as we told ourselves, always on the brink of collapse, yet never taking the hint.

Still, there were the little triumphs—the stray lambs Sophie and I would recuit, the Party growing steadily, the Soviet Union—with Stalin at the helm—pointing the way to socialism.

As for Sophie and me, the first political shadow between us fell in 1939, when we read in the headlines: "Soviets Sign Non-Aggression Pact With Nazis!" "How can they do it?" Sophie ranted at me. "How can they shame us this way?"

Astonished, I said to her. "Sophie, as Comrade Stalin pointed out..."

"What Comrade Stalin," she exploded. "Every time you say that at a meeting—once you actually called him 'the glorious leader of socialism'—people laugh behind your back. Maurice, listen to me, you are not in the Soviet Union. You are in New York, the center of world capitalism. People simply do not speak like pamphlets. Can't you understand that?"

That night, in our headquarters, oh, what a scene—comrades weeping, fainting away, some tearing up their Party cards. My wife, shocked and silent, stole out early, while I argued with the others not to swallow the bourgeois lies. "Give Comrade Stalin time," I begged. "He will explain."

Later, when the hall was empty, I stood before his portrait. Looking into his piercing eyes, I asked: "Joseph Stalin, why have you done this? Why are you breaking our hearts?" Never before had I been this close to utter despair.

It was at this very moment, Miss Snyder, that I began the first of my conversations with Stalin. Call them delusions, if you will, the crazed imaginings of a man on the brink of breakdown. But please believe me that I was then—and always after that—perfectly lucid whenever we conversed.

As I stared at the portrait, I saw his head turn toward me and his lips move. "Ah, young comrade," he said softly, in perfect English. "Did you think that the road to socialism was strait and narrow, without flip-flops, and painful reversals?"

Was I startled, Miss Snyder, when I first heard him speak? Not in the least. Only grateful that he was confiding in me in this moment of crisis. "Yes," I said, "I know that history is full of surprises—but for you to lie in the same manger as Nazi murderers . . ."

He shook his head sadly. "True, comrade, the train of history has taken a dizzying turn. But I beg you, Comrade Greenbaum, be steady, don't fall off, have faith. The revolution needs you." Closing the conversation with these words, he froze once again into his portrait.

Somehow or other, Sophie and I eventually made up our differences and continued, on the surface, as before. Looking back, though, I can see that for her the dew was off the red rose. Though she remained in the Party, little by little she withdrew from active participation.

Meanwhile, as the years slipped by, and we became increasingly estranged, the ties between Joseph and me became stronger. Interpret it as you want—a pathological obsession—he was now for me a father image, a confidant, a friend who could trust me with his most intimate thoughts. By now, too, I was an omnivorous collector of everything that related to Stalin, searching through bookstores, libraries and special collections for anything I could find. Not only his writings but letters, journals, observations by friends and political colleagues, interviews with famous people, photos from his boyhood days to his May Day appearances on the ramparts of the Kremlin. It's entirely possible that I know more about Joseph Stalin than anyone else in the world.

No doubt, Miss Snyder, you like the others have swallowed the vilifications of Stalin hook, line and sinker. What, however, do you really know about this son of a serf, this brilliant Seminary student in Tiflis, who served in jail, was exiled to Siberia, became a Bolshevik, fought at Lenin's side in the revolution, and built the first socialist state.

"Steel," that's what the word *Stalin* means—made of steel "that holds and molds the spirit of man!" And a splendid poet too—you weren't aware of that, were you? Here, I'll recite a few lines:

> Know well that those who once
> Fell to the oppressors
> Shall rise again and soar,
> Winged with hope, above
>   the holy mountain . . .

And this is the man who is supposed to be a crude and cunning power-hungry tyrant? Have you ever seen the film "Lenin in October?" No, how could you. They don't show Soviet classics these days. Anyway, there's this scene where Lenin—tired and ill—turns to Stalin and says:

"We must, at all costs, defend the people's revolution." And Stalin, his hand gently on Lenin's shoulder, replies: "With my life, dear Vladimir, every fibre of my soul." God, how I cried all through the rest of that film.

During this period these visual visitations I have spoken to you about were becoming more frequent—and more important to me. And what did we discuss? Oh, whatever was au courant: the new Five-Year-Plan, dialectical materialism, the treachery of Trotskyites, the Third International, the state of affairs in Bulgaria.

You want me to describe precisely what it's like to have such a visitation. Let's see. When I was a kid, my best friend would have these seizures. And once, when it was over, he told me what it was like. He would have this sense of being completely calm in the eye of a storm—a blinding flash, kind of, as if some great mystery is about to be revealed. This is how I feel when Stalin appears to me. Then, afterwards, everything is clear and light, as if the world's problems were lifted from my head.

There was one exception, though, and that happened in 1953, a day after Stalin's death. As I lay in bed, mourning, he put his hand over my mouth and whispered: "Comrade Maurice" (we were quite familiar with one another by then) "shattering events will take place in the coming months and years. Accusations will be made, crimes attributed to me so awesome they will shake the world. You must not believe them, Maurice. They are the acts of desperate traitors. Hold the line, my dear friend, steel yourself for the dark times ahead..." With these words, he disappeared.

Sad to say, Stalin's warnings were prophetic. Three years later, Nikita Khrushchev, that vulgar, shoe-banging kulak, delivered his infamous Report to the Twentieth Congress of the Party. Fortunately, Miss Snyder, your generation barely remembers that tissue of arrant fabrication. In it, my God, what unimaginable crimes Comrade Stalin is accused of: murdering his comrades, writers, doctors, a reign of terror and torture, imprisoning countless men and women in labor camps. I have myself never read these calumnious inventions... this sensationalist swill. It couldn't be avoided, sad to say, if you so much as glanced at a capitalist newspaper.

You can well imagine the disastrous aftermath in our Party. I will pass by the soul-destroying guilt, the quarrels, recriminations, the decimation of our ranks. My wife Sophie was even worse than the others. "They have lied to us," she raved at me, "betrayed our trust, destroyed our hopes and dreams. And you, Maurice, with your noble Comrade Stalin—that sadist, that dictator, that executioner of socialism..."

All through this hysteria she was packing her belongings into a small suitcase. Of course I tried to reason with her—to no avail. Later that night, without another word, she disappeared from my life. Shortly after that, she sent me a letter with quotes purporting to be Stalin's orders concerning the so-called Doctors' Plot: "'If you do not obtain their confessions, we will shoot you in the head . . . As for investigative methods, beat, beat, beat and once again beat.' If you are any kind of a Jew, how can you read these words and not condemn once and for all this antisemitic monster?" Sophie too was beyond the pale. My enemy, like the others. It saddened me to realize we could never communicate again.

With Sophie gone, my revolutionary optimism wilted like a dying flower. In a traumatic scene I left the Party, which had already been wiped off the political map. Who could put up with the bickering, the cross-accusations, the unprincipled dumping of Stalin. Oh yes, I made in the years that followed some efforts to regroup the scattered comrades still loyal to our leader. Gradually they had lost heart and fallen silent. In desperation I tried the younger radicals—the small sects that had sprung up: The Revolutionary Party of Workers. The Party of Revolutionary Workers. The Proletariat League for Revolution. The League for Proletariat Revolution. And so forth. What did I find there? Maoists, Trotskyists, assorted adventurers, anarchists, Third World terrorists—every species but unabashed Stalinists like myself.

At one point, I even considered, when all else had failed, seeking exile in Albania, where Comrade Enver Hoxha and his Party still kept aloft the banner of Stalinism. But then I thought. How could I be of service to the people of that poverty-stricken land? They needed an octogenarian ex-mink-matcher like a hole in the head.

And Stalin himself? He appeared to me during these years only in my dreams, no longer steel, a graying, bitter exile from his own land. Each visit the same: two aging men, with tarnished dreams, idly chatting or sitting in unbearable silence until he faded away.

I had by now quit my job and was living on social security in a tiny tenement flat near St. Mark's Place. Friendless, with no family, surrounded by photos of Stalin on my walls, I was beginning to look forward to death. And then, one evening as I dozed in the park, with my dirty sneakers and leather cap (someone had told me it made me look like an old Bolshevik), an astonishing thing happened. There, walking by the empty basketball court, was Stalin himself, in his military tunic, waving wildly in my direction. Luckily we were alone when he sat down beside me.

"Maurice," he said, "did you know that my daughter Svetlana is at this very moment living near the University of Princeton, in these United States?"

"Yes, Joseph," I answered. "Recently I saw her on television. She has turned her back on socialism and is spreading terrible canards about her father. It was so awful I had to turn off the set."

"Forget all this," Stalin said. "This is my darling Svetlana—the one person upon whom I lavished the greatest affection. Whatever her words—she was always a willful child—she is still her father's favorite daughter."

"And what," I said, "does all this mean?"

He put his hand on my knee. "Comrade," he said, "I want you to visit Svetlana at once. Talk to her, Maurice, explain to her that I cannot rest until I am vindicated and my bones lie where they belong, in the tomb next to dear Comrade Lenin."

Poor Stalin, I thought, could it be that being dead all these years has muddled his mind? "And what is it," I asked, "that I must persuade her to do?"

In the gathering darkness, Stalin's black eyes blazed at me like a cat's. "She must announce to the world—at a press conference which she has the power to convene—that Khrushchev and his cronies were the real traitors. She was there with me, privy to the facts. Till now, she has been silent. Finally, she has realized it is her duty to reveal the truth... her father is and remains to this day guiltless!"

I shook my head at Stalin. "How can I get her to do this? It would be a reversal of everything she has said and written."

Stalin seized me by the shoulders in an iron grip. "Do what is necessary," he said savagely—I could see why he had taken the name Stalin—"by whatever means that can succeed... Beg her, flatter her, make her feel pity for me, threaten her—if all other appeals fail. But make her change her mind about me!" Then, he rose from the bench, saluted me like the old soldier he was and said: "In the name of the revolution, dear friend, I order you to do as I say." Just as he dissolved into mist, I heard his firm voice: "With your help, Comrade, history will absolve me."

Returning to my flat, shaken to the core, I tried dispassionately to consider what was being demanded of me. Surely it was madness, this appeal to a woman who had chosen to exile herself in the fleshpots of capitalism. Still, I argued with myself, did overthrowing Tsarism with some motley workers make sense? Did defending the USSR against twenty-one armies make sense? Did defeating the mighty Nazi juggernaut make sense? Sense, in this instance, was a petit bourgeois fear of undertaking a revolutionary task. If it meant my life, I would risk it.

The next day, in Chinatown, I bought a cap pistol and a black mask if I should need to disguise myself. Then I took the bus to Princeton, and, as I leaned back, waited for a plan to reveal itself to me. When we had almost arrived, an academic type seated beside me pointed out the window. "See that big white house on the side road? Joseph Stalin's daughter lives there, in the Cummins place. Isn't it lovely?"

Yes, it was lovely, a gem of a house, God's little green acre in the suburban heartland of white-bread America. She had rich tastes, all right, Stalin's little daughter.

It was snowing gently when I stepped off the bus and trudged the dirt road until I stood at a low fence facing her house. No one was in sight. A light was twinkling at the window. I tiptoed to the embankment and, peering in, saw her reading, half-lying on a couch, in an elegant room. Moving to the other side of the porch, I tugged at a window and—what do you know, Miss Snyder—it had been left unlatched. Once I was inside, I slid the gun into my side pocket. As for the mask, I decided that dignity was preferable to concealment.

Stepping into her room, I said: "Svetlana Alliluyeva?"

She turned toward me and answered with amazing calm: "Is this maybe some kind of prank?"

"No," I said, "I'm deadly serious."

Svetlana rose from the couch. She looked me over carefully, head to foot. "Are you not much too old," she asked, "to break into people's houses like a chooliyagan?"

She was, I could see, an imposingly tall, sturdy woman, towering over my frail, five-feet-two frame. She had her father's dark eyes and curly hair, the same longish features, only more delicate, more kindly. Her accent—nervous as I was, I couldn't help noting—was broad, exaggerated, like the stage Russian of Greta Garbo in "Tovarich." I had the feeling we were engaged in some kind of farce. It was important to me to take command, to be masterly, like her father.

"My name is Maurice Greenbaum," I said sternly. "And I'm here as an official emissary of Joseph Stalin."

"Ah," she repeated, "a messenger from a dead man. That is most, how should I say, exceptional?"

Was she mocking me? "This is very serious business," I barked at her, fingering my gun and pointing it at her through the trouser pocket.

The outline of the gun directed at her didn't seem to faze her a bit. "Can't we be seated, and converse like civilized people?"

Across the table from her, face to face, I said: "Mrs. Alliluyeva . . ."

"No, no," she said, "I don't like formalities. My name is Svetlana."

"Very well, then, Svetlana," I said, "Comrade Stalin—yes, he is my comrade—has instructed me to request this of you—that you clear up his name, so that he may finally find peace."

She breathed heavily. "My father, the materialist, talks to you from his grave?" A small smile played across her face.

"Yes," I answered, flustered, "though it may seem odd to you, we communicate frequently at intervals."

"Uh, huh," she said, stroking her chin thoughtfully, "I see. But what you ask is impossible. Papa has already written his dark pages in history. It is too late for me—or anyone, for that matter—to rewrite those pages."

"No, no," I said, "Socrates, Dreyfus, others, have been found guilty too, and exonerated long after. Why not Joseph Stalin?"

"Because"—she searched for an answer—"he was not a very good person. I speak only as a daughter, who knows him better than anyone else." Her voice trembled with agitation. "How heartless he could be—how cynical and suspicious. I could tell you stories—the way he neglected my mother . . . she killed herself, did you know? drove my brother Vasily to an alcoholic death . . . refused to see his grandchildren."

"Stop it," I shouted, getting to my feet. Without thinking, I drew the pistol from my pocket and waved it menacingly in her direction. "I will not listen to these character assassinations, not even from his own flesh and blood. You are no better than the other renegades from socialism. You've bought the whole system . . . the luxuries"—I swept my arm around the room—"this easy, corrupting life."

"Very well, then," she said, holding a hand out to me. "Put away the gun. It makes me nervous. What do you want of me?"

"First," I said, "that you should believe your father was wronged. This man whom you call cruel, cynical, without pity. Do you recall what the great poet Pablo Neruda said at Stalin's death? 'In the darkness Stalin rose before my eyes, a good-natured man of principles, a titanic defender of the Russian revolution. When this Cyclops of the Kremlin died, it had a world-wide impact—the whole human jungle shuddered!' "

"Please," she said, putting her palms to her ears, "I cannot listen to this drivel. Tell me what I must do."

"Call the *New York Times,*" I said, "and inform them that you have a momentous announcement. You want a reporter, no, a group of reporters, to come here this evening, so that you can reveal the true story of your father."

The telephone was on a side table nearby. I thrust it into her hands. "Phone them, I beg you, in the name of Comrade Stalin. Tell them how Beria, Khrushchev and the other enemies of the worker's state plotted against your father . . ."

The gun was trembling in my hand—so close she could now make out the cheap lettering. "Why, Maurice," she said, bending toward the pistol, "it is a child's toy, like my son loved to play with." Suddenly, she tore it from my hand, pushed me heavily into the couch and, with her superior weight, pinned me against the cushions.

As I struggled half-heartedly, she shook her head. "It is of no use, Maurice, they would not have, for a moment, believed me."

I lay there quietly, all the fight in me gone. She was so close, she looked so much like her father, I had to resist the impulse to embrace her. After a while I said: "It's time for me to go."

"I'm sorry, Maurice," she said, regretfully, "I must call the security police, and inform them that a—how shall I say—deranged person—temporary, of course—has wandered by accident into my house. He is no criminal, I will assure them. Only he needs rest, help, quiet."

Then, holding me down softly with one hand, she dialed with the other: "Hello, this is Svetlana Alliluyeva. Someone has broken into my house. I need the security men at once."

While we sat there waiting, I said wistfully to Svetlana. "Comrade Stalin is my friend—you must understand he always will be. Surely there are some nice things you can remember about him?"

She thought for a while and said: "He loved me when I was a little girl—I made him laugh. Oh, he would say, you look just like your mother—red freckles and all. How tenderly he would touch my face. Sometimes he wrote little notes: 'I send you fifty peaches. How are your dolls? Why don't you answer my letters? You will never know how much your father misses his tiny sparrow . . .' "

"What else," I urged her, "what else like this do you recall?"

"Please," Svetlana said, "it hurts too much to remember."

"Please," I begged, "it will be the last time you tell these stories."

"Oh, Maurice"—she brushed her hair aside continued in a low voice—"Sometimes, at night, he would come into my room and, kneeling beside the bed, put his face up toward mine. 'Can you guess what I want?' he would ask. 'A song,' I would tease. Uh, uh, he would shake his head. 'A cup of tea,' I would answer. 'No, again,' he would say. 'A chocolate,' I would laugh. 'Still no,' he would shout: 'A kiss for Papa Stalin!' Then, when I leaned forward and pressed my lips to his, I could feel the sharp bristles of his mustache pricking my face."

Reliving the scene, Svetlana sighed and folded her hands into her lap. "The kisses stopped forever," she said, "at nineteen, when I married a Jew."

We sat in silence, then, a silence so deep, I couldn't bear her ending on this note. "One more memory," I cajoled her, "only one."

As she spoke, Svetlana looked out into space. "Once he told me about his dog, Trisha, when he was in exile in Siberia. Trisha—a little scrappy mongrel—and he were inseparable. They ate, slept and played together. When Trisha died, he couldn't stop grieving."

She was warming my heart, bringing tears to my eyes. Without my having to ask her, she was reminiscing on her own. "When he was a boy," she said, "and his father beat his mother, Joseph drew his knife and tried to kill him. He loved her very much, so much, he would have gladly given up his life for her.

"Before he died," she continued, her eyes clouding, "I spent three days at his bedside, experiencing the greatest pain and terror I have ever known. He had had a stroke and could barely breathe. Suddenly he moved his lips as if to disclose a great secret. 'Papa, flesh of my flesh,' I thought, 'speak to me.' But he never said another word again."

After this, she could not go on and we lay there in silence. In a while, two policemen knocked at the door. When they wanted to manacle my wrists, Svetlana told them, "No, no, he is a friend, a little confused, that is all. Treat him kindly, bring him where he can be cared for." And with that, she leaned over and kissed my cheek. "Take care of yourself, Maurice," she said, "and think always well of me."

The next day, a special police bus drove me directly to this hospital—and here I am, Miss Snyder, waiting to be released.

All through these sessions with me, Miss Snyder had been writing down, as quickly as she could, everything I told her. "Now that we have all the information," she said, "we can begin to treat you properly."

A few days later, the Chief Psychiatrist, together with Miss Snyder, talked with me in his office. "I have your case history," he said, studying her notes. "Unusual," he said, "most unusual."

"Don't you think," I said, "it's time for me to leave?"

"Very soon"—he hesitated—"only, we'll have to begin treatments first."

"Treatments," I asked, "what for?"

"Mr. Greenbaum, we can't let you go around believing you are in communication with Joseph Stalin."

"I am," I said testily. "I see and speak to him as clearly as I do you."

The psychiatrist threw up his arms. "Mr. Greenbaum, I'll level with you. You will have to be on thorazine—probably for the rest of your life. There is no other way to stabilize you."

"A comrade of mine was on thorazine," I protested. "He walked around like a zombie. No life force, no spirit, no spunk left for political activity. They have, in effect, silenced him."

"What can I say to you?" the psychiatrist said. "If you refuse, we'll have to send you to Bellevue, where there is no discussion on treatments. Well"—he waited for my response—"what will it be?"

I looked at Miss Snyder. She was shaking her head yes. "Yes," I said, "let it be thorazine."

I have been on thorazine now, for almost a month. Just like I said, it's a capitalist tool. I feel half-drugged, without will or energy to fight this system. On top of that, the visitations have stopped—stopped cold. At first, in the middle of the night, Stalin would vaguely appear—like one of those ghostly images between regular TV channels—flickering, no sound, then dissolving altogether. This week the hallucinations, yes, I have to agree that's what they were all along, have altogether ceased.

Yesterday, Miss Snyder informed me I would be discharged in a day or so. As I sat at her desk, the phone rang and it was—would you believe it?—Svetlana Alliluyeva. "Maurice," she said. "Is that you . . . are you well?"

"As well as an eighty-year-old on drugs three times a day can be. And you?"

"Fine, fine, Maurice. I just called to say goodbye. I'm leaving for the Soviet Union."

"What," I said, "you are reconsidering?"

"No, no, of course not. It's just that I am lonely for my children. They have offered to let me see them. After that, I will be living in England. So, goodbye, my friend."

"Wait, Svetlana," I shouted. "I want you to answer a few questions, without prejudice—as it really happened."

"What is it, Maurice?"

"Svetlana," I asked, "your father, Joseph Stalin, you swear he did what Khrushchev told in his Report?"

"Yes," she said softly, "everything, and much, much more."

"The two million sent to the slave camps?"

"Twelve million, he said, Maurice, twelve million."

"And his comrades on the Central Committee?"

"He had them murdered, every one of them."

"And the actor Solomon Mikhoels?"

"Yes, yes"—I could barely hear her—"run over by a car, on my father's orders."

"And the Jewish poets—David Bergelson, Samuel Halkin, Peretz Markesh, Itzik Fefer . . . and all the others?"

"Shot," she said, "in the back."

"And"—it was torture for me to get the name out of my mouth—"Leon Trotsky?"

"With a pick-axe," she said, "by my father's henchman."

"In the skull?" I finished for her.

"Yes, the photo was in all the papers. Trotsky's head on the table, blood dripping on his manuscript." Suddenly, her voice turned stern. "Enough, Maurice, please let me go."

"No, no, one more question . . . only one."

"Very well," she said, "only one."

"Knowing about these—Svetlana, these murders, lies, terrible crimes against humanity, can you have any feelings left for him?"

"I have to, Maurice, he's my father."

"Aha," I said, "so you still love him."

A long pause. "More than anyone else in the world." Over the wires, I could hear her weeping as if her heart were broken. Then *click*—she had hung up.

Throughout the conversation, Miss Snyder had been hovering at my side in rapt attention. When I put down the phone, she asked, "What did she tell you?"

"Svetlana? Oh, that she loved her father more than anyone else in the world."

"Oh, no," she cried, "not that antisemite, that monster Stalin."

I turned to stare at my psychiatric aide. "We all loved Stalin," I said.

She looked back at me with blank eyes. "Love him!" she spit out, "you've got to be kidding."

"Well, didn't we, Miss Snyder. Didn't we?"

Will the Morning Be Any Kinder Than the Night?

In the summer of his forty-second year, Allen Kaufmann has, out of the blue, fallen in love with a voice on the telephone. Though she exists, thus far, only as a disembodied image, Laura Myers has left him both elated and decentered. Allen spends his days now in a fever of expectancy. Waiting for her to call, he re-evokes her high-strung laughter, her sharp intakes of breath, her hesitations and silences. He tries to imagine how full her breasts are, the taste of her mouth, the heft of her thighs. His hands, on their own, touch his sex into a state of constant arousal.

"It's as if I'm being pressed" (he has this habit of conversing and thinking in well-turned hyperboles) "against the flame of my own want. Can this be the profound opening I've always yearned for?" At the same time, he feels his equilibrium teetering—as if he were on a tight edge, with little room to maneuver or breathe.

Allen has always been rejected as socially inept, even bizarre, by women to whom he is attracted. In one of his journals, he has scrawled this painful notation:

> I live desperately for moments of sexual release. For me, a hard-on is sacred and fucking is another form of prayer. The gratification I long for needs the mystical union of body and brains. Brains I have more than enough. But my body is gross, clumsy, yes, even disgusting. I feel cheated, ripped off, furious . . .

How ironic, Allen tells himself, that it is precisely his intelligence that Laura admires. She'd heard him, several nights' running, on a phone-in program sponsored by a radical radio station—WBAI. This is Allen's one outlet to the real world—a free-for-all arena for controversial subjects, where his well-honed intelligence is at its spontaneous best. He is known to his night audience as a diehard sixties person, a tenacious defender of all things marginal, utopian or unpopular. Free speech for Nazis, sadomasochism, pederasty, pornography, the end of compulsory education—these are among the issues he has upheld lucidly, with calm dignity, as indignant listeners called in frantically to object.

One night Laura had listened to him passionately extolling man-boy love: "What is behind the orchestrated attack by so many so-called radicals on man-boy love? It seems to me very clear. They are terrified by all that is unknown, liberating, primal. Because of this, they feel threatened by the erotic expression of love between older men and young boys. It can evoke in otherwise reasonable people a savage and punitive streak."

"Kaufmann," an irate man had called in to complain, "you are a menace to any truly civilized impulse. What do you do when you're not corrupting public morals under the guise of tolerance?"

"My only vocation," Allen had answered, "is to resist any effort by the social order to demean absolute freedom."

Moved by his eloquence, Laura had tracked down his telephone number. The next day she phoned and shyly introduced herself as a member and sustainer of WBAI. "You don't know me," she said, "but I want to tell you how really terrific you were last night."

"Oh," he had responded, stunned by the stranger's praise. "Then you agree with me on man-boy love."

"No, not really," she had stuttered. "I mean, I have no idea how I really feel about it."

"Then what is it," he had prodded her, "that you admire about me?"

A long pause while she considered. "Well—maybe because you're not afraid to take risks . . . go out way on the limb. Right now, nothing is working for me. I'm hung up, scared to death. I haven't the nerve to make a move. I guess what I'm looking for is answers. Crazy or not," she blurts out, "I have the sense you might have some."

The urgency in her voice startles him. No woman has ever responded so strongly to him. Surprising himself with his boldness, he cries out, "No, Laura, follow your instincts. It's not crazy at all. Maybe we can help each other find answers."

On this note begins a faceless liaison that keeps the wires humming between them with confidences, day after day, hours on end. Soon he learns that she is thirty-three, honey-blonde, once divorced, recently arrived from Providence, a fledgling editor, and dazzled by the tight world of the intellectual left. "What a drag," she says, "wasting my time and energy on idiotic books. It's a living, I tell myself. But that's a small consolation."

Of himself he reveals only the barest facts. He lets her know diffidently that he's a social critic, a cultural observer and a writer. Without consciously intending to, he leaves the impression that he is a beleaguered outsider in the movement, "such as it is." His role, he tries to explain, is to try to sustain a vision of existential possibility against the cynicism and resignation so rampant everywhere.

"I see," she says lightly, "a radical gadfly." Are her words mocking or in empathy? He wonders, uneasily, has he come off like some pompous ass?

When she asks what he looks like, he replies with a small pang of guilt: "Oh, brown hair, black eyes, pale skin, kind of chunky, nondescript." He resolves, then and there, to lose fifty pounds, become stylish, transform himself inside out.

The passing days settle into interludes, during which he lies inert on his bed, reading, day-dreaming, jotting down his impressions on the progress of the affair. When she calls, he cuddles his cheek into the curve of the receiver, drinking in her voice the way other lovers devour kisses. He thinks of Laura, at the other end of the wire, vivacious and warm, as if she were tied to him with an umbilical cord.

"My God," he writes in his journal, "haven't I had enough of this loneliness and loss. At forty-two I'm only a half-mensch. I have no job or future. I'm short on recognition, grace or guts. Deliver me from myself, darling Laura, so that I can escape the terror of time bypassing me, without hope, without love."

Each phone call has become a ritual in which they ardently share their sensibilities and ideas. Losing all track of time, they discuss art, politics, revolution, the counterculture, God, love, the state of society, their own moment in life.

"Who are your favorite authors?" she asks.

In answer, he reads her passages from Paul Goodman, Noam Chomsky, Simone de Beauvoir, C. Wright Mills and Kate Millet. He exhorts her to read books on philosophy, fiction, social theory. Carried away, he often delivers impassioned exegeses on writings he thinks will open her to new and subversive areas of imagination.

Laura, in turn, reads to him feminist literature which she has recently discovered. He listens, enthralled, to her excitement . . . her cries of delight . . . as if each insight revealed to her is a recognition of her own lived experiences.

At times, when she expresses admiration for his skill in cutting through complex ideas, Laura's breathy voice provokes in him a wave of erotic pleasure. He imagines Laura and himself living together in a full-fledged affair, their bodies lovingly entwined in bed. He has never before allowed himself to believe he is capable of such intimacy.

Laura has a fiercely independent mind. She resents the pressure of his talmudic harangues, his habit of turning her into a passive vessel of his wisdom. "For God's sake, Allen," she shouts, "give me breathing space. I feel as if you're crushing me under the weight of your male ego." Allen, abashed, promises himself again and again to hold back his torrential outbursts of words.

One night he reads to her from a newly finished essay:

> Early in the game, we are emotionally stifled, conditioned to a dehumanized and confining rut. Dreams, fantasies, glimpses of eternity are ruled out. Our stabbings for explosive sexuality and joy are repressed as dangerous. For myself, I cannot settle for this psychic torpor—the clinical death trap that goes by the name of everyday normality. I will never stop searching for experiences that take me beyond the expected, the known.

Allen is tremendously insecure about his writings. He waits, with trepidation, for her reactions. There is a long silence. "For you," she says, carefully choosing her words, "everything seems to be sheer black or white, without the slightest shading. Either life must be inauthentic, dull and trivial—or else, one has to cross the borders of sanity to reach for apocalypse and ecstasy. That's not the way things are, Allen. People—at least the ones I know—have careers, lovers, children, luxuries, fun. They travel, fuck off, watch dopey television, indulge themselves in the most vulgar narcissistic pleasures. And why not? I mean, radical or not, we have to make peace with the here and now—the unexceptional . . . even if the world is gruesome, even if we all blow up tomorrow. How about you, Allen?" she laughs uneasily, "don't you long for some kind of normal life in your own future?"

Laura's words—he reads them as a gently intentional put-down—have a lacerating sting. My perspective, he thinks, must seem off the wall, distorted. There is so little to balance or protect me. Without meaning to at all, she can break me like a twig. If only there were something deferential he could say to smooth over their differences. Instead, he hears his own voice, cool, faintly belligerent: "Assuming I wanted to be normal, I wouldn't know what it meant . . . even if it came up and hit me in the face."

"Ah, Allen," she says placatingly, "you know how fond I am of you.

Stay the way you are, always. I'll never have anyone else like you in my whole life."

After he hangs up, Allen tosses all night in his bed, turning over the nuances of her last remarks. It occurs to him that unless he does something drastic to change the situation between them, he will very soon lose whatever small connections he has with her.

Laura has come into Allen's life at a disastrous time for him. A few months ago he had walked into the living room to find his mother twisted into the shape of her death on the couch. One arm was flung across a pillow, pointing ahead, as if to show him a direction. A huge, exuberant woman—immortal, Allen had thought—she had simply let her heart run out, most probably out of exhaustion, without a fight. Allen sank to his knees and buried his head in her lap. "Don't leave me now, Mama," he sobbed, "Alone, I'll break like glass."

Allen's words were more than a figure of speech. Very early on, Mrs. Kaufmann had grasped that it would be her mission to devote herself body and soul to this splendid misfit who was her son. From the first, he had grown up absurd. The commonest activities—dressing, feeding himself properly, keeping clean—were largely beyond him. It terrified him to play rough games in the streets. He was too shy to make friends. School panicked and confused him. At camp his mere presence fanned whatever was malicious in the other kids. They devised ingenious ways to torment him—mocking his pedantic speech, his roly-poly waddle. They would wrap snakes in his blanket, hold him captive while they tore off his pants and poured ice cubes on his penis.

"Mama," he would weep to her over the phone, "take me home, I hate the kids—I hate everything here."

Heartbroken, she would try to console him: "Never mind the others, darling. Keep away from the bad ones. Here it's so broiling hot, the tar sticks on your shoes. Stay, stay, it's so nice in the country."

Stifling his grief, Allen would follow her advice and go off by himself. He would wander, in the evenings, to the lake, where he stared, trance-like, into the crimson sun. Trembling uncontrollably, he would fall into a strange ecstasy of self-loss. Even then, he understood, though dimly, that only by moving beyond himself into a transcendent space could he feel fully and palpably alive.

Allen's father, a small gray wraith of melting sweetness, was by turn awed and dismayed by his son. He watched him devour books far beyond his age and gorge himself into fatness. He listened to his little vunderkind hold forth like a blue streak on esoteric matters of world import. From all this, he sensed—like his wife—that they had been blessed . . . or cursed . . . with some kind of prodigy.

Others in the family took a less sanguine view of Allen. His aunt, observing how Allen's body trembled violently when he spoke, nudged her brother: "Take Allen to a neurologist. Can't you see how he shakes? There's something definitely wrong."

A brother-in-law, with three stunningly normal children, would on occasion warn: "Go ahead, keep spoiling him like a baby. Soon, it will be too late."

All this upset Allen's father, left his weak stomach aflutter. Still, he answered with false assurance, "Wait, you'll see, in no time at all he'll grow out of it."

But no, as the years passed, Allen grew even more into it. In his final year of high school, he refused flatly to attend classes. "They laugh at me," he said, "and the homework makes me sick." Soon he dropped out altogether, spending his days reading or walking the nearby park.

Mr. Kaufmann, realizing the implication of his son's act, put away the lion's share of his earnings to support Allen after his own death. A few years later, just as he had reached his goal, Allen's father suffered a stroke and passed away peacefully in the middle of the night.

At home, alone with an adoring mother, Allen made a virtue out of his almost total isolation, without friends, school or a job to fill his days, at the far end of the Bronx. He began to compose, in the bookkeepers' ledgers his father stole for him, the nervous, incandescent—and sometimes incoherent—essays which he considers his creative hallmark. His voice choked with exultation, he would read each outpouring to his mother, who listened in awe to her son:

> Everything around us conspires to rob the young of their dreams. We are trapped by school in conformity. Stifled and balked by society into half lives, the teen-agers display a superficial serenity. Underneath, they walk around seething with desire, confusion, envy. They move their bodies with inchoate passion, sexual madness. Many communicate their anguish with drugs and violence. Will they ever be free to express their mysterious, truncated yearnings?

Glowing with pride, Mrs. Kaufmann would desperately try to follow her son's meaning. "Oh, my God," she would whisper, "it's so deep, so beautiful."

After his mother's death, living on a modest trust, he keeps the same small apartment in the Bronx. Hopelessly incompetent, he lets books, newspapers, unwashed clothes and unopened boxes take over the space. In the sink the roaches run unimpeded over the moldy take-home food. The bedsheets grow grungier by the night. He no longer shaves, often forgets to wash. Gradually he settles into the live-in chaos with the benign indifference of a bagperson.

Curiously, though the grief at his loss lingers like an omnipresent aura, he is by no means unhappy. With his mother no longer around as ballast, he floats freely into an unfathomable space. Each morning, delirious with dream, he breaks out of sleep as if to another resurrection. Afternoons, he sits on a parkbench, notebook in hand, watching the winos, the old people, the children playing with their mothers in the sandbox. He sits, feverish, in the sunwashed air, experiencing everything around him—the gyrations of the ballplayers, the colors, the summer light, the shrill voices—with a piercing intensity. In this frame of mind a random incident can touch off in him a mystical release.

Once, while he lies reading on the grass, a group of young black men near him shatters the calm with their deafening radio. He cups his ears to hear the hard-driving music. "These sounds," he writes later, "are cries of pain, moans of heat, blasts of anger from the heart. Like them, I feel utterly alien yet at home in this oasis of terminal leave, where none of us works for a living."

Later in the day, still in this heightened mood, he calls Laura at work. As always, before she answers, a twist of anxiety knots his stomach. He is frightened at her power over him. At any moment, if he pushes too hard—lets his desire for her surface—she can say: "This ridiculous thing between us, I've decided to end it."

Instead her voice is genuinely affectionate. "I've been thinking about you all day. You're such an enigma, I can't tell what's going on with you. Are you okay?"

"I'm fine," he assures her, "but I miss you . . . terribly. I just wanted to make certain we're still in the same universe together."

"Of course," she laughs. "I'm hanging in, by my fingernails. Allen, Allen," she sighs, "my work is so deadly boring. Tell me something existential—that's your favorite word, isn't it?—Something that will transform my whole existence—psychic, physical, spiritual . . . the whole bit!"

Is she flirting with him, he wonders. No woman has ever come on to him before. Confused, ashamed of his awkwardness, he remains silent. He closes his eyes and imagines the two of them blind, sitting across from one another, each frantically trying to picture the other in the tone and timbre of their voices.

"Okay, Allen," she says, "you have ten seconds more to come up with the magic word."

Yes, *the word is love!* He remembers the line from a pop song he'd heard that afternoon in the park. It crosses his mind that this might be the time to spill out his feelings toward Laura.

"So sorry," he hears her say, "your time is up. I have to go back to work."

Before she can cut him off, he blurts out: "Laura, I miss you. Talk to me a while more. Make my day."

"Thanks," she says, archly, "it's nice to know you have such power."

"Laura," he presses on, "do you think of me fondly . . . very fondly?"

"Please, Allen," she says. "There's someone on the line." And clicks him abruptly off.

Allen sits with the dead phone dangling in his hands. The conversation, with its innuendos and evasions, recalls previous wild goose chases for love. What a freak, he thinks, never to have related intimately to a woman. Never fondled a breast, or lain next to a naked body. Only through his hand, through lonely self-love, to have had sex. If he could cry now—which he is too numb to do—grains of hot glass would pour out of the corners of his eyes. Lying in bed, a sheet over his head, he rocks himself into a numbed half-sleep.

Allen's one friend, Robbie, is alarmed at the tenor of their phone conversation. "I'm pissing away my life," Allen tells him. "Even with Laura, I can't think of a reason for ever getting out of bed."

Robbie has never heard his friend sound so dispirited—so close to hopelessness. He takes the long ride to the Bronx to prod him, if he can, out of his torpor.

To most acquaintances, Allen and Robbie seem spiritual twins. They think of the two as childishly impractical, often at the edge of euphoric unreality. Actually, Robbie negotiates his terrain quite well. He makes a living at odd jobs, has his own flat in the East Village, has ties with influential movement people, and has had stories published in small magazines.

Robbie is Allen's sole connection to the radical world. Allen sleeps over, on occasion, at his friend's apartment. They ignite each other with their extravagant and subterranean perceptions. They quarrel and laugh, until exhausted with elation, they give in to sleep. Robbie is profoundly in touch with the tenderness underlying his outlandishly inept friend. He considers their bond a precious gift. At the same time he is sadly aware that Allen, always hovering at the brink of breakdown, will be for him a heavy and lifelong burden.

When Robbie opens the door, Allen is lying inert in his unmade bed. Through the open top of his pajamas, his flesh billows at the waist and splits his crotch at the seams. Robbie takes in, without comment, the unbelievable dishevelment that confronts him. Long ago he stopped railing at Allen's blindness to external disorder. It is too ingrained, he believes, for change.

The two have been inseparable since they met in high school. Together, in the sixties, they had explored—with an exuberance they would never again feel—the cultural convolutions that were rocking the nation. Too timid to be full-fledged activists, they had nevertheless marched at demonstrations, shouting with the others revolutionary slogans. They have been shaped by the sixties—its hopes held out for human liberation. In its wake, they both feel, the vision has turned into a blind and a cheat.

Disillusioned but still inextricably linked to the movement, they try at every opportunity to express their indignance. On one occasion, they interrupt a radical conference to read a jointly written manifesto:

"All around us—here too—we see opportunism, self-aggrandizement, professional envy, snobbery and caste lines. How can we challenge the global death machine when we compete frantically for a piece of its action. Can our prattle about transformation and equality be authentic when we betray our deepest natures?"

There is a polite scattering of applause, a few boos, and they are promptly forgotten. Disconsolately, they sit back listening to the movement stars engage the audience with radical pieties. How much longer, they ask themselves, can they continue as opposition clowns in their own intellectual circles?

Over coffee, at the luncheonette near Allen's house, the two friends discuss his latest crisis. "It's hard for me to pin down," Allen explains, "except that I'm lost somewhere on a blue cloud, an amorphous angst, a free-floating discontent."

"Please," Robbie insists, "don't talk me an essay. Just tell me what's wrong."

Allen finds it hard to hold back his tears. "Really, I'm a total washout. Nothing makes sense—my writing, my ideas, the whole fucking world. In a few years I'll end up here in the Bronx, another old man shmoozing in the sun with dirty sneakers."

"What about Laura," Robbie asks. "A few days ago she was the love, the joy, of your existence?"

"Laura," Robbie groans. "An illusion, a farce like everything else I touch. You know what she thinks, Rob. I turn her on with words . . . mesmerize her with my ideas. A fine romance, huh? Two ghosts talking across a void."

"Listen," Robbie says, "there's a lot more than talk between you. You're exploding her mind . . . getting her off her ass. If you weren't something special to her, it would have been over long ago."

"You really believe that," Allen asks, pathetically eager to be convinced. "If we met, she might find me"—he searches for the words—"tolerable . . . maybe even attractive?"

"She's lucky," Robbie says, "to have a loving friend like you."

"I lied to her, by omission. She doesn't have a clue what a slob I am."

"Invite her out. Get some great new clothes. Take her to dinner—a movie or play . . . whatever she wants."

"What if she can't bear the sight of me?"

Robbie ignores the question. "When you see Laura, let her do most of the talking. Don't eat like a pig. Chew carefully, don't spit. Wipe the food off your mouth. And remember, keep things light."

"I'll think about asking her out," Allen says. "Seriously, I will."

All the way home, Robbie has serious misgivings about his advice. Has he pushed too hard? Maybe the telephone game—the farce, as Allen himself has called it—is all that he can expect.

Since Laura came to New York six months before—alone and in flux—change after change has shaken her life. She has gathered around her a circle of sustaining friends. She is in the first throes of a love affair with a young academic. As often as she can afford to, she sees a feminist therapist who urges her to discard any impediments—Allen, most of all—that needlessly drag her down.

"I know—it's a charade I should have ended long ago," she tells her therapist. "It's reached the point where I dread hearing the telephone ring."

"Make a clean break," the therapist advises her. "Tell him that the calls are oppressing you. You'll be doing the man a favor."

Again and again, Laura tries to explain her reluctance. "I've taken so much from him" . . . "How can I reject someone so vulnerable?" . . . "He's already falling apart" . . . "Maybe if I cool him out, he'll stop calling"..."It would be like"—she winces at the thought—"putting your old dog to sleep."

"All right, then," the therapist suggests. "Why don't you write him. He lives by the word. Maybe it's the best way to say goodbye."

That night, Laura sits before her typewriter, listening in her mind to the relentless rise and fall of Allen's voice. She tries to fill in the lineaments of a face that remains indelibly blank. She abandons herself, like a medium, to her fingers. They race, unhesitating, across the keys, composing their own story. When the typing stops, she reads aloud the rush of words on the page:

"Dear Allen, I wish I could say this without hurting you. I've decided it's no longer a good idea for us to be in touch. I'll always be grateful for your intellectual stimulation, encouragement and, most of all, your humane ethos—a social and spiritual vision that has deeply moved me. For my part, I hope that my affection for you and admiration for your writing will always be a reminder of the good things we had going. Someday, perhaps, under different circumstances, we may see each other. But, please, not now!

"Allen, don't try to reach me any more. It will only make things more painful. What you want from me—yes, it's time I came out and told you—sex, love, a continuing relationship—have always been out of the question. Since I haven't in the least encouraged you, they are even presumptuous.

"More than that, your unspoken demands, which are always there, have gotten to be intolerable lately. Your neediness makes me cringe, your demand for affection makes me hysterical. After each call, I feel creepy, put upon, used, worn-out, guilty—and very angry! Each of your phone calls has become torture. I take the phone off the hook, make believe I'm not at home, or simply stay away with friends. If you don't stop contacting me, I'll get an unlisted number.

"Find your own damned life, Allen, and—if you can—deal with it. Get yourself a real live person you can see and touch. But don't call again—ever! I beg you, leave me the fuck alone! Laura."

When she reads the letter aloud, her outpouring shocks Laura with its violence. Tearing the page into bits, she resolves to find a less wrenching means of cutting off their communication.

These days, it's become harder and harder for Allen to reach—or seriously engage—Laura. The phone is busy for hours. When he does get through, she's curt and distant...unwilling to converse for more than a few moments. If he tries to read an article, she cuts in sharply:

"It's much too complicated, Allen. I don't have the patience to follow it." Remarks about himself—his depressions, fears, highs—she quickly dismisses. "Please, we've been through that too many times before."

Allen has the sense she is being deliberately evasive—slipping through his fingers like a wary fish. He is, however, too insecure to articulate his feelings openly. Baffled, he calls Robbie to report on the dismaying turn of events.

"You swore you would ask her to see you," Robbie says. "Did you?"

"It's a bad time. Laura is very unsettled."

"Unsettled, crap," Robbie explodes. "Respect yourself, man. Tell her it's now or never. You deserve that much at least."

"If she says no?" Allen asks.

"Then do both of you a favor. Let her go once and for all. And Allen, don't dare call me with the same old boring complaints!" With that, he slams the conversation closed.

That night, lying in bed, Allen masturbates with his lips pressed against the receiver. Without Laura's image to feed his fantasies, he visualizes substitute faces, other bodies. "Laura, Laura, I need you," he moans. Licking the plastic grid, he reaches a quick orgasm. Magically, his melancholy immediately clears away. His mood has become untroubled, almost mystically serene. In this buoyant frame of mind, he calls Laura at midnight and finds her at home.

"Laura," he says, without his usual frenetic drive, "I have to see you. This can't go on, talking to disembodied voices out there in space. It's making me crazy."

"Allen," she says, fighting her anger, "I'd rather we didn't meet. It would only spoil things."

"Why? Is it something about me? Am I too much of a freak to confront in person?"

"Of course not. It's just the nature of our relationship."

"And what is," he asks, "the nature of our relationship?"

"You're pushing me"—her tone has become strident—"I don't like being pinned down this way."

"Three months we've known each other," Allen says. "That's a hellava long time not to see the woman who goes with your voice."

"I can't deal with you, Allen. It's as simple as that."

"It's inhuman," he persists, "to be shut out by someone you care for. I don't deserve it."

Laura's breathing is faintly audible. He is entirely in her hands—powerless as a child.

"For the time being," she says. "I want to keep it this way."

A pause. He wishes he hadn't forced the issue. There are no further arguments—no appeal—he can make.

"I'm sorry," Laura says. "I always react badly under pressure. It's not good, but that's how I am."

After she hangs up, Allen calls Robbie to report what has occurred. His friend is not home. Sitting at his desk, motionless, he considers his options. He can sift the cold ashes of his conversation with Laura. He can try to read, walk in the park, plunge into melancholy, or simply yield to the trance of time drifting senselessly by. His journal, opened to an empty page, reminds him that he has been too paralyzed for a long while to write. He scrawls as quickly as he can the unformed ideas whirling in his head:

> At times I willingly enter another dimension. Beyond psyche, reality, the passing of time. In the grip of this epiphany, I experience no loneliness, despair or pain. Precarious, uncanny, deranged. Swallowed up by nothingness . . . anticipating nothing. Wholly free of my body and senses, without desire for human discourse or attachments. If only I didn't have to return to this half-assed excuse of a self.

He closes the journal and hugs it to his chest. Its bulk, the smell of the leather binding, assure him he still exists. He wishes his mother were alive, her eyes ashine with wonderment as she listens to the marvels that bloom from her son's brain.

A few days later, Robbie calls, exultant with news. "I was at a party last night. Guess who I was introduced to."

An intuition answers for Allen. "Laura."

"Yes, your very own Laura, alive and very much in the flesh."

"Did you tell her you knew me?"

"Of course not," Robbie answers. "It's your chance to meet Laura on your own. She's coming to the BAI affair Friday night. If you don't want her to be invisible forever, you'll be there."

"What's the point in showing up," Allen says. "Laura doesn't care to see me."

"Listen," Robbie says. "I'm not going to try to convince you. If you chicken out, well, that's fine with me. Otherwise, be there Friday night"—he gives Allen directions—"at eight."

"What is she like?" Allen asks. A sudden montage flickers by. He's standing before a woman with ice-blue eyes. No, they're a soft melting brown. A glimmer of recognition. No, a blank stare past him. Laura comes eagerly forward. No, she strides coolly away.

"See for yourself," Robbie says.

"Robbie, if I come, what do I wear?"

"A great new wardrobe—whatever it costs."

"I'll be there," Allen says. As soon as the words are out, the surge of panic subsides.

"I'll be there, waiting," Robbie says.

On Friday morning, Allen buys—with the salesman's enthusiastic approval—a blue pin-stripe suit, a white shirt and a thin black tie. To complete the ensemble, he chooses Italianate black shoes that taper sharply at the toes. "That's what they're wearing these days," the salesman says. "We can hardly stock them, they go so fast."

At home, dressed in his new clothes, Allen examines himself soberly in the full-length mirror. A sallow, ill-assorted man, with a pear-shaped bulge of blue around the middle looks back. The two of them—he and his reflection—shake their heads grimly in unison. Somehow, when he sees Laura, he must make visible whatever grace—whatever largess of spirit—are hidden in this lugubrious figure of a man.

On the way, early that evening, to the taxi stand, Allen buys a bunch of blood-red roses. He watches, enthralled, as the vendor arranges the roses and ferns into a bouquet. His first gift ever—his first love offering—to a woman. He dismisses the stab of self-reproach at his small manipulation. In the cab, leaning back with his eyes shut, he lets the last of his anxiety and fear float free. He folds the flowers in his arms and breathes in the heavy scent of the blossoms. He lets himself be lulled by the weave of traffic. On the verge of losing himself, he sets in his mind the scene for his meeting with Laura:

In a little while, she'll look up at me with an expectant smile. We'll regard each other shyly, reach out, maybe even touch. I'll hold the flowers out. "They're for you," I'll say. It's possible—no, it's virtually certain—that the gesture will move her immensely. She'll accept the roses, remarking, "Oh, Allen, how perfectly lovely." Something magical—a recognition—will happen between us. Our voices, alive this time, making small talk, igniting laughter. Our presence, incarnate, face-to-face, finally a consummation.

Through the plastic barrier, a pop singer rhapsodizes the intoxication of love fulfilled. All through the long ride to Manhattan, swaying in the little womb of a back seat, Allen toys with the premonition that this very evening might well mark for him a turning point.

When Allen enters the auditorium, the huge crowd is a commingling of generations. Aging politicos, once New Leftists, left-over hippies, younger movement people, assorted dissenters and culture-seekers. Each with its unique signature. Beards, spiked hair, close-cropped, straight. Blue jeans, flowered skirts, antique outfits, eclectic inventions. A scattering of open shirts with gold chains dangling.

Garish with colored jells, slides flashing across the walls, the cavernous hall is aglow with a sixties' ambience. It's pure nostalgia, Allen fondly thinks, our yearning to recapture this wildness so long ago tamed. A slash of amplified guitars vibrates the hall. He recalls similar celebrations in the past—the ear-shattering rock, the communal spirit he had so desperately wanted to share.

From across the room, Robbie waves frantically for his attention. Making his way to Allen, he points out a group of three young people standing near the doorway. If he notices Allen's new outfit, he will not let on. "That's Laura," he says, "the one in the middle wearing a purple and gold dress."

At the sound of her name, Allen's body—starting at the hands and spreading to his shoulders—begins to tremble. Unless he can take hold of himself, his encounter with Laura will be a disaster.

Robbie throws both of his arms around his friend. "Cut it out, Allen," he orders. "For once, you are not giving in!" The trembling subsides. Gently, he pushes Allen in the direction of Laura. "I'll be here," he says, "near the stage."

Allen lets himself move slowly through the milling crowd. He knows he must hang on to the remnants of his high . . . not allow himself to slip into that solitary space which empties and dislocates him.

Nearing the doorway, Allen stands stock-still behind Laura and her friends. He observes, as from afar, the vivacious, elegant woman dividing her attention between an older woman and a young man. How cozily they relate, the three of them, how wrapped in one another. Suppressing an impulse to run, he taps Laura on her shoulder. She turns, hesitantly, toward him.

"Laura Myers," he hears a strained voice asking.

Laura furrows her brow. "Do I know you?"

It astonishes him that he cannot associate the voice he knows so well with this woman who looks dispassionately at him. "I'm Allen," he says, "Allen Kaufmann."

Laura fingers her string of beads nervously. A quick intake of breath. A quizzical glance at her two companions. "How did you recognize me?" she asks.

"My friend Robbie, he . . ." Allen breaks off midsentence.

"What do you want from me?"

"I thought," he says, "we could talk."

"Can't you see I'm with friends."

"Maybe we can have coffee afterwards," he pleads.

"Christ," Laura says, "you know I can't deal with you. I thought I made it clear." Her voice is high-pitched, exasperated.

People around them ignore the drama with the feigned indifference of strangers caught in the middle of an intimate squabble. Allen hears, without comprehension, the fragments of talk that rise and fall from the crowd like lapping water. Allen cannot take his eyes away from Laura—her scrubbed beauty, the thick hair piled carelessly into a bun, the swan's arch of her neck. Unaccountably he is flooded with a tenderness toward her. He must find a way to defuse her anger. Remembering the roses, he holds the bouquet toward her.

"They're for you," he says.

"Allen, Allen," she admonishes, almost in a croon, "why don't you leave me alone. I don't want to be violated this way."

Allen advances toward her with the flowers outthrust. "Take them, please," he cries out, with a violence that startles him. "I brought them all the way from home."

Laura pushes the flowers away. "I don't want them," she shouts.

Allen holds the bouquet to his chest. Like little live animals, his fingers take off on their frenzied dance—shaking, darting, whirling, whirring. Convulsively he stretches his arms high over his head. Laura leaps back. The bouquet falls from Allen's fingers to the floor. "Damn," he says, "all I wanted was for you to have them."

The young man, who has been observing the incident in silence, steps between Allen and Laura. "Is anything wrong?" he asks. He takes her hand and draws her toward him.

"Oh, no," Laura assures him, "a slight misunderstanding." She touches the young man's face gently.

It dawns on Allen that this tall young man, so attractive, so appropriate, is Laura's lover. My capacity for self-deception, he thinks, is infinite. "I'm sorry," he says, "if I embarrassed you."

"Not at all," Laura says, with great relief, as if the unpleasantness between them is finally settled. She turns away to her young man and the older woman.

Allen feels a trickle of sour sweat pouring down his armpits. What is he doing here in this black tie, pinstripe suit and stiletto shoes? He is a mafioso from a thirties gangster movie. He longs to be in his own home, his own bed.

A woman passing by stoops to pick up the fallen flowers. She holds them up to him. "No, no," he says, pushing the bouquet into her arms. "They're for you." When he looks up again, Laura and her friends are gone.

Allen clears a path for himself against the current of people still pouring into the hall. When Robbie calls out, "Wait for me," he races through the exit, down the stairs and into the night. Hailing a cab, he realizes he does not have the twenty dollars' fare home. He wanders through the checkerboard of streets until he finds a subway entrance. Entering, he takes the Bronx express. It is the first time he has ever been in a subway by himself after dark.

The train, half-filled, click-clacks on hypnotically over the tracks. When he shuts his eyes, Allen hears the wheels beating out, over and over, a two-syllable rhythm—Laur-ra, Laur-ra, Laur-ra. He compels himself to ignore the imagined sounds. Eyeglasses on his nose, he tries to decipher the welter of graffiti that obscure the walls. Baffled, he composes an essay in his head:

> These hieroglyphics are impenetrable to me, like the street kids themselves who spray out their life codes in rainbows of fluorescence. I identify with them—every shred of me does. Yet I am frightened in their presence. I am all underbelly—flaccid, wholly vulnerable. Sensing this, they would humiliate me, sharpen their contempt like knives against my person.

At 125th Street, there are only five passengers left—all of them remote, withdrawn into their own spaces. Allen is acutely aware that his aloneness is filling him with foreboding. He takes a book from his jacket pocket. It is, absurdly, *One Dimensional Man,* by Herbert Marcuse. When he opens the book, he cannot follow the convoluted text with its dense reasoning. Raising his eyes, he notes the lighted ribbon of advertisements that flow across the train. He abandons himself to their messages, with unwavering attention:

CRACK KILLS!

Below the text is the photo of a bereaved woman, overcome with grief. For herself, her son, the en masse victims? The finality of her is stunning. He is sorry that he feels nothing at all for her.

•

JUST IN CASE YOU'RE FACE TO FACE

The couple—young, suburban, no doubt—hold tablets of a mouth freshener for each other to suck. Their faces register delight, enchantment, desire. What about me, he muses. Will anyone ever want to be face to face with me?

WIN YOUR HIGH SCHOOL EQUIVALENCY DIPLOMA

A burst of white stars spangled on a red and blue background. An exhortation to enroll now and change your life. It's never too late, the caption cajoles. At forty-two? Oh, no . . . a stab of self-pity . . . not for me, not this hopeless dropout.

BE SMART WITH SEX . . . YOU DON'T HAVE TO DO IT

A sullen, beautiful woman stares stonily ahead. You don't have to do what? With whom? What does it mean to be smart? If only she weren't so cryptic. Is there a subliminal clue here that he can't get?

ALIVE WITH PLEASURE . . . CREATE YOUR OWN CAREER . . .
GET EVEN-TONED SKIN . . . WE HAVE YOUR TICKET TO PARADISE
. . . AIDS IS A HUMAN DISEASE

Allen's eyes move steadily across the ads, left, then right. He is awash in their blatant urgency . . . the promises they hold out . . . the disasters they portend. IF Y CN RD THS MSSG . . . No, he cannot read this message—not for another second more. He tears his eyes away and makes a pretense at napping.

At 209th Street the train emerges into the night and runs, block after block, alongside silhouettes of decaying tenements. Besides himself, there are only two passengers left—a sleeping drunk and a young woman. At the next station, three young men enter—one wearing a red cap, the second a green, the third an orange. In high spirits, they exchange obscenities, pummel each other playfully, jiggle and dance. There is nothing ominous about them, Allen thinks, only a raw, unselfconscious energy that permeates the train.

The three sit, their legs sprawled out, directly opposite Allen. They are regarding me with detached amusement, he notes, as if I were some kind of creature in a zoo.

When the train stops, Allen tries to rouse himself to leave. Pinned down by their gaze, immobile with fear, he watches the door slide shut. It is essential, he exhorts himself, to disappear into his own black hole, where he will be too distant, too inconspicuous, to engage their attention. He opens his book and turns deliberately to the last page. He has studied the paragraphs so often, he virtually knows them by heart:

> Underneath the conservative popular base is a substratum of outcasts, the exploited and persecuted of other races and colors, the unemployed and unemployable... Their life is the most immediate and real need for ending intolerable conditions and institutions... Thus their opposition is revolutionary, even if their consciousness is not... It is only for the sake of those without hope that hope is given.

From across the aisle, green hat calls out softly. "What'cha reading, man?"

Allen, looking up, holds out the book eagerly. "*One-Dimensional Man*," he says.

In one quick movement, the young man slides toward Allen, takes the book from his hand, and returns to his seat. A white-hot coal has begun to glow in Allen's chest. It's making him giddy, light-headed with fright. "Lemme check it out," says green hat. He riffles the pages and, holding the book out as far as he can, says, "Heavy reading, man, it ain't gonna do you a damn bit of good." Winking at Allen, he tosses the book toward the door.

As if on signal, red cap and orange cap cross to Allen's side. They sit, one on each side, hemming him in. "How much you got on you, fat boy?" orange hat asks, holding his palm up.

Allen draws a wad of crumpled bills from his back pocket. Blue cap scoops the money from Allen's hand.

"You ain't hiding anything?" the young man across the aisle asks.

Allen nods no. Orange cap runs his hands roughly over Allen's chest, then down both arms. He feels the bulge of Allen's wrist-watch. "Fucker, you are lying," he says. All three laugh uproariously. Deftly, orange cap removes the watch.

Red cap notices the silver ring on Allen's finger. "Hand it over, fatso," he commands affably.

"Not the ring," Allen pleads. "My mother gave it to me. She's dead now."

"Sheeit," the man across the aisle says. "What is that supposed to signify?"

Orange cap twists the ring off Allen's finger.

"I want my ring back," Allen says in a thick voice he cannot recognize.

"Let that man be," the woman at the other end of the train shouts.

"Screw off, lady," orange cap jeers back. He tosses the ring to green cap.

Allen, possessed, rises and takes two steps across the aisle.

"It's a gift," he repeats, "from my mother." He holds out his hand.

"Fuck off," green cap says. He slaps away Allen's hand.

Allen reaches out for the ring. Green cap pushes his shoe into Allen's belly. He catapults backward, falling heavily against a metal post. His reading glasses fly off, up into the air, and shatter on the concrete floor. A stream of blood drips down Allen's face, tasting of salt in his mouth. Leaning over, he picks up the glasses and puts them on. Through the shattered lens, he sees a latticework of distorted images. It's a scene, Allen thinks, from some old movie, clearly remembered, only in dimmer focus. Surely out there, somewhere, the real world must be going on its routine way.

When the train comes to its next stop, orange and red caps make a quick exit. For some reason, green cap—the one with Allen's ring—jams his body into the doorway. Shaking his head, he drawls at Allen: "Hey, man, you are one mess. Now why don't you just wipe up the blood." And suddenly, still holding the door open, he reaches down and slides the book in Allen's direction. "Don't say we never did nothing for you."

All at once—in this last split second—the unexpectedness of the gesture drains away Allen's horror and humiliation. "Is he playing cat and mouse with me?" he asks himself, "or really handing me back a piece of my dignity?" Removing his glasses, he peers intently at the young man's face through clouded eyes, as if to search for a clue.

"Let's go, man," orange hat urges from the outside, pulling his companion onto the platform. When the door closes, the three saunter out of sight, laughing raucously.

Allen sits back, limply, book in hand. He feels himself sinking into a bottomless pit of loneliness. Oh God, he prays, let me belong to someone—anyone! The woman at the far end, carrying two overflowing bundles, runs toward him. She takes a handkerchief from her bag and gently wipes away the blood. "It's only a scratch," she consoles.

Before she can draw away, Allen holds her hand to his face. "Stay with me," he pleads.

The woman lets her hand linger. "You be all right," she says, "soon's you get home." She is heavy-set, with a wide face and soft features. Her voice is burred, comforting. "Honey," she says, "you just hurry on to your family."

Allen is seized with an overwhelming impulse to sink to the floor and embrace her thighs. If he had the courage, he would pour out his gratitude . . . his love. He would beg her to take him home. Instead, all that comes from his mouth is a feeble, "Thanks for everything." He walks unsteadily through the train door, the length of the station, and gasping for breath, runs the four empty blocks to his house.

Reaching his home, Allen climbs the steps and unlocks the door. He undresses, letting his sweat-soaked clothes fall to the floor. Enwrapped in shadows, the room has grown sinister. Boxes and furniture dissolve into grotesque shapes. His throat aches with rawness, as if the air he is breathing were burning like alcohol.

Nauseous with memory, he stands naked amid the clutter. Laura shrinking back . . . the ring twisted from his finger . . . the woman's hand on his cheek—images unreel and die in his head. He stumbles to the couch on which his mother died. He sits stiffly, at the edge of the cushion, and hears himself asking aloud:

"Is this it, Allen Kaufmann, the whole existential sum of you, now and forever? Mr. Alienation himself. Nebbish extraordinaire. Oddball in residence!"

The words are hot stings across his face. He understands, with an unbearable poignancy, that he will never find a love of his own. There will be no ultimate revelations awaiting him under a stone. And no, the transcendent visions—the ones that had fueled his secret hopes—haven't the slightest chance of being realized.

From the bedroom, his mother's closet teases. It would be so tempting to close the door behind him (he has done it many times before) and burrow in like an animal. He could pile her dear clothing onto the floor. He could let himself sink into her dresses, coats, undergarments. The smell of her body oils, still clinging, would soon anesthetize. Buried in her depths, quietude would be no more than a closure of his eyelids away.

Allen leans back into the arm of the couch, as if to rein himself in. It strikes him with stunning force that he no longer wants to drown himself in sleep. The thought roots him to the couch. He waits for the trembling erupting from his body to die down. He surrenders to the center of an agony that drills like a living nerve. Staring at the window, transfixed, he listens—as if for an affirming message—to the muted sounds in the street. The hours move by, almost motionlessly, like clouds without a wind. He wonders, as the first glint of light streaks the window, will the morning be any kinder than the night?

Take Me Home

Not far from where I live, a pack of homeless men swarm around the entrance to Tower Records like bees around a syrupy sweet. Mostly, the way I see it, it's the swirl of energy in and out the revolving doors that attracts them—the constant drive of the music; the shoppers high on their new CD's and tapes; the jam-up of tourists, panhandlers and street vendors. The whole scene has the frenetic ambience of a medina in a North African town.

To avoid being hassled, I ignore the men who trot alongside me, reciting their scams as they jiggle the coins in their cups. I've learned how to look right through their imploring gazes, which are meant to elicit pity. What a horrible feeling—it makes me cringe—having to transform human beings into invisible creatures.

My next-door neighbor doesn't agree. "Like it or not, you've got to harden yourself," he tells me, when I mention the black men sleeping in a near-by alley, whiskey bottles in hand, staring off into space, pissing their lives away. In a city like ours, he insists, drowning in its poor, there's no other way you can survive without stewing in guilt.

There's one homeless man, however, who invariably catches my eye with a smile he beams at me like a searchlight. In his twenties, powerfully muscled, he looms over the other homeless. Classically aquiline, his features seem to have been hewn out of mahogany marble. His hair is tightly coiled into rows of blue-black ringlets. It's easy to imagine him strolling nobly through the throng, draped in a silken kaftan. Only his teeth, decaying along the gumlines, are bad.

At first I'm highly skeptical of the upstretched hands which he unfolds at me graciously like an offering. It's a con job, no doubt, a merchandising ploy to lure the guileless into believing they have been elected for his good graces. Con job or not, the truth is that Richie Johnson has charmed me out of my shoes.

It's awesome, the speed with which he's insinuated himself into my confidence. From the start he seems to have sensed all my soft spots and vanities, my half-truths and self-deceptions. One small example: The first coin I drop into his cup, he leans forward buddybuddy and points a finger at my leather captain's cap. "Hey, man," he says, "you a professor or a writer or something creative like that. Am I right?"

Well, yes and no. I'm actually a failed academic, who long ago yearned to be a standout English teacher in a small college. Occasionally I still teach a course in basic composition to high-school drop-outs. As for being a writer, less and less do I compose those little poems that for the most part I can't bear to read a second time. In all honesty, I should have disenchanted Richie then and there. Instead, sucking up to his flattery, I say, "How did you guess?"

Richie lays a hand on each of my shoulders and pulls me close until we are eyeball to eyeball. "Your two irises," he whispers, "are like crystal balls in which I can divine"—yes, *divine* is the exact word he used—"that you are a dispenser of holy wisdom."

For some reason, though it shouldn't be so, the crock he's handing out moves me immensely. Before I can comment, he slips a hand over mine and holds it like a vise. "White man," he says softly, his eyes glittery and quick, "from here on in, you and me are street brothers. And that ain't jive!" I reach into my pocket for a dollar. It's more than I intended, but that's okay. At a moment like this, anything less would be chintzy. When I hold out the bill, he pushes it aside and circles my body with both hands. We stand there, stock still, as if it were perfectly normal for strangers to be locked in one another's arms in the street. Vaguely it dawns on me, then and there, I'm making some kind of commitment.

The next time I see him, Richie has corralled two young women coming out of the record store and is breaking up everyone in sight with his super-hip spiel: "I'm here to tell you"—he lifts his cup high—"I ain't too choosy. Just hand over any dirty old assets you wanna unload. Some CD's, friends, blue chips, Treasuries, tax-frees, junk bonds, whatever. How about it, peoples, confederate bills, gold coins, a tenspot, a fiver, a buck, a half?" No one makes a move. "What d'you say"—he snaps his fingers—"my bank closes in a few minutes."

I can see how hard he's working at being clever. The hand in which he tightly clasps the paper cup is trembling. A rivulet of sweat is running down the front of his neck. As he slowly sweeps the cup around, three or four onlookers drop in small coins. Each time he bows slightly and says, with what seems to be the smallest hint of irony, "God bless." By now it's so painful I turn around to leave. As I do, he catches sight of me and shouts out gleefully: "Hi, Professor. Don't forget. You and me got a date for later in the evening."

Sure enough, when I return from class after dark, Richie is parked near the door of my building. (For fifteen years I have resided here in a small loft, with a platform bed, tiny toilet and minimal kitchen. The rent is so miraculously low, I can manage to subsist on social security, a half-pension and my part-time teaching job.)

Somehow, Richie's presence at my doorstep, without an invitation, strikes me as a small invasion. I'm a very private man. Only in my own space, alone, am I wholly at one with myself. Susan, my woman friend of six years' standing, once confessed she doesn't feel entirely welcome in my loft. How does Richie know where I live? Has he been following me? One of these days, can I expect him to ring my buzzer in the outside hallway?

Again, Richie has read me. "How the hell do I know where you live?" he mocks at me. "I got my spies everywhere. You can't make a move without me hearing about it."

Without meaning to, I stiffen at his little joke. Richie picks up my reaction at once. "C'mon, guy," he chides, gently jabbing at my ribs with his fist. Unwittingly it enters my mind, could I handle him if he turned violent? "Nobody wants a fucking thing from you," he says. "If you think I'm bugging you, just say the word, man, and we are forever strangers." He turns, halfway, as if to leave. "That what you want?" he asks, glancing at me sidewise.

Without bargaining for it, I have me a proud, sensitive new friend—is that what this homeless man is?—on my hands. I reach out to him and tousle his thick, wiry ringlets. It's the first time I have ever touched a black man's hair. "I'm starved," I say. "You like hamburgers?" He faces me, puts his hands on hips and arranges his face into one of his dazzling smiles. "Only if you let me treat," he says.

I let his offer go unchallenged. How am I to know the proper etiquette between the homed and the homeless?

In the nearby McDonald's we sit face to face, biting into ketchup-sogged burgers. Under the garish lights, Richie's luminous skin seems toned down to ashen gray. Staring at him, I feel curiously shy, as if we were on a first date. Don't ask too many questions, I warn myself, let him reveal himself at his own pace.

I don't have to worry. Soon enough the revelations come in a rush. Richie daubs his lips delicately and waves his napkin at me. "You probably curious," he begins, "how come a man like me is on the streets." (I note from the first his odd mixture of correct and garbled grammar.) "Strictly for the education," he goes on, "that how come. Sure, I could've gone ahead in college, studying some bullshit or other. Not me—what I want is real learnin', out there in the streets"—he points at the window—"the university of the homeless, that's where it's at." He slides his hands forward on the table. "You dig?"

In this closed space, Richie's voice is shockingly resonant. As he speaks, his fierce energy pulses palpably across the store, rousing the few diners slumped over in their booths. It bothers me dimly that anyone who recognizes Richie could mistake me for one of his homeless buddies. "In six months," he says, "I got me an awesome fund of street-smarts. I mean, man, I just don't barely survive—I truly thrive! It's all stored here"—he taps his forehead—"where to shower, shave, trim my beard sharp. How to dress cool. Eat good. Keep warm. Stay fit in body and mind. No drugs for me," he intones, "no alcohol, no evil thoughts that kills the others." He's watching me intently as if to measure the impact of his words. I nod brightly, without dredging up anything relevant to say.

Reaching behind him into his back pocket, Richie pulls out a handful of coins and a few bills. He plunks them on the table. "I don't need to beg for these nickels and dimes." He pushes the pile toward me. "Here, I'm paying you back for the burgers and coffee." I sit glazed, ignoring the scattered money. "When I finish my learning," he says, "I got me a dozen options. My dad is real well fixed. I can go into his business. Or, if I want, I can work in a bank, sell just about anything, operate a computer, be a construction foreman, a fine carpenter. Let's see, what else? Oh, yea"—he makes a chopping motion with his left arm—"teach karate." He grins. "If I had to, I could deal crack."

Suddenly he seems to have run out of his torrent of words. He leans over and breathes heavily. "Shit, man, I do go on, don't I? And I ain't even found out your name."

"Steve. Steve Klein."

"Professor Steve Klein," he corrects. "Yea, you a writer." He looks at me quizzically. "What kind of writing you do anyway?"

"Poetry," I say.

"Poetry? Now ain't that something. I read some cool poetry in school. Hey, do you know the cat who wrote about the black bird? How does that damn poem go?" He closes his eyes and waits for the words to come. "Man," he says, "it's on the tip of my tongue. You know which one I mean."

I don't want to showboat or upstage him, but I can't resist. "It's 'The Raven,'" I say, "by Edgar Allan Poe," and recite at random:

Leave no black plume as a token of that lie thy soul hath spoken!
Leave my loneliness unbroken! Quit the bust above my door!
Take thy beak from out my heart, and take thy form from off my door!
Quoth the Raven, "Nevermore."

"Above the door . . . Nevermore! Man, that's beautiful," he says. "It ain't rap, but it's beautiful."

When I get up from the table, Richie sweeps the pile into his palm, rises and tries to pour the money into my coat pocket. I back away but he pulls me toward him almost angrily. "I said it's my treat," he half-shouts. People across the table are staring at the two of us. I let Richie slide the money into my pocket. He smiles broadly, takes me by the arm and swings me lightly with him through the door.

Susan, my live-apart lover, is disappointingly negative when I tell her about Rich. "Are you sure you want to be this involved?" she asks. "With a homeless man you know nothing about?"

Susan is a psychiatric social worker in a private hospital. For more years than she cares to remember, she's worked with any number of psychotics, suicidals, nervous breakdowns, criminally violent. One of the things I admire about her, she maintains her humanity despite all the horrors she has to deal with.

That's why, frankly, I'm so dismayed at her reaction. I thought she might understand a rare friendship that can spring up between unlikely people. A kind of mystical bond, if you will, that draws them together across their differences in age, race, circumstances.

"My gut reaction," I try to explain, "tells me he's a terrific guy—smart, funny, resilient. With help, he could be off the street in no time."

Susan shakes her head sadly. "Look," she says, "do you have any idea how much has to go down before a guy ends up in the street? You name it—childhood trauma, abandonment, mental illness, drugs, poverty, crime, worst of all, demoralization. It's a long fall for a guy like Richie—and neither you nor I are going to stop it."

"If not you and I," I deliberately misquote an ancient Hebrew proverb, "then who else?"

"Oh, Stevie, Stevie," she says fondly, "my sixty-year-old innocent, my babe in the woods. How do you intend to help him?"

I hadn't really given that a thought. "Well," I improvise, "encouraging him. Giving advice. Hearing him out. Who knows, maybe just laughing at his jokes."

Susan sees I'm hurt; she slips her hand into mine. "Of course, darling," she says, "be his friend. Relate any way you want—it's your privilege. But please, Steve, I've had lots of experience with people like him. Don't let him pull you in over your head!"

I draw my hand away from her sharply. Now I'm really bugged. For me, condescension like Susan's ends all communication. The rest of the evening I mope. Our dinner is a charade of stiff, overpolite chatter. In bed, later, I lie with my back to Susan. When she tries to embrace me, I breathe heavily in mock sleep. For hours I lie awake in a funk, wondering: Who is this complex, baffling man—this black Gorki searching for wisdom in the lower depths of yuppie Manhattan. Why am I attracted to this homeless stranger? What, under it all, is my motivation?

I drift gradually to sleep with the persistent echo of his laughter following me in my dreams.

At times, unseen by Richie, I stand nearby watching him tease handouts from passersby who can't resist his flamboyant presence. Other homeless, I've observed, work on your compassion, or else through flattery, or even subliminal fear. Not so with Richie. His is pure performance, a persuasion so amusing it removes all traces of the real needs behind his begging.

On this cool afternoon, Rich is delivering short raps to crowds of tourists who are idly shopping Noho. As he recites, he snaps his fingers to set the rhythm and undulates his long stretch of a body with surprising agility:

> Now, folks, you can spend your bucks today
> on junk you'll only throw away,
> or do your soul a real good favor—
> give till it hurts to your homeless neighbor.

After each stanza (they seem endless), Rich takes a small bow to a burst of applause. On the wave of appreciation, he walks his cup through the audience, milking each of them with a little amusing aside. More times than you'd think, they drop coins into his cup.

Richie has his regulars, too, whom he greets vociferously, as if they were long-lost friends. (It stung a little when I discovered I wasn't the only one.) His arms extended up and out like a huge bird, he sidles up to them and whispers intimacies in their ears.

"Exactly what is it," I once ask, "that you tell these people?"

"In this racket," he explains, "you gotta size your client up quick and apply the right psychology. With a banker, I come up with finance shit. With a lady, I feed her sweet talk. Everybody's got a weak spot for a touch. That's part of my street learning, Steve."

It distresses me, not only his gross and crafty manipulation, but the intense pride he takes in it. Oh, what the hell. Who am I in my safe little cocoon to be so uppity moral. Selling himself could mean the difference between a hot meal and an empty belly.

Walking with Rich later, in the direction of my house, I blurt out: "How about a poet like me, Rich, what psychology do you use on him?"

The usual smile on his face dies quickly. "For you," he says, "I don't want nothing but a little friendship. For that I don't need any fucking psychology."

When he turns from me with a curt goodbye, I grab his arm and swing him around. "Hey, Rich," I cajole, "I was only kidding. How about giving me five?" I lift my hand and hold it out, poised. Rich hesitates, then raises his too. We brush fingers, once, twice, three times and slam our palms together hard, like black brothers. It's nineteen sixties style, but it feels fine anyway.

It used to be whenever I passed Richie, I would instinctively fumble in my pocket for some change. Seeing my hand move, he would pull his cup away and shake his head no. "Man, I don't hustle a buddy." Finally, after talking it over, we have some kind of agreement. I drop a dollar bill into his cup every few days. Although I do it as offhandedly as I can, I always feel awkward. Could be he does too. In any event, it's no longer an issue between us.

For his part, Richie is always trying to even things out with small surprises. Each time it moves the hell out of me. Once, he asked me if I liked nuts. When I said, "I sure do," he presented me with a big cellophane bag of honeyed peanuts (which, incidentally, I detest). Another time, it was an expensive pen, still in the original case. "You gotta write great poems with this," he said. "The point is pure gold."

The gift I like most, though, is a tape of two Mozart quartets. "I figured you go for this cat," he said when he handed it to me.

"Do I ever," I said. "He's by far my favorite."

"Think of Richie," he said, "whenever you play it." After I thanked him, he pointed a finger at me. "Don't ever forget, man, I didn't steal that tape . . . I bought it with my own money!"

Each time I hear the heart-breaking slow movement of the D Minor he gave me, my eyes film over. I don't know whether it's the soaring music, or thoughts of Rich, or both.

Last weekend I walked Susan past the record shop just to introduce her to Rich. "Susan," I said, "this is my good friend Rich Johnson."

He took off the fez he sometimes wears and made a sweeping bow almost to the ground. "You are one lovely lady, Susan," he said "I truly hope he takes fine care of you."

"Steve can't stop talking about you," Susan said. "I see why."

Rich's eyes lit up. "The both of you," he said, "don't make a move. I'll be right back." With that, he raced to the Korean store on the corner and came back with a long-stemmed rose. "For you, ma'am," he said. "I gave it magic instructions. If you add an aspirin, it will last forever."

We did, in fact, throw an aspirin into the water, but the rose wilted into an ugly brown within a few days.

Mornings Richie often waits for me near my house when I come down to do my chores. Over coffee, in a little restaurant, he fills me in with his complex perceptions of the terrain in which he wheels and deals with such élan. My role—which he seems to want me to assume—is to ask him naive questions that require his setting me straight.

"Rich," I might ask, "is there any close relationship between homeless people. Do they help each other with money, food, whatever?"

"Man," he answers, "it is so brutal out here, you don't have the time or inclination to be thinking about anything but you. Yours truly, Steve, that is the name of the game. If you don't play it real mean, you gonna go under real fast." A wicked grin. "Course, there are exceptions, like guess who?"

Rich prides himself particularly on his knowledge of street people's psychology. "People look at a guy with his cup and they're thinking—these poor blacks, you can't tell one from the other. Bullshit, man, they are so different under that skin . . . clown types, victim types, Tom types, I-am-a-piece-of-shit types, you-owe-it-to-me-types, scare-the-hell-out-of-you types. There ain't any end to it."

"How do you see yourself," I once kidded him.

He took me quite seriously. "Me, I'm the cool, controlled type. I may seem frantic out there, but baby, you better believe I am busy observing every goddamn minute."

Sometimes Richie urges me to help him write a book about his adventures out on the streets. "There ain't anything like it," he says. "With my know-how and your writing skill, we got a good thing going."

"I'm a poet," I object, "not a journalist."

"Shit," he counters, "you can put one smart word after another, can't you? That's all we need for a big-seller."

As he pours out his street lore, Rich trembles and his eyes have this ecstatic glow. In his presence I'm almost ready to believe that the persona he presents to his tight little world—the college-educated son of well-to-do parents on leave from his comfortable life—is an actuality rather than a devious invention.

One thing for certain, the way he maintains his dignity in the naked, down-to-the-bone existence out here—without a home, job or supportive network—makes my own life pale by comparison. I must admit how childishly flattered I am to be the one who shares the confidences of this star in the firmament of the homeless.

A disturbing footnote: Some people have observed how close Richie and I seem to be. A neighbor of mine asks me, one day in the elevator, "Klein, what do you and that tall black man discuss so seriously whenever I see you together?" I give him a mysterious smile, but don't answer. Oh, yes, when I was standing near the record shop recently, a homeless guy shouted out to Richie, "Hey, Johnson, your boy's looking for you." *Your boy*—what am I, some kind of joke among them? Do they roar and slap their knees, when they're drinking in the alleyway, about this white asshole who thinks he's penetrated their inner sanctum?

Once, when Rich mentions in passing he's just turned twenty-five, I buy him a denim jacket and a black turtleneck sweater. "Here," I say, handing him the elegantly wrapped gifts, "what the best dressed street person will wear."

Rich doesn't laugh, nor does he thank me. Instead, he stands immobilized, the packages grasped to his chest. When he raises his head, I can see tears glistening in his eyes. Then, in an abrupt change of mood, he lifts me high above the ground in his thick arms and shouts: "Steve Klein, I ain't ever gonna forget you, and you'd better believe it."

Shriveling at his ostentation—at the public announcement of my name—I twist myself loose and steal away as quietly as I can. At my last sight of him before I turn the corner, Rich has slipped the gifts out of their wrappings and is holding them out to passing strangers. "For me," he says over and over, "compliments of my pal Steve Klein. Ain't they something!" Oddly enough, the strangers are stopping to "ah" and "oh" enthusiastically over the gifts.

What strikes me at the moment is that I don't know whether to be touched or embarrassed. I have to face it: whatever is between Rich and me, it arouses on a very deep level a chorus of conflicting emotions—fascination, shame, contempt at my snobbery—that I can't seem to control. It must be in the nature of the beast.

Late one afternoon in November, Rich and I are stretched out on the grass in Washington Square Park. The quality of fall light is rare for New York . . . lucid, even transparent . . . making each scene around us stand out in precise detail, like finely focused snapshots. Nearby, a juggler tosses and retosses his white clubs with exquisite patience. A benchful of old people doze off, read or speak idly under the cool lemon sun. Their backs against a tree, a young couple on their bright-orange blanket are locked, shamelessly, mouth to mouth.

Away from his high-tension hustle, Richie is surprisingly mellow. Hands folded under his head, he rambles on freely about his plans for the future. "I don't like winter a damn," he says. "No matter what I wear, I can't keep warm. Hope I can hang on till spring before I cut out. I figure by then I'll pick up all there is to learn."

"And after that?"

"Like I told you." He shrugs his shoulders. "Whatever I feel like doing—computer work, I guess. Or else, I may just lay around in my mom's house, not doin' a fuck-all. She's got a beautiful big place in Connecticut."

A beautiful big place in Connecticut! This is the most specific he's ever been about his pre-street existence. I try to conjure him up, in a sports jacket and loafers, on the veranda of a country house. The picture doesn't ring true.

"You gotta visit us one day," Richie urges. "Mom likes me bringing white folks to her place." I blanch at the invitation. He sounds all innocence. Still, I wonder, is this a little jab at me for not asking him up ever to my loft?

We lie lazily, barely awake, listening to the muted strains of rock music floating across from the fountain. It occurs to me, with a stab, how grotesquely—even obscenely—unequal our relationship is. In all this time—over three months—we've had something that approximates a growing friendship. Rich and I have talked, walked, dined and laughed together. We've shared thoughts and opinions; exchanged confidences and gifts. I'm certain, at least I hope, he sometimes thinks fondly of me. And yet, when we say so long, outside my hallway, I go upstairs to my cozy loft and he disppears into the night.

What is it really like for him on the street? Is it true, as he keeps insisting, that he's mastered all of its hardships? Is he a loner? Is he ever lonesome? Is there a lover anywhere around? Does he hang out with other homeless? Where are his belongings? He says he eats three squares a day. Where—in the Third Street soup kitchen? In cheap coffeeshops? From throwaway plastic bags outside supermarkets? And how does he keep his clothes so clean, his face almost always shaved, his little triangular beard so neatly trimmed? Occasionally, when I try to pump him for information, he laughs or clams up or turns the question away. I haven't even a clue where he sleeps—in welfare hotels, a city shelter, the streets?

Relaxed and close as we are this moment, perhaps it's the time to ask: "Rich," I say, "would you mind a personal question?"

"Shoot," he says, "we'll see if I do."

"I haven't the slightest idea where you sleep? Where do you?"

He looks at me oddly. "Why do you want to know?"

I hesitate before I answer. "I guess I worry about you. It would make me feel better if I could locate you in my mind." God, how lame and inauthentic I must sound to him.

"I know just where you sleep," Rich answers, a sharp edge to his voice, "and it don't make me feel any better."

Suddenly there's a chasm of silence between us, the most tense moment I can recall. Looking up at the sky, I note that the sun has surrendered to the clouds. The park, with its few stragglers, is gray and desolate. A chill in the air foreshadows the end to a long Indian summer.

On the way back, passing an alleyway where crack-smokers hang out, we see a man lying face down in his own pool of urine. Rich stands, hands on hips, staring at him with disdain. "If we leave him this way," he says, "the piss is gonna burn his face bad."

After we drag the man to dry ground, Richie can't hide his contempt. "No goddam self-respect," he spits out. "Before I let it happen to me, I slit my throat!"

I remember wondering, at that moment, why he was so unforgiving of a homeless man like himself.

The weather has, without warning, turned biting cold. When I leave my house, this evening, clouds of powdered snow are swirling down the avenue. The few homeless still around are huddled against the buildings, hands buried in their sleeves. The only time they come to life is when they pounce on passersby with mumbled and menacing entreaties.

I don't run across Richie anywhere as much these freezing days. Each time I do, it's clear that he's losing his ebullience . . . the extraordinary verve that lends him his magnetic aura. It saddens me to observe how much of his sharp edge of neatness is gone in so short a time. More and more he's unshaven. His beard is growing scraggly, undefined. The fez has been replaced by an ill-fitting cap that covers his ears. Worst of all is his oversized sportcoat which swallows him in its bulk without being nearly warm enough. Of course Rich can't even begin to think of his appearance. Every ounce of energy has to go into keeping warm and getting through the day. Still, as an ardent fan of his, a believer in his own mystique that nothing can faze him, I am rooting for Rich to sail through the winter with his usual high spirits and style intact. I'm afraid things don't augur too well for my expectations.

As I walk east, Rich unexpectedly hurries out of a doorway to greet me. He looks so forlorn, I invite him to a Chinese dinner in a place I like in the East Village. A hot meal, I figure, might cheer him up, but Richie is more sober—melancholy, is more like it—than I've ever seen him. He has in fact, for this moment, wholly dropped his mask of insouciance.

Rich gulps his food down without seeming to enjoy it. Then, over tea and orange slices, he begins to pour his heart out. "I figured things were going to get tough," he says, "but Christ, not this ball-breaking."

I listen with a mixture of unease and empathy. Of course I want to help in whatever way I can. The one thing I can't allow myself, however, is to be swamped in the flood of his despair.

"Nothing is going for me," he continues. "I'm always freezing cold. There ain't enough money in the streets. All those deals I used to count on are dead." (Deals? . . . What does he mean by that?) He tugs on the collar of his ragged sweater. "I can't even find the energy to get me heavier clothes."

I slip my hands over his on the table. "Look, Rich, if you're that hard up, I can spare the cash. Pay me back when you can."

Rich's reaction baffles me. "Fuck, no," he says. "If I needed bread that bad, I could take a run home and pull it out of my stash."

His stash? What stash is he talking about? Susan and I have discussed his stories about rich parents and country homes. She thinks they're not so much lies as tightly woven illusions he needs to sustain his damaged sense of self. The whole invention, she predicts, will unravel as soon as he can't support himself on the street. "So what?" I answer, "don't we all have our patterns of lies and illusions?" "Sure," she agrees, "but they don't usually lead to our physical self-destruction."

If Richie won't accept money, at least let me try one more suggestion. "Listen, Rich," I urge him, "my friend Susan tells me most guys on the street are on welfare. You get ninety-nine dollars in food stamps a month and spending money as well. All you do is show up at the Welfare Office with identification."

Richie recoils as if he's been slapped. "Hey, man," he shouts, "Rich don't take welfare, now or ever. Nobody's gonna hook him on that corrupt charity system for lazy niggers. Have them run my name for all time through those goddam computer chips? You gotta be out of your mind!"

As he rants on, I can't help wondering why this frenzy over welfare. Is it his pride? A fear about exposing himself to authority? Or just sheer paranoia? Whatever it is, the evening—which was supposed to lift his spirits—has gone down the drain.

We sit back, the two of us, in strained silence. After a while, we put our coats on, still without a word. Outside, in the covered doorway, Richie shuffles his feet slowly without moving. I can see that he's begun to shiver. On impulse, I blurt out: "Do me a favor, Rich. I've got thirty bucks with me I don't need. Take it and get yourself one of those padded coats in the Salvation Army. They are toasty warm."

"Forget it," Rich barks out. He leaps into the street, stumbles a few feet forward and stops, his back to me, half-crouched. Abruptly, he turns and comes slowly back. "I'll take that, man," he says, holding a hand out. I fumble in my pocket, find the three tens and hand them to him. Richie snatches the bills without a thanks or a smile. Turning away, he weaves unsteadily south until he disappears down the block into an alleyway. It's known as a hangout for gang fights, knifings, robberies and, most of all, heavy crack-dealing. I have a sickening premonition that the unraveling Susan talked about has already begun.

The ring, ring, ring of the phone that yanks me out of sleep in the middle of the night is hardly unexpected. I've been waiting for—and dreading—Richie's call since our disastrous Chinese dinner. I haul the phone over, bleary eyed. Sure enough, as my gut told me, it's him.

"That you, Steve. I gotta speak to you real bad." The voice I hear is hoarse, phlegmy, barely recognizable.

"Speaking," I answer.

"Can I come over to your place?"

My heart begins to trip violently. "No, Rich, you can say what you have to on the phone."

"I'm real sick, man. I mean, I been puking my belly out. My body hurts all over. And I've been thinking crazy thoughts again. Steve, I can't stay where I am much longer."

I don't ask where he's calling from. How come he's so sick. What he expects of me. The truth is, I don't want to open the floodgates. "If you're feeling that bad, Rich, maybe we ought to get you to a hospital."

The blast of his voice is so harsh I have to pull away from the phone. "No," he shouts, "no damn hospital. I need to go back home."

"Well," I say, "why don't you call your mom?"

"Won't do me no good. I tried calling. She won't listen." A long hesitation. I can guess what's coming next. "Steve," he asks, "will you call her for me?"

"Tell her you're very ill, Rich. She'll be glad to have you. She's your mom."

"It don't make no difference." I can hear him beginning to sob. "She'll only hang up."

"Why do you think," I ask, "she'll listen to a stranger?"

"You tell her you're my friend. A professor, see? She'll believe you. She'll say for you to come on bring me home."

"Richie, she'll think I'm off my rocker."

"I never asked you nothing, before, you hear?" He can barely get the words out. "I'm begging you now. Please, baby, please!"

He has me trapped. I can't get out of this. "Okay, okay, I'll phone. What's her number?"

Slowly Rich counts out a seven-one-eight number. Seven-one-eight? That's a Brooklyn number. So much for the Connecticut bullshit. "Rich," I say, "I'll call in the morning. You get back to me by twelve."

"Thanks, friend. You are one prince, one real prince of a guy. I knew you were my man."

I barely sleep the night, twisting and turning, until ten. When I call Rich's mother's number, the answering voice, "Who there?" is prickly with suspicion.

"You don't know me, Mrs. Johnson, I'm Steve Klein, a friend of Rich."

"You got the wrong number."

"Please, Mrs. Johnson, I'm a good friend of your son."

A long, exasperated sigh. "What's he done now?"

"Nothing, Mrs. Johnson"—somehow I've got to disarm her resistance—"He just lost his apartment, so I'm calling for him from my place."

"Who you kidding, Mister? He's out on the street and now he's in big trouble again. Well, you just tell him for me he ain't welcome."

"He only wants a place to rest. There's no trouble at all."

"No trouble? He tol' you how he stole my money, tore up my place? How he frighten the other children with his crazy talk? He tol' you the times he go to the hospital, come back and start that same shit all over? He say that to you too?"

"Mrs. Johnson," I plead, "Richie is not acting crazy. He isn't feeling well. All he needs is rest, a little attention, a little love."

"Uh, uh, Mister, I gotta think of the others."

Another tack: "He's your child too, isn't he?"

"You a white man, right?" I can hear her thinking over the wires.

"Yes."

"You got a job, a home too?"

"Yes, I do."

"And you his good friend?"

"I am."

"Then you give him a home, and attention and a little love."

I've run out of words. All I can do is wait for the denouement. Mrs. Johnson's voice softens. "When you speak to Richie, tell him his momma say to take good care. Tell him I'll be praying for him. And, Mister, don't you ever call back."

At twelve, when the phone rings, I brace myself for another punishing call. "Sorry, Rich," I say, "your mom says no go."

"Goddamn," he cries, "why not?"

"She says she's been through this scene many times before—and it doesn't work. She's gotta think of her other children."

"You explained to her? You told her how fucking sick I was?"

"I did my best, Rich, I really did."

"You couldn't have tried a fuck-all, man." I can hear him breathing hard, holding back the tears. "You're no friend of mine," he shouts and slams the phone down murderously hard.

I lie back, the phone irreversibly dead in my hands, wallowing in a pool of guilt, pity . . . anger, too, that blots out everything but the image of Richie sinking in his quicksand as I stand by helplessly watching. For days afterwards I'm so disjointed I can't teach, can't write, can't make love, can barely do my daily chores, until very gradually my sense of proportion begins to return.

All that week, while the bone-chilling weather continues, I can't find Rich in any of his usual haunts. None of the homeless on my block have any idea where he's gone (at least that's what they say).

Susan, who has followed all the highs and lows of the Richie story, believes his unreal and escalating demands on me were inevitable. "Most likely," she explains, "he's manic-depressive on the down phase. When they are that desperate, they'll pull you down as deep as you let them."

"Who wouldn't be depressed," I argue, "out on the street in the winter, sick and cold, with no money, no home and no prospects in sight?"

"Okay, Steve. What do you intend to do. Take him home with you?"

"No," I answer, "but I certainly don't want to abandon him."

"So, where does that leave you?"

"First," I say, "I'm going to find him."

"You're a sweet, caring guy," Susan says—she knows just how to avoid provoking me—"but please, do yourself a favor. Let your friend make the next move. He knows where you live."

Susan makes sense. If I were in my right mind, I'd sit back and wait. But I can't help imagining him sprawled somewhere in his own piss like that pathetic drunk. Finally here's my chance to let go of the black tiger I've had by the tail. Why, then, do I still hang on?

Two weeks have gone by and still no sign of Richie. His prolonged absence fills me with a mounting apprehension. Nights, lying sleepless, I often get horrendous images of him stretched out in a gutter or in some city morgue. At the same time I experience each of these fleeting pictures with a leap of joy (and shame too) as if his death will free me from the drag of his continuing existence.

I suppose I should, as Susan urges, do nothing till he comes around or else definitively fades away. But the idea of making no effort to find him strikes me as utterly heartless. Richie and I do have something going between us and there has got to be a way I can track him down.

Dressed in my shabbiest clothes, early in the evening, I make the rounds of a few homeless hangouts nearby. At the Third Street Shelter, I line up against the wire fence with the others waiting for a meal. "I'm new here from Chicago," I tell the man in front of me. "Where do I sleep around here. A welfare hotel?"

"You kiddin," he answers, "those crack-men, they steal your clothes right under your bare ass. And if you fight back, you be taking your life in your hands."

"Where do you sleep, Mister?"

"When I got enough bread, one of them fleabags on the Bowery. It's cheap and a little safer."

"Thanks, man," I say. As I walk east, I note with dismay how seamlessly well I fit in with the homeless.

Along the Bowery, I walk from sleaze hotel to hotel, looking for Rich. The shoddy lobbies, crowded with dozing men, reek of urine, sour clothes and disinfectant. "Five bucks a night," the clerk yells out when I approach the desk. "I'm looking for a friend of mine, Richard Johnson," I explain. They don't even search through the register. They shrug and turn the other way.

It's begun to sleet. I'm tired and depressed. A few more tries, I decide, then I quit. In the Sunrise Hotel (the sign is actually a yellow neon circle, with a blaze of red rays circling it) a man in the lobby hears me inquiring about Richie. "That the big skinny guy with a red fez and a beard?" he asks.

"Yea, that's him."

"I seen him last night. He's sleeping in the Houston Street subway."

"Is he okay?"

The man looks me over carefully. "Why you asking? You a social worker or something?"

"Hell, no," I say. "We're friends, for a helluva long time."

He shakes his head. "He's on something and he don't look good."

"Thanks, mister." I pump his hand. "I appreciate this."

It's agonizing, that short walk to the subway. At the West Houston station I climb down the slippery stairs into a maze of connecting tunnels. Near a brightly painted mural showing black and white workers vivaciously interacting in a communal scene, a panorama of sleepers stretches out, wrapped in their blankets, knees drawn up, and coiled into their dreams. When the train screeches to a halt, nobody stirs and nobody wakes. From the broken glass gratings above, the melted sleet drips slow, muddy tears onto the concrete where the homeless are sprawled.

Knowing Rich, I wouldn't want him to see me observing him in his public bedroom. I search from body to body, barely able to make out the faces. In the dim light, a distance away from the token booth, the rows of sleepers seem to have flowed together into yellowish funeral mounds. Even if I were to stumble over him, it doesn't seem likely I could recognize Richie. But there—alongside the steel bars that separate the subway platforms—I see a lanky man on his back, legs spread apart, head fallen over to one side. It's him, all right, half covered with a thin plastic cloth.

I can't tell, from where I stand, whether it's the shadows or ravage that have created dark splotches on his face. Terrified that he will see me, I carefully move closer. Now I can make out a bloody scab on the corner of his mouth and ugly bruises under his eyes. Poor Rich, what has he done to himself?

Squatting beside him, heartsore in this dank, dark tunnel, I watch my sick and beaten friend vibrate as the train whooshes by. Why am I here? Now that I've found him, what's my next move? Do I awaken him, comfort him in my arms? He stirs—has he sensed my eyes on him?—and begins to moan. In one moment, if he awakens, he'll surely see me. All it would take is for me to reach down and stroke his face. Stifling the impulse, I get up on my feet and look at him one last time. Then I pick my way through the sleepers and race up the subway stairs.

Outside again, I walk completely disoriented through the almost deserted steets until I come to an elegant Japanese restaurant on Lafayette Street. Once, in a flamboyant mood, Rich had promised to treat me, when he was flush, to the most expensive meal in the place. "From sushi to sake," he had bragged, "and it's all on me."

Through the window I can see the diners around the red satin tablecloths, faces glowing in the candlelight, silver in their hands, the ritual of eating carried on with such assured, unhurried pleasure. A man gestures exaggeratedly with his fork; the woman opposite throws her head back with what I imagine to be a delicious peal of laughter. How many evenings have I dined out like this? So why then does this pantomime so disconcert me?

One time, when I'd asked Rich what he hated most about the streets, he never even hesitated: "The way these fuckers pass you by, when you're out hustling, like you were dirt, an animal that don't belong on the planet with them."

Taken aback by his burst of anger, I hadn't commented. "Here, Steve," he had said, thrusting his coffee cup at me, "you wanna find out what it feels like to beg? Get out there, like me, and start begging!"

Well, Rich, I didn't have the guts then to take up your challenge. But tonight, I have a hand for a cup, I'm out here alone on the street and something impells me here and now to find out what it's like to be in your shoes, hustling for coins. I pull my hat down and wait against the wall, far enough from the lights so that I won't be recognized. Okay, Rich, what do I say when someone comes along? Yea, yea, I know—something pitiful. Guilt-provoking. With a heartfelt ring. Haven't I been at the giving end a thousand times?

Across the street, three men slide out of a cab and begin to walk toward the restaurant. I have only a few seconds to check out my feelings. Curiously, I'm not embarrassed at all, but rather demeaned, unworthy—no, completely at their mercy. Here they are, the young trio in sleek leather coats ambling by. My open hand shoots out. "Sir"—the words come spilling from my mouth by themselves—"I'm out of the hospital today. Can you spare . . ." Before I can finish, the three of them sweep, without even a glance at me, into the entranceway of the restaurant.

My God, the bastards, that hurt! Breathing heavily, I regroup and move closer to the corner. This time it's an elderly couple, arm in arm, walking by. They have, I can see, gray hair like mine. They have sweet faces, anyone can tell that, and most probably, compassionate hearts. "Please," I mock-whisper, "I'm real hungry. Anything will be appreciated." The man slides his hand protectively around the woman's shoulder. He holds the other hand out before him, stiffly, like a fullback, and hurries her past me.

My hand is limp; my mouth cottony dry. Help me, Rich, I'm no fucking good at this! Ah, swinging up from Houston come two well-dressed women, fur coats, stiletto heels. "I'm cold and starving," I spit out, with more force, even maybe a little disguised venom. They keep on walking. I come out of the doorway and hurry to their side, my hand held close up to their bodies, as I've seen the more aggressive homeless do. They begin to move along faster on their unsteady heels. Now I pick up my own pace in rhythm to their gait, my arm almost surounding them. "Only a quarter," I shout, "a dime, any goddamn thing, please!" One of the women hurls my arm out of her way and they race click click along until they turn the corner.

Ah, here I am on Bond Street, no more than a hundred feet away from my house. I lift the brim of my hat, pull down my collar and compose myself. Key in hand, I step into the doorway, open the front door and enter. There, thank God, on home ground, in the warm glow of the hall lights, I've finally found myself again.

It's wrenching, despite my efforts to drown it out, the thought of Richie lying in a heap every night in the deeps under West Houston, less than a block away from where I live. Most likely he's too ill to care for himself. Who feeds him? Where does he wash his mouth, his body, his clothes? Where does he defecate? He could so easily die on his back, with the other homeless carrying on their lives around him unaware that he's dead until the stink of decomposition sets in.

Susan says my morbid imagination is running rampant. She's dealt with his type before—on and off drugs, in and out of hospitals, hopeless when they're rock bottom, resourceful on the upbeat. "You'd be amazed," she assures me, "how many times I've seen them come out of it unscathed." Besides, she says, they are part of a social pathology and not one's personal problem. I've done far more than my share, she insists. For the sake of my mental health, I need a saner perspective of this bizarre entanglement with a homeless man.

I have indeed been trying to separate out what is genuine in my relationship with Richie—and what is some hyped-up neurotic attachment between a hip young down-and-outer and a middle-class, middle-aged—let's face it—voyeur! It was heady, I now understand, crossing so many barriers, breaking taboos, under the illusion that an authentic friendship was burgeoning in this most unlikely of milieus. One fact alone—that he has no roof over his head, while I have a cozy roof over mine—should have been enough to make a mockery of my pretensions.

For all of this, I still like to envision Rich and me in my loft some afternoon in the near future, with the sun pouring bars of light over the two of us as we loll back on the couch. He is, of course, in my mind's eye, impeccably dressed, from the Frye boots (the ones he always admired back then) and slim-line jeans, to the trim denim jacket and black turtleneck sweater (my gifts) that set off his proud ringleted head so handsomely. There we are, sipping wine and remembering old times, he without a trace of rancor, only the enticing smile of his that makes it possible to believe that his existence and mine have, for these few moments at least, come beautifully together. Rewriting people's lives in my head, the way I want them to be, is one of my more sustaining weaknesses.

Richie is back! He shows up one night, sprawled across the entranceway to my house, his head against the glass door, his long legs blocking anyone who might want to enter. Standing over him, I'm assaulted by the stench of stale sweat and aromatic piss, the shit-stink and underwear rot that rise from his unwashed clothes and body. Oh, Rich, I had hoped it would never come to this, you like the stupefied drunks spilled on the sidewalks along the Bowery, all pretense of your humanhood almost wholly gone.

I bend down and run my fingers across the tracks of his burning brow. Rich stirs and opens salt-encrusted eyes. Seeing me, he wipes the snot bubbles from his nose with a sleeve. He lets a ghost of a smile flicker across his face. "Where you been all this time?" he asks. "Your pal Rich is counting on you."

Counting on me? I allow the significance of his remark to go by. "Rich," I say sternly, "you are seriously ill. I've got to get you to a hospital."

Richie shuts his eyes and, lying back, begins to drift away. Is he on something, or is it just the high fever? "Listen, Rich," I tell him, "I'm calling an ambulance."

Richie rolls his head from side to side. I can see him trying to pull out of the deep space he's fallen into. "No way," he whispers, "you gonna get me to a hospital while I'm still alive."

"Sorry," I say, "you are burning up, probably dehydrated and God knows what else. You need medical care."

Rich jams his feet against the doorway and struggles laboriously up to a half-sitting position. Reaching out with his hand, he carefully circles my wrist. There's no power in his grip, nothing like the old Richie. "Steve," he says, "you hear me?"

"Yes, I hear you."

"Man," he says, "know how many times I been on that hospital trip—Bellevue, Staten Island, Rockland, all the pits. I been shot up, zombied with dope, been tied into bed, lay in my own dirt, had the shit kicked out of me for talking back. And what for, all they do is dump you back on the street sicker than before."

"Rich," I say, "there's no other choice. I can't take care of you."

In the hallway light that streams through the glass behind him, I can see under his bundled-up rags how emaciated he's become. He sways toward me, his palms locked together in a gesture of prayer. "You my friend," he intones, "my white soul brother, ain't that so?" My eyes lowered, I let his words wash over me as if I were nowhere in sight.

"A friend's for taking care of you when you sick, yes or no?" His voice has risen to a thin whine. "Well, I want you to put me up in your place till I get better. You don't have to do a damn for me, understand?, only a little bread and soup, and let me sleep my sickness off. Ain't too much to ask a pal, is it, Stevie boy?"

I hold my hands up and outward toward him without answering. Considering my words carefully, I let them come out of my mouth one at a time. "Rich"—long pause—"that is simply not possible. I'm not prepared for guests. It's a tiny space. Barely enough for one."

"Don't need much more room than a dog. I can sleep anywhere. On the kitchen floor, in the outside hall, the toilet, the tub if I have to."

"Forget it, Rich," I say. Somehow, I think, I've got to put an end to this. "I'm calling an ambulance."

Richie's body begins to twitch. His face contorts. Tears—of rage, I think—flood his eyes. "You're ashamed for me to be in your house. You don't want a dirty nigger man around."

Richie pulls himself up to his feet. "Fucker," he shouts, "you owe me one!" He slips his arm around me and pins me against the door. I feel myself suffocating in the soggy-crap odor of his clothes. Twisting away, I disentangle myself and hold Richie off with one arm. At close range, I can see the blaze of fury in his eyes.

"It's out of the question," I say, "either you go to a hospital, or you walk off on your own."

"Open that door," he spits out, "and take me upstairs, or"—he raises a foot—"I'm kicking this fucking thing in . . ."

I circle Richie's body with my arms and try to calm him down. By now a small crowd has gathered around. They watch us silently, enthralled. "Call an ambulance," I yell, "this man is very ill." A woman races over to the nearby street phone and throws a coin into the box. I can hear her clearly enunciating the numbers of my street address.

"No fucking hospital for me"—Richie is sobbing now, huge insucks of air, each one drowning out the other—"you motherfuckin' whitey, you piss-ass ofay, you dumb-bastard old honky, how you any different from the rest?"

Stung, I put my hand over his mouth. Rich pulls away violently. Wheeling, one foot out toward the door, he loses his balance. Face forward, he falls hard against and through the glass.

I stand paralyzed for a moment, then pick my way through the shattered pieces. Opening the door, I lift his body into the hall. In this one instance, at least, Richie is in luck. All I can see on his face is a slight scratch, but there's a bloody and deeper gash on the underside of one thumb. I lay his head on my lap and wrap a handkerchief around his thumb. "Need any help?" someone asks. "No," I answer, "we'll be fine." The crowd, one by one, drifts away, until we are alone. Rocking him gently, I try to comfort Richie. "You'll see," I say, "this time it will be different."

Richie isn't listening. He has slipped off into some fantasy of his own, humming an odd little tune I can't recognize. Between bursts of song I hear him carrying on a conversation in a voice I can barely make out, with someone far away and long ago: "I'm gone be fine, Josie, loose as a goose and ready to fly, you just bet I will."

It doesn't take long for the ambulance to arrive. The two attendants lift him onto a stretcher and into the ambulance with bravado skill. I step into the back with him and hold his face with both hands. "You gonna visit me, right?" he says. There is not a hint of anger in his eyes, only trust.

"First thing you have to do," I evade, "is to get well."

Richie takes my right hand, turns it over and plants a soft kiss in my palm. "We are street brothers," he says, "now and forever, ain't that so?"

I back up and step down from the ambulance. The driver regards me strangely. "You a priest or something?" he asks.

"Do I look like one?" I snap back.

He shrugs his shoulders. "You never can tell." The ambulance takes off, its warning siren shrieking, and zooms down Broadway.

There is no way I can sleep by myself this night. When I call Susan, she picks up on my voice and asks: "Is something wrong, Steve?"

"I had to send Rich to the hospital. It was gruesome."

"Grab a cab and come right over. We'll talk about it later."

"Be there in a few minutes," I say gratefully.

"Hurry, darling," she whispers. "I'll have a place all warmed up for you in bed."

Already the sound of her voice is making the nightmare of Richie recede. By the time I hail a cab and sit back, breathing again and relaxed, I have recovered enough of myself to anticipate the balm of Susan's sweetness.

All term long, in my composition class, the students have been curious about my poetry. I hadn't intended to, but when the session ends, I decide, on the spot, to read aloud from a poem entitled, "To Richie." Shortly after that dreadful episode in front of my house, I wrote it with the gold-tipped pen Rich had given me. It's thoroughly third-rate—maudlin, manipulative, saccharine. If I wasn't entirely aware of this before, I can tell from the forced tremolo in my voice as I read the ending:

> "I who hoped there might be room
> in me for this one homeless man,
> had I so soon betrayed
> the empty chambers waiting
> for him in my heart?"

"Any comment?" I ask.

Instantly my brightest student rises to her feet. "It's great," she enthuses. "I mean the way you show we have to open our hearts to the people without homes."

After her critique, a young man slowly gets up to his feet. "I don't know"—he shakes his head from side to side—"pitying those guys ain't gonna buy them the cheapest apartment in town."

I'm tempted to explain that my poem was meant as an extended metaphor, not as a call for social action. Instead I thank the class for listening and wish them the best for the new year.

Afterwards, on the steps of the school, I remain motionless, my head blanked out, waiting for an omen to direct my feet. A mile or so south is my house. In the other direction, about the same distance, is Bellevue Hospital. What am I confused about? Haven't I promised

—no, sworn—to Susan, I would not visit Richie? Haven't we agreed that it would be destructive to me and pointless, even cruel, to him if I suddenly showed up?

Yes, of course, I've promised, sworn and agreed. Why, then, are my feet, with a mind of their own, taking me to the corner and swinging me north, block after block, in a steady, unrelenting pace, until I reach the gate of the hospital and follow a family of five up the curved cement path through the entry door into the lobby?

Inside, at the information desk, a clerk looks up from her papers. "Mr. Richard Johnson," I say. She checks the file and, handing me a pass, points to the elevator. "Psychiatric Ward, C3, Room 432," she directs.

The elevator door is open, about fifty feet away, but I can't seem to negotiate the distance. I make a detour and slump down in one of the benches. The visitors, almost all black, sit around disconsolately, in the defeated posture of the poor. Conversations, hushed and properly tragic, sink midstream of their own weight. I have got to pull myself together.

On the bench near me, a man with blood-engorged eyes, wearing a bathrobe, is heaving up long, desperate sobs into his friend's chest. The friend, stony faced, pats him clumsily and turns his face away, past the other man's grief.

I feel faint, as I sometimes do when my dentist shoots my gums up with anesthesia. My pulse has gone crazy skipping beats. If I don't do something, I'll pass out in a minute. I put my head down between my knees. There, the spasm of nausea is over. All I register now is a faint twinge of self-loathing.

I take the elevator to the third floor and walk down the gleaming tile corridor. At Ward C, I turn right past the nurse's desk. She does not even bother to glance up at my pass. Inside the long room 432, painted a light bile-green, the mental patients lie sleeping or sleepless in their beds, drowning in the folds of their white linen. And there, ten beds down on the left, is Rich, propped up against a pillow. His face gaunt, gray and blotched, he stares ahead with fogged eyes, as if he's searching for someone lost in another dimension.

As I lean against his bed, I see that Richie hasn't as yet noticed me. Maybe I'll be lucky . . . maybe he'll be too zonked out to be aware of me at all. Instead, dammit, his head makes a slight movement toward me. Now, without any doubt, he makes the connection that it's me. I can tell by the way his eyes glitter and his lips begin to mumble.

God, what's my next move? I've nothing but free-floating anxiety in my head, as if my slate of intelligence has been wiped clean. Any moment now I will have swum clearly into his focus. I've got to invent something, anything, cheerful to say. Turning toward me, he holds his hand out until, tenderly, he finds mine. As he pulls me toward him, I feel my whole being trapped in the clutch of his fevered, clammy grip.

"Steve, baby," he whispers in a choked, sandpaper voice: "I been waiting to hear from you." His eyes are loony with love. "What's the good word, friend?"

The good word? Oh, Rich, you poor bastard. How the fuck am I supposed to know?